# GOING WILD

AN OAKLAND HILLS NOVEL

GRETCHEN GALWAY

ETON FIELD

GOING WILD

Copyright © 2017 by Gretchen Galway

Eton Field, Publisher
www.gretchengalway.com

Cover design by Gretchen Galway
Stock art images from Depositphotos



ISBN (eBook): 978-1-939872-17-3
ISBN (Print): 978-1-939872-18-0

v.20170601

Jane maneuvered her minivan carefully up the narrow, private road, searching for house numbers. Markers along the wooded hills were hard to find, as if rich people in Marin County, California, didn't want to encourage visitors.

Understandable. Someday, after she'd amassed her own fortune, she'd mark her remote estate with just enough signage to ensure UPS drivers could deliver her Amazon packages. The rest of the world could get lost.

She was smiling at the daydream when she spotted the number she was looking for on a black iron gate.

"Thank God," she said aloud. Only six minutes away from running late, she wanted to make a good impression.

She drove up the hill past horse stables, grapevines, apple trees, tennis courts, a guest house, three fountains, an herb garden, and two pools, trying to take it all in as she maneuvered the gravel drive already lined with cars, searching the shoulder for a space large enough to park her bulky vehicle. But soon she saw that the drive was blocked, a dead end; she'd have to back up.

Maybe it was because she was rushed, maybe it was because she was distracted by the ostentatious surroundings, but when Jane threw the van into reverse and hit the gas, she felt the sickening jerk of impact. Too late, she pressed both feet on the brake pedal, a bubbling brook of profanity pouring out of her mouth.

Not now. Not today.

A quick, cringing glance told her she'd backed up into a black SUV. How had she missed it?

Muttering another soothing curse, she opened her door and braced herself for an apologetic confrontation. The guy climbing out of the SUV was tall and broad, heavily bearded, and wore stained khakis over muddy boots. He regarded her with steel-gray eyes that didn't blink.

She recoiled involuntarily. He looked like a macho, old-fashioned type who made insulting jokes about women drivers. As she walked over, she was suddenly conscious of her sheer summer dress and dainty kitten heels, which made her feel more vulnerable.

"I'm very sorry," she said quickly but firmly, turning her gaze to his SUV, then her van. She'd backed into him at an angle, denting the right side of hers and the front bumper of his. "I'll get you my insurance information."

He bent over and rubbed his hand over the dent as if he could wipe it away. "Hm."

Her hands shook as she returned to her van for her purse. Silly to get so upset about a fender bender, but she hated making stupid mistakes. And her coworkers—or worse, boss—might've seen her get into a car accident at the front door like a stoned high schooler without a license.

The man's brow furrowed as he looked around the crowded driveway. "What's going on?"

"Mr. Whitman invited us up for a barbecue."

One eyebrow lifted. "The old guy's throwing a party?"

Mr. Whitman, the estate's owner, had founded the boutique accounting firm in San Francisco where she worked. "It's a business function."

"That makes more sense," the man said. "Let me back up so you can get out."

"Here's my information." The card she held out to him had her name, insurance, license, plate, and phone number. Every year she printed out a few copies for her wallet, just in case. It was the first time she'd had to use one.

"Don't worry about it," he said. "It was my fault."

"No, it wasn't," she said. "I backed right into you."

"I shouldn't have been in the way."

Was he kidding? "Please take it." She pushed the card at him. She would never damage somebody's property and not pay for it.

He rubbed his beard, which was fluffy as a poodle, and took the card. His fingernails were rimmed with dirt, his knuckles chafed and raw. "I'm not going to fix it. I don't mind a few dents. That's life." He held it out without looking at it.

"Hold on to it in case you change your mind."

Ignoring the card, he crossed his arms over his chest. "You work at Whitman?"

She nodded. "Several years now."

His eyes drifted down her dress to her heels and back up to her face. "Do you like it?" He seemed genuinely curious.

She was too surprised by his question to respond right away. "It's a good job," she said finally. Whitman had a better work atmosphere than the Big Four firms. She'd tried that right after college, before getting her CPA, and had burned out on the hundred-hour workweeks.

"That doesn't mean you like it."

Her mouth fell open, uneasy with how quickly and obliviously he'd struck at the heart of the matter. "I love being an accountant." She surprised herself by adding, "I don't always like the travel and unpredictable hours." And she was overdue for a promotion.

He nodded. "I was never any good at math."

"It's about the only thing I am good at," she said.

"I doubt that."

"You doubt I'm good at math or—"

His smile warmed his gray eyes. "I doubt that's all you're good at."

"You say that to the woman who just backed into you."

"Nobody's perfect," he said. With a wave, he started to turn away.

"I'm not going to let you leave unless you let me compensate you for the damage somehow," she said. Even aside from the risk to her reputation with the Whitmans, she couldn't bear to walk away from any accident she'd caused without making amends.

"You're not going to let me? What are you going to do, lie down in the dirt behind my wheels?"

"If I have to." She reached into her purse and pulled out her wallet. Because she liked the security cash could provide, she always took out the maximum at the ATM. She pinched a thin stack of twenties between her fingers and pulled them out. It was only a few hundred, but it would buy him a new pair of jeans. A haircut. Maybe even a manicure. Hadn't he ever heard of gloves?

His face was pained as he looked at the money in her hand. "Please put that away. I don't need it."

She reached up and stuffed it into the chest pocket of his button-down shirt. Faded chambray, frayed at the seams with a tear at his left shoulder. She hoped he'd buy himself a replacement. "I insist." She turned and hurried back to her van, averting her gaze from the nasty gash in her van's side. Poor thing. She offered a silent apology to her big four-wheel baby as she climbed in and waited for the guy, who had stared after her for a moment before giving up and climbing into his SUV to get out of the way.

When he finally rolled out of sight, she backed up, more carefully this time, around the curved, crowded drive until she had room to turn around. Belatedly she saw a bald man in a white shirt waving at her from the lawn, gesturing for her to park in the grass next to a few other cars she hadn't seen earlier.

Within two minutes, she was jogging up the steps to the house, hoping nobody would notice she was late or that her dress was glued to her backside from stress sweat. She paused, picked at it in an attempt at ventilation, took a deep breath, and went in.

The property was equally stunning on the inside. Italian tile; earth-tone walls; abstract paintings in gilt frames; a cool, fragrant breeze wafting through the open floor plan; armfuls of lavender in copper pots flanking the French doors to a courtyard.

It would be easy to write the ad copy to rent a place like this. Not so easy for her stucco box in Oakland. Nothing she could do about the tile or French doors, but she could get some lavender. It grew all around box store parking lots; how expensive could it be?

"Did you get lost?"

Jane spun around and smiled at Sydney, her favorite coworker. "Worse. I'll tell you later. Has anyone noticed I'm late?"

Sydney gave her a pitying look. "Mr. Whitman is going around with a clipboard, taking names. He was just asking if all the seniors were here."

Jane's heart jumped. She scanned the several dozen bodies mingling outside in the courtyard, searching for the eightysomething founder of the firm.

And then she remembered whom she was talking to. Jane snatched the cocktail glass out of Sydney's fingers and drained it. Vodka. Nice and strong. She felt her shoulders loosen a little.

"Clipboard?" Sydney shook her head. "Seriously, Jane. You believed that?"

"He might have a clipboard," Jane said. "He used to be quite a dictator in the old days." She'd worked there long enough to remember seeing him at the office a few days a week. Now he came less often but still had an office and refused to retire completely.

"These aren't the old days," Sydney said. "Unless you mean he's old, because that he is. Poor dude is asleep under a tree in the garden. I wish somebody would roll him back into the house and let him rest."

"He'd kill us if we tried," said a man behind Jane.

Jane and Sydney shared a despairing look before slowly turning around. It was Troy, officially a senior manager, unofficially the boss. He was a grandson of the elderly sleeping dude, the man Jane had just called a dictator.

This day was only getting worse.

Jane commenced groveling. "Troy, I apologize. That was out of line. I never should have said—"

"Me too," Sydney said. "So, so, so sorry, Troy. Troy Whitman. Mr. Whitman."

"Relax," Troy said. "It's just me, guys. Thanks for making the trip up here. Is something wrong?"

Jane and Sydney looked at each other. Troy was a nice guy, not even thirty yet, but everyone knew he was the heir to the throne.

When his grandfather finally retired (or died, which seemed more likely), Troy would be the Whitman on the letterhead. Jane had never seen any of his brothers at the office in San Francisco.

"Uh—" Sydney said, scowling at Jane as if it were her fault for inspiring her comments about Troy's grandpa.

"He can be a tyrant," Troy said, sipping his wine. "Nobody knows it better than his family. Please chill. I'm not going to fire you for making a joke. That's why I wanted to have everyone up here, so we can get to know each other, relax, eat, drink, have a few laughs."

"Team building," Sydney said, nodding.

Troy made a face. "I hate buzzwords, but yeah, something like that."

"Well, thanks," Sydney said. "Jane took my drink, so I have to go get another one. OK?"

"Of course, of course," Troy said. "Please. Go."

Sydney walked away, glancing over her shoulder to wink at Jane behind Troy's back.

Jane wished her own glass wasn't empty. Sydney had already consumed half before Jane had stolen it. But talking to Troy was good career politics.

"So the party was your idea?" Jane asked.

"Another reason to hate me," Troy said with the smile of a man who knew very few people in the world were capable of hating him. He was the type of person who shot rainbows out of his ass, even early on Monday mornings.

Well, maybe Jane was capable of hating him a little bit. The man was just too nice. And with golden-boy, killer good looks, he could've gotten away with murder if he'd ever wanted to hurt somebody, which of course he never would.

Jane couldn't relate to that. Her dark side could swallow stars.

"Why don't you go pay your respects to my grandfather?" Troy asked. "I get the feeling he's woken up."

Jane looked through the doorway into the crowded courtyard. "How can you tell?"

One corner of his mouth curved. "He's like a flame surrounded by moths. See how everyone has kind of turned in that direction?"

She did see. Once again, she looked mournfully into her empty glass. Ah well. Best to be sober for the formal greeting and then indulge afterward.

She thanked Troy and meandered through the crowd to the center of the action. The partygoers had turned to face Mr. Whitman, but everyone except a brave few had kept a safe distance, drinks in hand, polite smiles in place. Those brave few lining up to chat with the man in the chair included Jane's supervisor, Nicole.

Jane wasn't an emotionally expressive person like her sister, but it had taken years of practice to hide her dislike of Nicole's company. After a moment of intense concentration to make sure the mask was in place, she strode through a gap in the bodies and approached.

Nicole was reminding the man in the chair of who she was. "That's right, Mr. Whitman. Nicole Timney. A senior manager." She noticed Jane. "And my subordinate, Jane Garcia."

*Subordinate. Servant. Groveling half person.* With great force of will, Jane prevented her eyeballs from rolling upward. Although Jane did good work at the firm, she and Nicole had never gotten along. No drinks after work, no shared memes on social media, no personal chitchat.

Jane stepped closer to Mr. Whitman's chair with her hand outstretched. He favored a strong handshake, even among women, and she was already tensed and ready for his crushing grip.

"Mr. Whitman, thank you for inviting—" she began.

"Jane Garcia?" Mr. Whitman sat up taller.

"Yes, sir. You have a lovely—"

"What are you doing here?" His thick white eyebrows drew together over the bridge of his nose. "You're fired!"

2

---

ane's smile was too carefully constructed to falter even a micromillimeter. The man had been sleeping outside in a chair and was in his late eighties; he was bound to get confused now and then. "No, Mr. Whitman, not fired. I'm here for the party." She jutted her hand out again. "Jane Garcia."

"I know who the hell you are. I thought we fired you." He looked up at Nicole, who had been frowning at Jane.

Nicole frowned at everything. Probably frowned at teacup poodle puppies.

"Didn't you fire her?" Mr. Whitman demanded.

"I beg your pardon," Nicole said. "It was Lorraine McNeil who left. Same department."

"Damn it, I'm not confused," Mr. Whitman said. He rubbed his eyes. "I remember the name."

"You may recall," Nicole said, "we had a meeting about that, ah, client and—"

"And we decided she had to go. This one. Why is she still here?"

During this exchange, Jane felt the muscles that had been

10

holding her cheeks in the unnatural smile begin to cramp. Both corners of her mouth began to sag. Clamping her jaw shut failed to slow their descent.

Lorraine, the newest hire, had been let go with severance because their department was contracting. That was what Troy and Nicole told them, although there had been rumors about performance problems. Jane's reviews had always been stellar. Even after that problem in the spring.

Nicole moved between Jane and Mr. Whitman. "Could I get you something to drink, Mr. Whitman?"

"You're trying to change the subject." He began coughing violently, his face turning red.

"Would you like me to get Troy?" Nicole asked. "Your grandson?"

"I know who the hell he is," Mr. Whitman barked. "And I know who the hell *she* is. Garcia. Jane Garcia. I want her gone. Out of here. Fired." He doubled over with more coughing.

"Yes, Mr. Whitman, of course." Nicole took Jane's arm and pulled her away. The gaping crowd closed in, blocking his view of Jane. "We need to get you out of his sight. I've never seen him so upset."

"But I have no idea why! Do you?"

Without a word, Nicole led her away through the courtyard, into the house, and out the front door, then down the steps to a spiral rosemary topiary set in a stone urn.

"Jane, I think you should go home," Nicole said.

Jane was too blindsided to think, let alone argue coherently. It had all happened so fast.

"And I don't think you should come into the office on Monday," Nicole continued. "In fact, you might want to brush up your resume."

Jane gaped. "What?"

"I'm afraid he's serious about this."

"But *you* can't be," Jane said.

"You'll have to talk to Troy," Nicole said. "I don't have the clout to oppose Mr. Whitman."

"He must've confused me with Lorraine."

"I don't think so. He was too angry."

"There's no reason for him to be so upset—" Jane stopped. Nicole knew about the problem a few months ago and that everything Jane had done had been by the book.

Nicole adjusted the chain around her neck. For such a tall, thin woman, she had a rather chubby throat. Her favorite necklace was too short, and she was always pulling at it. "I'm afraid there's nothing I can do."

"So that's it? I'm fired?" Jane had that weightless, out-of-body feeling you got when you were living a moment you'd never forget.

"I don't know."

"This is crazy," Jane said. "I'm a fabulous employee. I have great annual performance reviews."

"I know that. I gave them to you."

*Grudgingly,* Jane thought. "Do I get severance?" She heard the submissiveness in her voice and shook it off. "I'll need severance."

"It's too soon to talk about this," Nicole said.

"Now it's too soon? I just got to the party, was fired within the first few minutes, and I'm being hasty?"

"Calm down. Nobody can do anything right now. It'll have to wait until next week."

"Nicole, I just bought a house."

"You inherited a house. You refinanced. Not quite the same."

"To the bank, it's the same." Jane clasped her hands together to stop the shaking. "I owe them quite a bit of money. And now I don't have a job, apparently. Suddenly. For no reason whatsoever."

"Don't overdramatize. Nobody has died. You'll do fine."

Nobody had ever accused Jane of being dramatic. To hear her cold boss say that to her now, when she was being quite insanely calm about being shit-canned in front of her colleagues at a work party in a Mediterranean villa in Marin after getting into a car accident at the front door—

Well, it was enough to make Jane want to gather that tight gold chain around Nicole's neck and choke the life out of her.

Thinking like that wasn't good. It was definitely not good. She prided herself on her calm, her reason, her long view thinking. Murdering Nicole wouldn't look good on her resume unless she was applying for work in the criminal underground, or maybe corporate lobbying, and she had no interest in moving to Washington. She'd begun the process to build a separate entrance at her house in Oakland—

She spun around on her heel to lose the view of Nicole and her coral-pink silk blouse and too-tight necklace. Now the work on the house would have to wait. But the whole point of doing the remodeling was to have paying tenants or Airbnb guests to cover her new mortgage.

"Really, Jane. I'm surprised to see you be such a drama queen about this," Nicole said behind her.

To soothe herself, Jane stroked the soft pleats of her dress as if it were her cat waiting for her at home. That gold chain was short, but it was thick and ropey, probably a thousand dollars' worth of twenty-four karat, more than strong enough to cut off the air supply to an icy-hearted woman who probably didn't have any arteries, because that would involve a heart, and Nicole had demonstrated no such thing in the two years Jane had worked for her.

She turned to face Nicole again. "I am not being overly

dramatic. I've had a shock." She kept her voice low and world-weary, like a heavy smoker with five ex-husbands who'd lived long enough to give absolutely zero fucks. Not like some young, lonely little girl who was afraid and wanted to cry. "If you were in my shoes, you'd be hysterical right now."

"I strongly suggest you not burn any bridges with me," Nicole said. "You might need me to write you a recommendation."

Jane reached into her bra and pulled out her car key fob. She hadn't wanted to carry a purse around, and sometimes there were advantages to a D-cup. "I think I'd better leave. We can discuss this later. Email my personal—"

"You shouldn't do anything in writing," Nicole said. "Certainly not with me. You'll have to clear this up with Mr. Whitman when he's up to it. From the sound of that cough, you'll have to wait."

"Maybe instead of waiting, I'll start looking for another job."

Nicole shrugged. "Your decision. But you know as well as I do that leaving now will slow down your career."

"I'm not leaving voluntarily."

"Then be patient." Nicole raised a sculpted eyebrow. "Or don't you have enough of a financial cushion to survive a sudden end to your direct deposits if Mr. Whitman follows through on this?"

The implication that she, Jane Garcia, of all people, was irresponsible about money was too ridiculous to take seriously. "We'll talk later, one way or another." Jane turned and walked down the steps to the circular drive.

She held her temper as far as a trio of Teslas before she began swearing under her breath. She began small, with entry-level swear words her mother had used around the house when she was little. Damn, shit. Just the basics. But by the time Jane was fifty yards away from the front door, she'd moved on to the really bad ones that even her sister, no prude, didn't approve of. And she wasn't whispering them, either.

"I hope you're not upset because of me," said a voice behind her. A man's voice, one she'd heard for the first time less than an hour ago.

Belatedly she recognized the black SUV she'd most recently walked past during her verbal tirade, the one bearing a fresh dent in the front bumper.

She was too numbed by the soothing balm of profanity to care. She turned and gave him a polite wave. "No, not because of you. Sorry about that."

"Did you used to be in the navy? My grandfather swears like that, says he learned it all there."

"Listen, uh—" She hesitated, realizing she'd never gotten his name.

"Grant," he said. "Grant Whitman."

"Grant, I've had a really bad—" At last her brain processed the sounds that had just come out of the bearded, scruffy man's mouth. "Whitman?"

He closed his eyes for a moment and offered an apologetic shrug.

"You live here?" she asked.

"No, just visiting."

"You're Troy's brother."

"Yup," he said.

"Why didn't you say something?"

"I was kind of embarrassed," he said. "I'm not always good with people. I could see you were a little tense already. Didn't want to stress you out more."

"Right. Fine. OK." She massaged her temple. "I gave you a wad of twenties."

"I told you not to."

"You're a Whitman," she said, suddenly angry with him as if everything that had just happened was his fault. She scowled at his old vehicle. "Why don't you drive a nicer car?"

"Not my style, I guess."

She rolled her eyes. "Great. Just great."

"Sorry."

After a split second, she managed a weak smile in spite of herself. It wasn't this guy's fault. Twice now she'd run into him, first with her car, then with her temper. "No, I'm sorry. I just got fired. Sort of." She took a deep breath. "I don't know what, exactly."

"Just now? At the party?"

She nodded.

He didn't say anything for a moment. She thought he might ask her a question, but all he said was, "Sorry."

"Not your fault."

"Still, I'm sorry."

"Thank you," she said. "Well, I'm out of here. Sorry about denting your car."

"It really doesn't matter."

Nothing seemed to. She walked away, thinking of all the hours she'd worked late, the Sundays spent in airports on business, the coffee she'd fetched, the email she'd answered, the reports and spreadsheets and presentations, the—

All for nothing.

She kept her swearing silent as she marched the rest of the distance to her van.

3

Grant watched Jane of the Impressive Vocabulary disappear behind the row of parked luxury sedans, hybrid hatchbacks, and SUVs. He didn't turn away until he saw her minivan pull onto the asphalt and drive out of sight.

He wondered if she swore around her kids like that. Maybe it was bad of him, but that was something he'd like to see. They were probably used to it. The woman obviously had a temper.

Smiling, he got the bag that he'd forgotten to bring inside earlier and slammed the tailgate. Out of habit, he'd locked the doors, although nobody was likely to steal anything up here, certainly not out of his '94 Land Rover. Far better pickings in the new BMWs.

His amusement vanished as he remembered she'd just been fired. So soon after arriving at the party. Sounded like his grandfather's style, indifferent to people's feelings. When Grant was younger, he'd disliked his grandfather intensely, had even imagined he hated him for what the eldest Whitman had done to Grant's father. Now that he was in his thirties, Grant still didn't understand the man very well but he respected him and in an odd way, loved him.

Maybe Grant was just getting old and sentimental. Grandfather would say he'd spent too much time alone in the woods.

Walking into the house, Grant endured the suspicious glances the guests lingering in the foyer shot his way. He probably didn't look like somebody who should be walking in the front entrance, especially not during a party. He'd been hiking Mt. Tam that morning and was sweaty and coated with grime. Again he thought of poor Jane and her dented minivan. She'd naturally assumed he was a manual laborer or something, to push that money on him, and now she was the one without a job—

He wished he'd made her take the money back. If she'd argued, he would've insisted, pointed out he was one of the Whitmans, and she would assume money was the last thing he needed.

More assumptions.

Truth was he had to finish his book soon or his publisher was going to give up on him and demand he return the advance. The manuscript was already late, very late, and getting later every second. Although his first and second books were best sellers, the demand for outdoor creative nonfiction wasn't guaranteed. He wasn't a movie star with a drug problem and photogenic abdominal muscles. If so, he could've published a fifty-word stream-of-consciousness poem about banana slugs and, if sprinkled with photographs of his famous abs, sold ten million copies in a month. Forget book signings without anyone showing up; he'd need a security detail. An entourage. There would be groupies.

Grant was headed back to see his mom in her cottage when Troy, one of his younger brothers, bumped into him carrying a box of Band-Aids and a bottle of hand sanitizer.

"Who's bleeding?" Grant asked.

"One of our guests cut his hand on the suit of armor," Troy said. "Grandfather told him to get a tetanus shot on Monday, just in case."

"Dad always did hope one of us would become a doctor," Grant said.

Troy cheerfully lifted his middle finger off the box and aimed it at his big brother. "It was that one at the bottom of the stairs with his foot sticking out, like he's trying to trip everyone."

Their grandfather had amassed an odd collection of all kinds of old stuff over the years: suits of armor, medieval swords, muddy portraits of English dukes, frayed tapestries, uncomfortable mahogany chairs you weren't allowed to sit in. In no way did the collection match the Italian-inspired architecture of the house and grounds, but Grandfather couldn't care less; he just went out and bought another lance and nailed it right on top of a hand-painted Venetian mural.

"Sounds like there's a lot of bad luck going around at this work party of yours," Grant said. "I've already seen one woman let go."

"That'll be me if this guy bleeds to death in front of Grandfather," Troy said, holding up the box of Band-Aids.

"Seriously. A woman in the driveway just told me she'd been fired."

"What?"

"You didn't know about it?"

Troy let out a pained sigh and gestured for Grant to follow him into a quiet corner off the foyer. "No. I didn't know. His cough got worse, so Rachelle has been giving him a new medicine. It makes him a little groggy and pissed off."

Rachelle was his health-care aide. "Sounds like he'd be better off in bed," Grant said.

"I couldn't stop him from joining the party." Troy gazed off into space. "I'll have to find out what happened. What did this woman look like?"

Grant's thoughts immediately flew to Jane's body, full and lush in that almost-see-through yellow dress, one erect nipple standing out more than the other, which he'd tried not to wonder about too deeply. Her legs had been something else too, with dimples at her knees and curvy ankles and a hint of soft, soft thigh.

"Brown hair," Grant said instead. "Drove a minivan."

"A minivan?" Troy looked perplexed. "You aren't giving me much to work with."

"Her name was Jane Garcia." He still had her card with insurance information.

"Jane? Garcia? Oh no." Troy signaled to a random guy across the foyer, thrust the Band-Aids and hand sanitizer at him, gave some hurried instructions, and turned back to Grant. "Where is she? I should talk to her."

"She's gone. I saw her drive away."

"I'll have to talk to Grandfather," Troy said. "Too many people around right now, though, and he won't move out of that chair." He put his hands on his hips and stretched his back. "Who knew throwing a little barbecue would be so hard?"

"She was really upset," Grant said. "You should talk to her."

"I knew he blamed her, but I didn't think he'd do anything at a work party."

"Blamed her for what?"

"We lost our oldest account. Her name came up. He got wind of it last week and has been fuming about it for days."

"But you don't think it was her fault?"

"No," Troy said. "But the politics are tricky."

Grant imagined Jane going home and telling her family she'd lost her job, hardly what she'd expected when she got dressed that morning. "I think you should talk to her."

"He's still the boss. I can't do anything just by snapping my fingers." Troy sighed. "But you're right. We have to do something."

Grant didn't like the word "we" in that sentence.

"I can't leave the party, but you can," Troy said.

"Since when do I get involved with company business? Never. I never do." Like his father, Grant had needed to take a firm stand against Grandfather's pressure to join the family business. His sanity depended on it. "I need to write this afternoon."

"You need to take a shower and help me. I can't leave the party. You can drive to Jane's house and apologize for our grandfather's behavior this afternoon and…"

Grant waited. He didn't see how Troy could fix the problem without openly defying their grandfather, which Troy wouldn't do.

Troy held up a hand. "And ask her to wait a few days, maybe a little longer, until I can figure something out." He frowned. "I wonder if she'll buy that. Jane likes to do things by the book."

If that book has lots of swearing in it, Grant thought. "Why should I put myself in harm's way?"

"I won't tell Grandfather you're involved."

"I'm not involved."

"Great," Troy said. "I'll get you her address."

Grant watched Troy take out his phone and begin to tap and scroll. "I haven't agreed to do this."

"You'll do it, or I'll tell Grandfather you've changed your mind about working at the firm."

"He'd never believe you," Grant said.

"I'll tell him you've got writer's block on your new book and you've run out of money."

Grant whistled. It was close enough to the truth to hurt. "You're getting cutthroat in your old age, little man. Is this how you'll be when you make partner at Whitman?"

"Please, Grant. I can't ask anyone else."

"Surely she has a manager or someone who can go instead of me."

"I don't want to get into the gory details, but there's a story here that could be really upsetting for Grandfather. We've got to try to keep it in the family." Troy continued tapping on his phone. "There, I sent it to you. She lives in Oakland."

A pair of women waved at Troy from the doorway to the courtyard, calling him over, something about a toast. Then a preppy guy in a white-and-navy-striped sweater joined them, adding to the chorus.

Grant took pity on his little brother, who had all the responsibilities of running the family business without any of the power. "All right, I'll go."

She had said she liked working there. If she might be able to save her job, she should know as soon as possible.

And he'd have the chance to give her the wad of twenties back.

Troy flashed him a grin, patted him on the arm, and dove back into the party. Grant started to walk out to his Rover, but then, acting on an impulse he didn't investigate too closely, he went out back and down the outside steps to the basement room he'd been crashing in since returning to town.

It wouldn't kill him to clean up a little before he went to see her.

4

Ten minutes after she got home, Jane opened her laptop to update her resume. Shadow, her long-haired black cat, jumped into her lap and blocked Jane's access to the keys with her voluminous tail.

Jane stared at the screen. Was she overreacting?

Mr. Whitman had obviously been confused. He was elderly, he had health issues, and all the guests crowding around him had upset him. Other accountants at Whitman could explain why she wasn't to blame for what happened with Frank Bostock. Well, maybe she was to blame. But she'd had no choice.

If she stuck it out, she'd finally get the promotion she was due, putting her in line to make partner sooner. If she left now and went to a new company, she might be at the bottom, right when she hit her early thirties and planned to start a family. She'd need all the benefits and savings she could get.

She closed her laptop, gently set Shadow on the floor, and stood up to explore the front bedroom she'd decided to rent. The sooner she got a tenant, the better. Or guests, if she did

Airbnb. As long as they gave her money, she didn't care what she was supposed to call them.

The bedroom was small but there was a private bathroom in the hallway and a tiny kitchenette she'd installed in the closet. For clothes, she'd gotten an IKEA wardrobe that was in excellent shape, and nobody would ever guess she'd bought it for fourteen dollars from a neighbor's yard sale.

She fluffed the pillows and smoothed the quilt on the bed. Gray squares with faint peach accents, which she hoped was gender neutral, a little sophisticated. They could bring their own blanket if they didn't like it.

The sound of the doorbell made her jump. For a moment she imagined it was somebody coming to look at the room, maybe even move in. Unlikely, since she hadn't listed it yet.

Getting fired had made her edgy.

When she opened the door, the first thing she noticed was a stack of twenty-dollar bills in a man's hand at eye level.

Then she saw the man. He'd cleaned up. Rust-orange sweater, dark jeans, no visible grime under his fingernails. And his beard no longer implied it could provide habitat to an extended family of marmots. Still thick, but clean.

"I meant to give this to you up in Marin," Grant said.

"I meant for you to keep it," she replied.

"Can I come in?"

Shadow appeared at their feet and rubbed against his shins, making the odd growling noise she did to express social stimulation. It sounded a lot like barking.

Jane stepped aside but peered past him at the dented SUV. "Just because you're a Whitman doesn't negate the damage I did to your vehicle."

"Nice cat." Bending over to pet Shadow, he stepped into the house, glancing around, seeming to be searching for something. Then he placed the money on the pine drop-leaf hall table, one of the few pieces of her grandmother's furniture she'd kept. "That's not the only reason I'm here."

"I figured." She decided to ignore the stack of bills. It was kind of ridiculous to continue to insist he keep the money given his vast resources and her (especially presently) humble ones. "Troy sent you?"

He bent down and took off his shoes, clean, sporty oxfords with green and orange accent stitching. "You're quick."

"You don't have to take off your shoes."

"Old habit. You mind?"

"No, of course not," she said, admiring his colorful socks. They were striped with skinny bands of pink, black, white, and yellow. The toes and heels were purple. "I've never seen men's socks like that before."

"Really?"

"Really," she said.

He grinned. "Yeah, I know. I made these."

"Right."

"Seriously. Helps pass the time. Good for stress reduction."

"You *knit*?"

"You don't?" he asked.

She didn't know if he was joking. "I don't."

"You probably don't have as much time on your hands as I do," he said.

Even when she was in grade school, she preferred math homework to craft projects. Her choice of career hadn't been a coincidence. "That's not what's stopping me." She gestured behind her toward the kitchen. "Would you like a cup of coffee or something?"

He agreed and followed her and Shadow down the hall. "I don't have kids, so there isn't any finger painting or crayons or Play-Doh to satisfy that part of my brain."

She noticed again how he seemed to be searching for something. "Is something wrong?"

"It's just… your house is really… neat."

"Neat as in cool, or neat as in tidy?"

He grinned. "Both, of course."

"I don't have much stuff. I like it that way."

"I don't have much either, but I don't have a family." He frowned at the small café table and pair of stools she used for all her fine dining, which usually consisted of cheese and crackers, fruit, and takeout.

"I have a big family," she said, "but none of them live here, not since my sister moved out to live with her boyfriend." Now she was just one more happy cat lady.

"But— Oh, of course. I thought—your— Do they—" He cut himself off. "None of my business, sorry. I'm here because Troy wanted to apologize for our grandfather."

Some of the tension drained out of her shoulders. Troy was already trying to help her, and had sent his brother to tell her. Maybe everything was going to be all right. "Thank you for making the trip. You probably got stuck in traffic on the Richmond Bridge like I did."

"Saturday in the Bay Area. Nothing I'm not used to."

"You said you were just visiting…"

"Right," he said.

What harm was there in being nosy? "So, where do you live?"

"Nowhere, as it happens. Or everywhere."

"Wow. Sounds spiritual," she said.

He snorted. "I wish. I've been on the road— Well, so to speak—researching a book. I haven't figured out where I'm going to settle down yet."

Jane vaguely remembered one of Troy's brothers was some

kind of writer. Outdoor guides. "Are you the Whitman who writes hiking stuff?"

"Is that how Troy puts it?"

"No," she said quickly. "I only have employee gossip to go on. I'm sure it misrepresented your work."

He rubbed his face with both hands and sighed. "Actually, you got it exactly right. Staying under my grandfather's roof has made me overly sensitive. Yes, I'm the one who writes hiking stuff."

"That's why you drive an old SUV," she said.

"Yeah. I do a lot of hiking and backpacking. I park the Rover at the trailhead for weeks at a time. It's generally safe, but I don't like to tempt people with a cherried-up new truck. I kind of like having my wheels waiting for me when I hike out."

The thought of living in the wilderness for weeks made her shudder. The thought of spending the night outdoors—or, God forbid, peeing without a toilet—inspired her to walk over to her sink and wash her hands under the warm running water with lilac hand soap. "I'll get the coffee going. Full octane or decaf?"

"Full octane. Thanks."

She let her hand rest on her coffee maker, her favorite appliance. How could he endure all those days and nights without the basics of living? She peeked at him over her shoulder. He'd looked rough at the party, but pretty good now. He must've shaved and bathed before coming over. Should she be flattered?

"I'd assumed you had kids," he said. "Because of the minivan."

She smiled. "Is that what you were looking for when you came in?"

"Afraid so. Legos, Barbies, bulk diapers, you know."

"It's confused people before, the van. No, no kids."

"Married?"

"No. Just the cat," she said. "You? I mean, I assume not, unless she travels with—"

"Not married," he said.

What a life that would be, trudging after him in the freezing mud, up and down mountains, trying to pee standing up, sleeping on rocks. He was cute, but not that cute.

"Thank you for coming over," she said.

"You seemed really upset. I felt bad."

"Thank you, but I'm all right now. I don't know why I got so upset. It's not like me. Shock, I suppose." She got out two coffee mugs and her grandmother's retro sugar bowl. "How long before Troy can clear things up?"

"You'll have to talk to him about that."

"But he sent you," she said. "What did he say? He must have given you some kind of message."

"He wanted to apologize for our grandfather's behavior."

"But…" That could mean anything—his tone, his timing, his choice of words. "Am I really fired?"

"Honestly," he said, "I have no idea. Please don't ask me."

Her spirits tanked again. "You don't look like you think it's really going to be OK, or you'd say so."

"Troy wanted me to ask you to wait until he has time to talk to you," he said. "I'm sorry I don't know anything. I've never been an accountant. Please ignore whatever I look like."

That wasn't possible. He had a preppy lumberjack thing going on that was distracting. Her last boyfriend had been strictly graphic T-shirts and khakis, and would've slit his wrists before wearing plaid or growing a beard. Andrew hadn't a tenth of this guy's appeal, one reason his infidelity had been such a shock to her. What were the odds he'd find another woman who'd sleep with him?

Thinking about Andrew made her spill coffee grounds onto the counter. She swore and turned away for a dishcloth.

"I was imagining the vocabulary your kids must have," he said behind her. "Your imaginary kids."

"My imaginary kids have wonderful vocabularies," she said, smiling.

"Colorful."

"Swearing is a sign of intelligence," she said. "Especially in women."

"No shit."

Laughing, she glanced at him over her shoulder. "Read it on the internet."

"Then it must be true."

"Glad we can agree." She finished preparing the coffee and handed him a cup. "Do you take anything in it?"

"Just my lips."

She couldn't help looking at those lips as they puckered, preparing to sip his drink. The hair on his upper lip was carefully trimmed, providing plenty of coffee-to-mouth clearance. No handlebar mustache was going to take a swim.

"What's so funny?" he asked, eyeing her over the rim of the cup.

"How long does your beard get when you're in the wild?"

"I try keep it short, actually. Otherwise it's too hard to keep clean."

"You shave out there?"

"It's not Antarctica. I bathe, too."

She felt her cheeks warm. She lifted her own mug to her lips, hiding behind it as she pushed away the vivid image she'd had of his bare, muscled butt cheeks glistening under the spray of a mountain waterfall. Like a Norse god. Getting nice and clean. Nice and clean and wet.

What was the matter with her? She turned away and

mentally slapped herself. So he slightly resembled Chris Hemsworth. That didn't mean he actually was a god, or even a movie star. He only looked like one.

*Even better*, she thought.

They sipped their coffee in silence for a few minutes.

"Look, if you think Troy might not step in and clear this up, please tell me now. I can't afford this house without a guaranteed income." She set her cup on the counter. "I was getting the front room ready for a tenant, but I don't even have the permits yet for a separate entrance or the other things I need to do for Airbnb. I thought I had some time. But if I'm laid off as of yesterday or even next week, I—"

"You're renting out a room?" He looked unreasonably curious.

"I was. Eventually. But it's not ready yet. I can't count on that income either, not for at least a month." And even then, the amount would hardly cover her living expenses.

"What else do you have to do to get it ready?" He set down his mug and started to leave the kitchen. "Let's take a look."

She groaned inwardly. Why did men get so excited about thinking they could fix things with their hands? The last guy to help out with the home improvements had gotten engaged to her sister, which was how Jane had ended up owning the house by herself. "Listen, I'm sorry I mentioned it. If you want to help, talk to your grandfather."

Grant stopped in the hallway and gave her a sad smile over his shoulder. "That wouldn't help. Definitely a bad idea."

There was obviously a family story there she didn't want to get into. "Fine, then Troy. Tell him I can't wait more than a week to hear if I'm let go." She wanted to show she was reasonable but not a pushover.

He disappeared into the front bedroom without replying.

When she caught up to him, she found him opening the closet and pushing the buttons on the microwave.

"Nice," he said.

"You don't drag a solar-powered microwave with you into the woods?"

"Nope." He lifted the electric kettle, popped the lid, and peered inside. "You could make ramen in here like a boss."

"No, you could use the bowl and lid provided. Otherwise everything else you make in it will taste like MSG."

"There's a bowl and lid provided?" He opened the top drawer on the compact storage bin she'd put on the shelf above the mini fridge. "Aha, so there is. And spoons. And knives. Even forks."

"Maybe you should hit the road now to avoid the traffic," she said. "Saturday night can be worse than Saturday afternoon."

"What about the bathroom?" he asked.

"Don't worry about the bathroom."

"I saw one right out here in the hall." He strode past her and out of the room.

Once again she chased after him. "Please, I don't need your help with the rental. If you would just please tell Troy what I said about contacting me as soon as possible, maybe point out I'm in a delicate financial situation at the moment and—"

"This is perfect," he said, sliding the new glass door over the tub back and forth. "I don't understand what else you have to do. Why not get somebody in here right now?"

"I need a door put in. This bathroom is right next to my kitchen. They'll need their privacy."

He frowned, wiggled past her—close enough for her to notice he smelled like shampoo and men's cologne—and looked out into the hallway. "It's miles from the kitchen."

"I hope your hiking guides are more accurate," she said. "It's precisely eleven feet."

"And your bedroom is at the opposite end of the house, right?"

She nodded. What else could she do, push him out the front door? He was too big. She'd have to trick him somehow. Food? She'd found men surprisingly easy to lure around with aromatic snacks. Perhaps she could order a pizza and have them leave it on the front step.

He put his hands on his hips and smiled. "This is excellent. And the street parking isn't too bad up here, is it? And your driveway is big enough for a second car. BART is a short drive, the park is right there, it's close but not too close to the rest of the city, a great view…"

His positive description of her house made her forget for a second about kicking him out. "I was going to put all that in the listing. I also just had the floors refinished. Aren't they nice?"

"Very nice. Original?"

"Yes," she said proudly. "They were under this nasty carpeting you'd have to see to believe. My poor grandmother had cats, and as she got older, she had problems… Anyway, it's all been redone."

"So why wait? It's nicer than most of the other places out there. Hotels cost a fortune, and housing is scarce."

"I can't have strangers in here without a door between me and them. That's just how it is."

He looked at her, the front door, the hallway, then nodded. "Right, that's reasonable." He rubbed his beard. "In the meantime though, you could live without one. If you knew the person."

Numbers were her specialty, but she wasn't a complete

idiot about people either. She eyed him warily. "What are you suggesting?"

"I need a place for three months. Six at the most. I'll pay up front."

Although her practical, calculating heart warmed at *pay up front*, she didn't want to live with anyone she couldn't escape from with a lockable door.

"I'll pay twice whatever you were thinking," he added.

"But why? Why would you want to live here?"

"I'm writing a book. Or I'm supposed to be. I moved in with my mother and grandfather thinking it would torture me into getting the fucker—sorry, the manuscript—finished. I told myself I had to live there until it was done. That was a month ago, and I've written, let's see, nothing. Not a damn word."

"So get an apartment."

"I was thinking about it," he said. "But I don't want a long lease."

"Write in your tent, then. Close to the inspiration."

"Where do you think I just was? I had a solar generator and told myself I'd starve or finish." He rubbed his stomach. "I did neither. My campsite was just close enough to a Jack in the Box that I could hike out, drive down for a burger, and get back just in time to crawl into my sleeping bag."

"Maybe you don't want to write the book."

"You think?" His eyes twinkled.

"So why do it?" she asked.

He stared back at her. "That's a reasonable question. I can't explain it if you don't already understand."

"Fine. You're a special snowflake. I'm only an accountant."

"Do you like your job? Love what you do?"

She lifted her chin. "Yes, I do, actually."

"So do I."

"But you don't," she said. "According to you."

"Lately it's been a struggle, but I just have to push through it." He pointed at the entrance to the front room. "There. I can do it in that room. I can feel it."

Jane wasn't the touchy-feely, creative type and was skeptical of people who were. "How do you know you're not just engaging in another elaborate delaying tactic?"

His gaze fixed on hers. "That is an excellent question. I don't know. But I have to try."

Every instinct in Jane's body was shouting *no*. Something about him made her nervous. What if he couldn't write here either and took off next week? What if he used his family ties to her job to pressure her for free meals, annoying conversations, no-strings sexual pleasure?

*Would that really be so bad?* a tiny voice asked in a corner of her brain. Well, not her brain.

She swatted those thoughts away. Jane was practical above all else.

She turned away from him to collect her thoughts. Her career was more important to her than anything except family. To make partner, she'd need a lot more money in the bank than she had at the moment. Just a few more years climbing the same mountain she'd been climbing and her plans would be in reach.

And she had a foothold at Whitman. The firm was small enough that she hadn't needed to specialize too soon. Of course, tax season was crazy, and she had to deal with Nicole, but summer wasn't bad.

If she did have to find a new job, having a solid pile of cash in the bank would make the process less stressful.

Either way, having a tenant move in now, paying up front, would give her breathing room. She wouldn't have to change her plans if she got fired. Grant would be helping her meet her long-term goals. And what could be more important than that?

She turned. "All right. But don't be offended when I have the door put in."

"I'm never offended," he said. "Can I move in tomorrow?"

5

Some people found comfort in foods other than cheese. Jane didn't understand those people. If she ever went vegan, she'd have to make an exception for cheese. But then what would be the point? People would see her eating cheese and think her whole life was a lie. Which it would be, because she really, really loved cheese and would never give it up. Cream cheese in particular. She bought the big blocks at Costco and hauled them home in her minivan. By spoon or by knife, plain or mounded on a cracker, the creamy goodness made its way into her mouth.

Especially when she was stressed.

As she listened to Grant hauling in another box from his SUV out front, Jane peeled open a fresh tub—she switched to whipped cream cheese like a cigar smoker switching to vaping —and thrust the spoon into its beautifully smooth-yet-swirly surface.

She was trying to wipe out the memory of how she'd thought he was the gardener. When she'd backed up into him, she'd seen the dirt and the beard and the flannel, completely missing the high-tech GPS watch on his wrist. Not to mention the strong resemblance to his brother. The gray eyes were the same color, the same shape. The calm, laid-back expression was his alone, however.

Shadow kept prowling back and forth between the kitchen and the front door, watching the intruder for signs of danger, food, or lap opportunities.

Jane scraped the surface of the cream cheese, watching it mound like snow on her spoon. She would forgive herself for being distracted that day. She had just rammed into the man at her employer's party. Financial matters affected her more deeply than other people.

"Jane?"

She pulled the spoon out of her mouth and stood up just as Grant peeked his head around the doorway.

She gulped the mass of cream cheese like a rattlesnake with a chicken egg. "Yes?"

"Sorry to bother you."

"It's all right," she said, making another mental note to install a door.

Grant smiled faintly, creasing laugh lines at the corners of his eyes. For the first time, she noticed how deep the lines were, as if he spent a lot of time laughing. A vivid image popped into her head of him laughing as he jumped naked into a mountain stream.

Oh God. Not again.

"I was wondering if you could help me," he said.

She walked over, glad he wasn't, in fact, naked but instead wearing an outfit like the one he'd been wearing when they'd met: stained button-down shirt, faded khakis, dusty boots. "Of course. What do you need?"

With a frown, he glanced down at her body. "I was going to ask you to help me carry something."

Years of diligent trips to the gym had given her strength

she was proud of. She'd never be thin, but she could kick ass. Or at least kick the empty air during cardio classes, which was a lot harder than it looked. "Sure," she said, rubbing her hands together. "Is it outside?"

"Are you sure?" He rubbed his chin, casting a skeptical gaze over her again.

"Of course. Just because I'm a woman doesn't mean—"

"It's not that. I knew you were a woman before I— Well, obviously I did. It's your clothes."

"What's wrong with my clothes?" She wasn't wearing anything unusual.

"Nothing. That's the problem," he said. "They're pretty."

Just like that, she felt her face set on fire. "Thanks," she said, unable to stop herself from grinning like an idiot for a second. "But they're nothing special." She'd always liked to dress up a little more than was necessary. Ironed jeans just looked so much better than wrinkled ones, especially if you used a little starch. And why wear a cheap, see-through, clingy T-shirt when a nice button-down top was so much more comfortable and flattering? It didn't have to be tailored, but she did like fabric that held its shape.

"The TV's dusty. You'll get dirty," he said.

She was halfway down the hall to go out to his SUV when she realized what he'd said. She turned. "You brought a TV?"

"Is that a problem?"

"Don't you spend most of your time backpacking in the wilderness?" she asked.

"If I can," he said. "Why?"

"I just— I thought—" With Grizzly Adams moving in, she'd thought she was off the hook about buying expensive electronics. "I'm sorry. I should've bought one. I didn't think you'd use it."

"Why not?"

"Aren't you like Grizzly Adams?" she asked because, honestly, wasn't that exactly what he was like?

"No." His laugh lines were nowhere to be seen as he turned and walked to the front door. "The TV's in the Rover."

She jogged after him, regretting her joke that wasn't really a joke, which only made it worse. "Sorry. I shouldn't have said that." What had come over her?

He stood at the back of the SUV, the hatch hanging over his head. Other than a pair of bright yellow hiking sandals and a wrinkled tarp, only a large rectangular box remained inside. One end jutted out the back several inches. It was a very large TV. "It's not your fault. I'll kick Troy's ass later."

"No, please. This isn't Troy's fault. He never called you Grizzly Adams." Not even noon yet and she was already tempting fate with her boss.

"He's definitely called me Grizzly Adams," Grant said. "But maybe not to you."

"Definitely not to me. Please believe me."

"You came up with it all by yourself?" Leaning against the box, he crossed his arms over his chest and regarded her under a raised eyebrow.

Now what could she say? Either she got in trouble with her (she hoped he continued to be) employer or with her tenant.

Not a fair contest.

"I did," she said. "Because of the flannel and the beard and the living-in-the-woods thing."

"I hardly ever wear flannel," he said. "And half the men on this block probably have a beard."

Given the current fashion for facial hair, she thought he might be underestimating. "You're right. I apologize. Let's get the TV inside."

With a grunt, he turned away and slid the box out the rest

of the way, taking the far end for himself. Only as she lifted her end did she notice the box had never been opened. She herself kept the original packaging for most of her valuable electronics for moves just like this one, but this TV was brand new.

"Did you get this at the store?" she asked.

"No, I made it out of bark and deer pellets." He moved past her until he was the one in front, walking backward up the path to the house.

"You're going to be difficult about the Grizzly Adams thing, aren't you?"

"It might come up now and again."

"Watch your step," she said. "They aren't completely even."

His eyes met hers. He flashed a one-sided grin. "Thanks."

"I don't have cable."

"Dish?"

"No."

"Shit, really?"

"Sorry," she said.

"Mind if I set it up? I'll pay all the fees and costs and whatever."

"You're only going to be here a few months," she said, although he'd paid her for six. And twice the amount she'd stated. "Aren't you used to living without it?"

He walked into the house, maneuvering through doorways, and carried his end over to the only empty space in the room—where the desk used to be. They set it down at the same time, straightened, and stared at each other.

"If you have some kind of moral problem with me watching TV," he said, "maybe we should rethink this arrangement."

"I don't have—" She wiped her hands together. The box, new or not, had been dusty, just as he'd warned. "Watch whatever you want. But if you set up cable or a dish, don't get me locked into a long-term contract or anything. I'm on a budget. Try streaming over the internet like I do. The Wi-Fi password is in the little binder on the dresser." She'd filled it with all kinds of useful information, even street-cleaning days, when she'd been anticipating Airbnb guests.

"Sports are on cable. The Whitmans don't pay you enough to cover cable?"

"Don't bring your brother into this."

"I'm not." He began opening the box. "I was bringing my grandfather into this. The old cheapskate."

"The firm pays me plenty." Again, she hoped they would continue to do so. "I'd love a raise, of course, but I'm very happy there." She pointed at him. "Very. Happy."

"But you'd love a raise."

"Maybe we *should* rethink this arrangement," she said grimly.

He burst out laughing. "Are you kidding? I haven't had this much fun in months." Still chuckling, he pulled out a block of foam packaging, then caressed the shiny black plastic of his consumer electronic device. "Maybe we should agree to keep everything between us. Not a word to my brothers."

"I only know one of your brothers, and I never talk to Troy about anything except work."

"That's really sad. Never?"

"Why is it sad?"

"Troy's pretty cool. You should talk to him sometime."

"You were just saying *not* to talk to him."

"About *me*. But you should talk to him about England. He's really into English shit."

"Like Miss Marple?"

He gave her a withering look. "Like William the Conqueror and Vikings and Saxons and what have you," he said. "Caught the virus from my grandfather. Didn't you see the suits of armor at the house?"

"I was too busy getting fired."

Grant frowned. "Hopefully that'll get cleared up."

"Hopefully," she said feelingly. "I think we'd better stick to work talk."

"Suit yourself. Just don't talk about me," he said.

"Of course not," she said. Getting personal would only make her job situation more complicated.

"Absolutely. I'm glad we're on the same page. So when Troy corners you near the watercooler and asks how my book's going, you're not going to say a word."

"Unless my job gets reinstated, I won't be anywhere near the watercooler."

"Assuming it does."

"Then I'll be too busy working to chat at the watercooler with anyone," she said. "How would I know how it's going anyway?"

"You might see clues."

"Clues?"

He licked his lips, looking around the room. "Maybe we don't have to worry about that. I have a good feeling about this room. I'm going to be a writing machine."

"I noticed you took out the desk. Where did you put it, by the way?"

"It's under the bed. I took out the screws and the dowels. They're around here somewhere."

She stifled a groan. Particleboard furniture never reassembled well. "Before you flatten any of the other furnishings, will you let me know? I can move things to other rooms in the house."

"Just kidding about the desk. It's in the garage."

"Why did you lie?"

"I don't know." He ran a hand through his hair. "Something about you makes me want to ruffle your feathers."

"Yeah, I get that a lot."

"Maybe it's because you're so…"

She crossed her arms over her chest and waited.

"Not Mary Poppins," he continued, "but someone like that. Put together. Anal. Perfect."

"You're still hurting about the Grizzly Adams thing."

"Maybe a little," he admitted.

6

*G*rant waited until he heard her footsteps at the other end of the house before letting out his breath.

What was he doing? Not only was she not his type, she was a Whitman employee and his temporary land-lord. And Troy would kill him. He was already annoyed.

*Told you to TALK to her, not MOVE IN with her*, Troy had texted an hour earlier, adding a screaming-guy emoticon and several totally extraneous exclamation marks.

*Paid up front. Covers her mortgage and buys some time to wait for you to grow a pair.*

Radio silence after that. Grant took that as tacit agreement that his plan was a good one. For everybody.

He looked at his laptop bag, wedged between the bed and a case of trail mix. It had been three days since he'd even glanced at his email. When he finally sat down and checked in with his editor and agent, the reunion wouldn't be pretty.

Everything he did other than writing was an act of desperate, pathetic procrastination.

And that included a clean-cut babe with warm brown eyes. In fact, she was at the top of the list. It was a long list that included sports, politics, literature, technology, current events, friendship, family, exercise, sleep, eating, and breathing.

He had to write. All day, all the time, until it was done. His grandfather was just waiting to see him fail. Just as his father had failed, according to the old man.

Not according to Grant. His dad had lived life on his own terms, a creative, loving life, and Grant wanted nothing more than to be just like him. Except for the part about dying in the prime of life in a car accident. He could do without that.

After he'd gone outside to lock up the Rover, he settled on the bed with his laptop, a bag of trail mix from the case, and a bottle of water he'd filled from the filtered water pitcher Jane had provided. The house was quiet, his room lit by the evening sun. Not very optimistically, he began to write.

And two hours later, he'd more than doubled the pages in his manuscript.

"Holy shit," he said aloud, gaping at the word-count tally on his screen. The chapter that had bogged him down for months was now done. He wrote creative nonfiction, so it wasn't just a matter of describing the road to the trailhead, the campsites, the geography. Other hikers, store clerks, park rangers, hunters, locals, and even friends populated his stories. Some chapters were told from a shy black bear's point of view. Some were from his father's. Some were even his own.

If he hadn't been born into a wealthy family, it wouldn't have been possible to create the life he had, and he was always reminding himself how lucky he was. Although he lived off his writing—and teaching writing—pure luck had made that first book such a best seller. He'd only been able to take the time to write it because of the money his father had given him.

Not his grandfather. He'd refused to take money from the man who'd disinherited his own son just because he hadn't joined the family firm. Grant felt it was his responsibility not to go back to his grandfather and grovel for cash, which would prove that his father had made a mistake forty years ago in carving out his own life. Grant's failure would reflect badly on his father's memory. And Grant couldn't live with himself if he let that happen.

But he was feeling pretty damn happy now. He couldn't stop staring at the word-count window on the screen. The room had grown dark around him, lit only by his laptop and the streetlights outside. He could hear footsteps on the other side of the house, music, talking, maybe a TV. Except she didn't have cable, so maybe she was watching a VHS tape from the late 1990s.

He'd set up cable or a satellite dish and pay a year in advance. They'd wire the whole house.

Smiling, he backed up his work in three places, put away his laptop, and stood up to stretch his stiff muscles. His stomach growled, reminding him for the millionth time of the futility of relying on peanuts and chocolate for dinner.

It was still early enough to go out. One thing he craved almost as much as a mattress when he was backpacking was Chinese food. The good kind in Oakland or Berkeley or San Francisco, the kind you just couldn't get in an hour's drive from most trailheads.

On impulse, he knocked on the wall outside the kitchen. "Jane?"

She was obviously awake. He'd offer to bring her something. Just out of courtesy, a thank-you for taking him.

She stepped into the hallway from the far end looking not like a woman in for the night, in her pajamas, but as if she were going to a tax audit—sharp-looking khakis and a tight black sweater that he appreciated as discreetly as he could. Her cat peeked out from behind her legs, its gold eyes gleaming in the hall light.

"Yes?" she asked. "Is everything all right?"

She was even wearing shoes.

To hell with it. He was in too good a mood to stick to protocol. "I'm going out for Chinese. Want to come? My treat."

Her eyes dropped to his midsection. Then lower. He wore cutoff sweatpants and a T-shirt that had fit him better when he was in high school. "Don't worry. There's no dress code," he said.

"Aren't you uncomfortable?"

"Aren't you?"

"No," she said.

"Me neither. Hungry?"

"I am, actually," she said.

"Mind being seen with a slob?"

She smiled. "No."

"Then you should come. This place has the best Mongolian beef I've ever tasted."

After a slight pause, she nodded. "Sounds fantastic. I'm game. Thanks for asking."

* * *

PERHAPS JANE DID MIND a little bit that her companion looked exactly like who he was: a man who frequently slept outside without access to running water. But the restaurant he drove them to in Oakland's Chinatown looked almost as rough from the outside as he did, framed with graffiti and wedged between an adult bookstore and a discount carpet emporium with rusty metal bars over the plate glass windows.

*Emporiums aren't what they used to be,* she thought, climbing out of the SUV and following Grant to the restaurant door.

As he was opening it for her, she was struck by an enormous yawn. Normally, she'd be in bed by now so she could get up at five and hit the gym before work, but the first night with a new tenant in the house—and no dividing door—had made her just uncomfortable enough to delay her transition to pajamas. Add a bad night's sleep the night before, and she was starting to fade.

"You're tired?" he asked.

"Didn't sleep well last night."

The thick, spicy aroma of Szechuan struck her in the face. The place was much nicer inside than out, with bamboo tables and brick-red walls dotted with modern paintings. You'd never know it was so close to an emporium.

Nevertheless, she yawned again, this time long enough to make her jaw crack.

Grant picked up a menu by the door and handed it to her. "We'll get it to go."

She couldn't hide her relief. "Are you sure? I'll be fine once we sit down."

"That's not what happens to me when I'm that tired. Getting off my feet only makes me sleepier."

He was right, but she'd agreed to come and didn't want to be rude. "You sure you don't mind?"

"I usually get it to go. Then I can order like a pig, and they'll think I'm providing for my large family at home." He flashed a grin.

*Nice guy.* She accepted the menu, picked out the spicy eggplant—as if oil-soaked vegetables would negate the cream cheese—and in a remarkably short amount of time, they were returning to the car, their arms heavy with takeout containers in two reusable bags Grant had brought with him. She shouldn't have been surprised he would be environmentally minded, but she was. Messy people didn't usually plan ahead in her experience.

Her stomach was looking forward to a cream-cheese-free dish, but she couldn't stop yawning. Three hours of sleep used to last longer. Another reminder of her advancing years. Thirty was just the beginning of the Big Slide into Death.

She sighed. She often got morbid when she was tired.

When they were halfway home on Park Boulevard, her cell phone rang. A reluctant glance—it wasn't common, but corporate accounting emergencies did occur occasionally— told her it was only her sister Billie.

"Are you all right?" Jane asked without preamble. Billie was usually the texting type.

"Oh Jane! I have huge news!"

Jane assumed she knew what that news would be. Or at least that it would involve Ian Cooper, Jane's own former high school boyfriend and now future brother-in-law. He and Billie had announced their engagement a month ago.

"You've picked a spot for the wedding," Jane said.

Billie laughed. "No, that would be much too practical. We keep putting it off."

If Jane were engaged, she'd love to look at wedding desti-nations. She'd love all of it—the dress, the flowers, the food, the music. "Would you like me to find you guys a place?"

There was silence over the phone. No matter how often Jane said it, people didn't believe she was cool with her child-hood ex getting hitched to her sister. But she and Ian had only been kids when they'd dated, and she was a different person now. Much smarter, for instance.

"No, Ian hired a planner. She's going to do all the work for us. But thanks."

Ian was a fabulously wealthy investment fund manager. He

could afford to hire an army of planners to put on the party of the century. "So what's your news?" Jane asked.

"Don't you want to guess?"

"I already guessed."

"Guess again," Billie said.

Little sisters could be annoying, but because Jane loved her so much, she played along. "You found a house." Billie and Ian were shopping for a place up in the hills, not far from Jane. Neither one of them wanted to commute from the suburbs or exurbs—life on the freeway didn't appeal to either of them, and they had jobs and school in the East Bay.

"No!" Billie exclaimed with glee. "Excellent guess. Yet another thing that would've been much, much more practical than reality."

"Then what? And please don't make me guess again. I'm exhausted."

"I know it's late for you. Actually, I thought you might be in bed. But you sound like you're in the car."

"I'm in the car." Jane glanced at Grant, who was pretending not to listen. She wouldn't tell her sister who she was with or what she was doing. Billie might think there was something intriguing about her getting takeout with her tenant, a man whose last name was the same as the company where she worked. It had been three months since Jane had broken up with her last boyfriend, and her sister seemed to think it was time she dated again. But Jane was finally, happily single and refused to screw it up.

"I should call you back," Billie said. "I don't want to cause an accident."

Jane would've been alarmed if her sister didn't sound so happy. "I'll pull over. There. I've pulled over. What is it?"

"You don't sound like you pulled over."

"It's really windy," Jane said.

"It *is* windy. Do you think we'll have another El Niño year?"

"*Billie...*"

"OK, OK. I guess I'm nervous. You can be scary—"

"Stop saying that or I'll kill you."

"See? That's—ouch!" Billie's voice moved away from the phone. "Why'd you do that?"

Jane heard a man's voice, low and calm. Ian was with her.

"He's probably telling you to hurry it up," Jane said.

"He is. I'll let him— No, he won't take the phone. OK, here goes." Billie paused. "I'm pregnant!"

7

*J*ane's breathing stopped. Her mind blanked. But while the rest of her organs locked up, her heart took off galloping like a spooked racehorse.

"Jane?" Billie asked.

She still couldn't breathe. Billie? A mother?

It was all wrong. It was too soon. It wasn't what she'd planned.

"You don't even have a wedding date yet," Jane finally managed to say.

"Good thing, because we'd have to move it up. Or out. Think of the cute little outfit we could put the baby in. I could carry it like a bouquet."

"A baby isn't an 'it.' It's—I mean, *he* or *she* is a *he* or *she*."

"It's so funny that's your objection," Billie said, "and not that we totally have to get married before it's born. And I'm calling it an it because I don't want to be narrow-minded and pigeonhole the poor thing before it's even breathing."

Speaking of breathing, Jane was still struggling with it. She was going to be an aunt? Her mother was going to be a grand-mother? Her father a grandfather?

It shouldn't have shocked her. Although younger than Jane, Billie was in her late twenties, engaged, and she'd always been great with kids, volunteering with a community homework club at the library after work, attending all their half-siblings' birthday parties and graduations…

"Are you still there?" Billie asked. "I'm sorry. I should've told you in person. I was going to, but I couldn't wait. I'm so sorry."

Jane cleared her throat. "No, it was just a backup on the freeway. I'm fine."

"I thought you'd pulled over."

"Wow, Billie." Jane's voice cracked. "Congratulations. How do you feel? Are you OK? Any nausea, fatigue—"

"No, nothing. I'm fine, totally fine. Great."

Jane relaxed. She could never stand the idea of Billie in pain. "When is— How far— Do you have a date yet?"

"Not yet. I just found out tonight. Haven't even been to the doctor yet."

"But you're sure?"

"I'm sure. I never miss a period. I bought two kits, and then Ian went out and got four more. All positive." Billie let out a squeal. "I can't believe it!"

Imagining serious, thoughtful Ian running out to the store and buying an armful of pregnancy tests made Jane smile. He must be very proud of himself.

But then Jane frowned. Had he rushed Billie into this? "What about school? What about your career? The house-hunting, the wedding—"

Billie laughed. "Yeah, it's crazy. I messed everything up again. I never seem to be able to do what I'm supposed to do, do I?"

"Takes two to tango," Jane said.

"And a broken condom and antibiotics," Billie said. "So more like four. Takes four to tango."

Jane was cool with Ian and Billie being in love with each other, but she didn't appreciate being forced to imagine the gory details. "Have you told Mom? Dad?" Their parents had each remarried and had more children. There were lots of people who were going to be excited about a new generation.

"Not yet," Billie said. "You're the first."

That touched Jane so much that tears formed in her eyes. Blinking them away, she swallowed hard and said, "You might want to wait a few weeks, make sure…"

"I know, that's what Ian said. But I don't know if I can. The longest I think I can last is a week. Maybe two."

"Good luck with that." Jane tried not to laugh. Billie tended to act on impulse. "Good luck with everything. Thank you. For telling me. And tell Ian…" She trailed off.

"He knows. I know. You love us both and can't wait to meet it."

"It's *not* an 'it,'" Jane said.

Billie laughed. "You said it too. Well, I should go. I'm going to eat for three in case it's twins. Starting right now. I thought pregnant people got nauseous, but I'm as hungry as ever. Bye!"

"Bye." Jane lowered the phone to her lap and stared at it. Her world was rocking. There had been so much upheaval this year. Her ex cheating on her, her grandmother dying, Billie and Ian getting engaged, taking on a mortgage for her own house—it was so much.

"Are you all right?" Grant asked.

"My sister's pregnant."

"Sorry."

"Why are you sorry? It's wonderful to bring life into the world, isn't it?"

Grant signaled and turned onto a side street. "I don't know. Is it?"

"Of course it is. Billie will be a great mother."

"All right."

"What do you mean? Don't you believe me?"

"Look, it's none of my business."

"That's right, it isn't," she said.

The lights of oncoming traffic lit up his smile. "Help me navigate? I forgot to turn on the GPS. I'm useless without it."

Regretting her rudeness, she forced herself to sound more cheerful as she instructed him through the twists and turns to the house.

"I'm sorry I snapped at you," she said as he pulled up to the curb. "You can park in the driveway. There's room for two cars."

"This is fine," he said. "I don't want to block the garage."

"There's nothing in there. It's totally empty." She'd thought about renting it out too, but there wasn't a parking shortage up here, so far from apartment buildings, jobs, restaurants, retail, and freeways. "You can park inside it if you'd like." She was trying to make up for taking out her bad mood on him.

But why should she be in a bad mood? She was going to be an aunt. Billie would be a fantastic mother. Everyone would be ecstatic for her and Ian.

Even more ecstatic than they were already.

Was she jealous?

"I don't need to park it inside." Grant opened the car door. "It's used to being abused by the elements."

"Just like you, right?" She would be cheerful if it killed her. She climbed out onto the sidewalk.

"Exactly."

As they walked up to the house, Grant held out one of the bags. "Thanks for your company. I hope you like the food."

"I'm sure I—"

He put a hand on her shoulder. Something about his posture, hard and alert, made her freeze in alarm.

"What?" she asked.

"Somebody's there," he said, squinting into the shadows. The bulb over her front door had gone out, and the new one she'd bought hadn't fit inside the fixture, so it was dark.

Great. One poor retail decision was going to lead to their brutal deaths.

Again the death. She really needed to get more sleep.

"Jane?" The violent killer's voice drifted down the steps through the darkness. And his voice was familiar.

"Kill me now," Jane muttered. But there would be no such release with this visitor.

"I'd rather not," Grant replied, just as softly. "Although prison might be a good place to write a book."

"Jane, is that you?" the man asked again.

"What are you doing here, Andrew?" Then to Grant, she added, "My ex. Very, very ex."

Andrew crept down the steps as stealthily as if he were actually trying to do her harm.

A few months ago, he'd harmed her plenty by sleeping with their dentist. Not surprisingly, Jane had found somebody else to clean her teeth. She didn't know if Andrew had. He probably found it weird to have his girlfriend drilling into an orifice. Now he'd know what it felt like to sleep with him.

"Hello," Andrew said, holding out a hand to Grant. "I'm Andrew Puckett."

Grant paused before taking it. "Grant."

Jane was grateful Grant had left off his last name, which Andrew would've instantly linked to the firm where she worked. The last thing she wanted was her ex thinking she was having some kind of relationship that involved her career. He'd once admitted to the nasty, ignorant belief that women could get ahead in business more easily than men because they could sleep their way to the top. It had been the worst thing he'd ever said out loud, not long before he'd cheated on her, and it was one reason she was so quick to move on and never look back.

"Are you two dating?" Andrew asked in that cold, unemotional tone of his that she'd first mistaken for intelligence before realizing it was because his heart was a charcoal briquette.

Although she wanted to tell him to fuck off, she didn't want Grant to get drawn into anything awkward. "He's renting a room," she said. "Go on in, Grant. You don't have to wait outside with me."

"Why would he?" Andrew stepped aside, crossing his arms over his chest.

Her taste in men had always been flawed. She knew this. When a person focused on school and work at the expense of social relationships of any kind, that person made mistakes. Andrew, as only her third boyfriend ever, was a rookie's mistake. The problem was that the mistake had turned her off dating altogether for the indefinite future. Developing better skills in the romance area just wasn't worth the risk.

"You know me," Grant said. "I prefer the outdoors." He stayed at her side.

Nice of him. "I'm waiting to hear why you're here," Jane told Andrew.

"It really would be better if we could talk alone," Andrew said.

"Then you should've used the phone," Jane said.

"You changed your number."

So she had. "And why do you think that might be, genius?"

"I sense you're still angry."

"I sense you're still a sociopath."

Andrew shot an annoyed glance at Grant before moving closer to her. "I've been talking to somebody."

"Welcome to the human race. Most people don't have to make an announcement about basic social contact."

"I mean a professional," Andrew said tightly. "I'm learning a lot about myself."

"And?"

He blinked. "And I can share it with you."

"I don't want you to share it with me," she said. "I know more than enough about you already."

After a pause—was he doing meditative breathing exercises?—he said, "My therapist said you might react that way at first. I'm prepared to accept it. I forgive you."

"You forgive *me*?"

"For pushing me away. For not giving me a chance. I'm learning to understand and not let it bother me."

All her life, Jane had been told she was the calm, cerebral type. But at that moment, she was experiencing the overwhelming urge to dig her thumbs into Andrew's eyeballs like the hero in a violent action movie. Normally she couldn't stand the sight of blood, but in this case she'd find a way to work through it. Maybe the loud screaming she'd be doing as his fluids spurted over her hands and trailed down her forearms would give her strength.

Grant's deep voice made both of them look at him. "Sorry to interrupt, but Jane's dinner is getting cold." He held up one of his reusable bags. "And so's mine."

It gave her just the break she needed to retract her thumbs into her fists, stride past Andrew, and unlock the front door without once cursing or crying or even rolling her eyes. She was an ice queen. She would let it go. Without singing the song.

"Come on in, Grant," she said. "I'll bring you another set of plates. I forgot to put them in your suite earlier."

Grant was thankfully right at her side, following her and lingering just enough to block the doorway in case Andrew tried to rush in.

But Andrew wasn't the rushing type. He stayed where he was on the sidewalk, staring up at them with a sour scowl on his face, as if he'd done what he was told, it hadn't worked, and somebody was going to hear about it.

Not her. Oh, how could she have wasted so many days of her life with that toad?

"How could you have dated that guy?" Grant asked. "Not to be rude, but…"

"Excuse me, I've had a long day. Good night." She went through the door and left him there with his ecologically aware bag filled with lukewarm Chinese food that would never recover from the delay in eating it.

8

olding the bags of takeout just inside the front door, Grant watched Jane stride away and disappear at the far end of the hallway.

"Jane," he called out as he kicked off his shoes. "I can't eat this all by myself."

After a pause, her voice returned, "Sure you can."

He looked into his room, then back down the hall. The cat sprawled halfway between them, licking herself.

To hell with it. There wasn't a door yet. "I'm putting yours in the kitchen. And I'm leaving it on the table, so you better come get it." It took him a few seconds to find the kitchen light switch, an old-fashioned one that made a snapping sound. He reached into the bags, found her containers, and arranged them on the table.

Her voice grew louder. "Put it in the fridge— No, just leave it, I don't want you coming into my—" She cut off. A moment later she appeared in the doorway to the kitchen, her cheeks flushed and eyes bright. "Please don't come into my side of the house."

"It would be a crime to waste Szechuan eggplant this good."

"You could've eaten it yourself."

"Eggplant gives me loose stools," he said.

She pressed her lips together, and he wondered if she was truly angry or maybe, just maybe, trying not to laugh. "I did not need to know that."

"Apparently you did." He turned to the cabinets. "Where are the plates?"

She walked over and swatted him between the shoulder blades. "I can get my own plate."

"Did you just hit me?"

"I told you, I need my space. You're invading it in a big way, and I need it now more than ever."

He didn't really want to know about her sister or her ex-boyfriend, because that would be too personal and he had a book to write, but he hated seeing anyone suffer alone. And she wouldn't get her food. Thinking about that would make it impossible for him to sleep or get another writing session done.

"I was looking for a plate for myself," he said. "You were going to get me—"

"Oh, right, so I was. Sorry." She reached past him and took a few dishes out of the cabinet. "You can keep these in your kitchenette when you're done. I put dish soap in the cabinet beneath the microwave."

He took the dishes from her, three heavy plates in bright primary colors. "Are you going to eat? It really isn't as good as leftovers."

She gave him a pained look, glancing at the door, still unhappy with him being there. "I'll enjoy it more tomorrow. Thank you, Grant."

Convinced now that he'd done his best, he nodded and left

the kitchen with the plates and the remaining bag of takeout. "Sorry to bug you."

After a moment, she followed him into the hall. "I'm sorry too."

"For what?"

"I'll have the door put in. Then we won't have any misunderstandings."

"I understood you," he said. "I just didn't agree you should waste good Chinese food, no matter how bad your life is."

"My life isn't bad."

He cleared his throat. In the day and a half he'd known her, she'd lost her job, been forced to rush a tenant into her home, and found her creepy, stalkerish ex-boyfriend lurking at her front door.

And she was jealous about her sister being pregnant. If he were wrong about that, he'd lick the seat of a campground pit toilet.

"Let me know if my check doesn't clear," he said with a smile and strode to his own room.

Just as he was closing the door, he heard her say, "It better. It's paying for that door."

JANE WOKE up Monday morning at her usual time, climbed out from the covers, and made the bed as she always did—replacing the midnight-blue velvet throw pillows that spent the night on the chair next to the bed and smoothing out the folded faux-fur blanket at the foot—and went into the bathroom to complete her full routine of self-care.

Shampoo, shaving, moisturizing, clipping and buffing, brushing and drying. The only step she skipped on her days off was foundation and eye makeup. After breakfast, she'd put on lipstick or gloss, and if she went out, she'd add a few quick swipes of mascara.

At six forty-five, she was ready for the day. If it were January instead of July, it would still be dark. Then again, if it were January, she'd still have a job to go to and being up would be necessary.

She walked to the kitchen with Shadow mewling at her heels for her breakfast.

What was she going to do today? It was too early to call Nicole or Troy, and she didn't go to the gym on Mondays. She didn't want to call her brother-in-law-to-be about installing a door because…

Because he was going to be a dad. With her sister.

She wasn't ready to see them just yet, all happy and stupid with their unplanned joy.

She filled Shadow's bowl and watched her dig in. She always attacked her food like a stray dog, not the pampered kitty she was. She smiled down at her, enjoying the show she didn't usually have time to watch.

Now would be the perfect time to make a full breakfast, not just a quick spoonful of cream cheese and a travel mug of coffee. That would take some time, and she could make extra, share it with Grant—

Only if he barged in and asked for some, which he probably would. She'd make a plate and put it aside as thanks for the dinner last night. It had been excellent. And it had not, knock on wood, given her the runs.

Shaking her head, she got out the flour container and other ingredients, laughing silently. The runs. Very funny. She was pretty sure he'd been joking about that to cheer her up.

Making waffle batter was her specialty, and she could get it together without even consulting a recipe. Soon the first waffle was steaming away in the waffle iron and she was lifting her first cup of coffee to her lips.

Before she tasted it, her phone chirped with a text message from her mother.

*Don't ruin this for Billie*, Mom wrote.

To Billie, Jane was the perfect, brilliant older sister who achieved great things and could do no wrong. But to their mother, Jane was the most insensitive, stubborn, and generally difficult of all her children.

*Ruin what?* Jane texted back.

*If you can't be happy, find an excuse for the party.*

Jane sighed. *What party?*

*I'm sending invitations this week*, her mother wrote. *If you can't find a date, I think you should send your regrets. Out of love.*

Jane knew her mother didn't mean to be cruel. In fact, she wasn't being mean at all. They both knew Billie was the sweet, emotional one in the family, who would be crushed if Jane couldn't be happy for her. Jane could be happy for her—she would—but she understood why her mom would worry.

But Jane wasn't going to make it easy for her mother to treat her callously, not when she had real problems of her own —even if her skin was thick enough to handle it.

*What party?* Jane repeated. *Which event shall we be celebrating?*

*Oh, Jane!* Her mother texted. It wasn't enthusiasm but a rebuke. *Ian is going to be a wonderful father.*

Jane flinched. Yeah, her high school ex probably would be a good dad. And he and Billie adored each other. The kid would be very lucky. That wasn't the issue.

Jane's shit life was the issue.

*So it's a baby shower?* Jane texted.

*If you can't show up with a smile, don't show up at all. Please, sweetheart.*

The endearment was a nice touch. *Sweet. Heart.* Her mom didn't associate Jane with either one.

*Wedding AND baby? Just need to know if I bring one gift or two,* Jane replied.

*Don't be stingy.*

Jane swore and set the phone on the counter. God damn it...

She unfurled a few choice curses—verbally, where her mother couldn't read them or screen-cap and send them to her friends as an example of how difficult her eldest daughter was.

And the dig about bringing a date...

"Fuck!" Jane shouted. Muttering more curses, she picked up the phone and stabbed in her reply.

*I will bring my new bf and many gifts. Looking forward to it. xoxoxo*

And then she turned off her phone, shoved it in her pocket, and noticed the waffle was smoking.

"Damn it, damn it." She pierced the burned waffle with a fork and flung it onto the counter.

"You're kind of like Gordon Ramsay," Grant said behind her.

"Fuck." She poured fresh batter into the iron and banged it shut. "What the hell are you doing in here again?"

"I'm sorry. I was just bringing you the paper." He held it out.

"You just wanted to see what I was swearing about this time."

"I figured it was because of whatever was on fire."

"It wasn't on fire," she said.

"Smoking, then."

She paused, then went over and took the paper from him. Andrew had mocked her for having a subscription to a physical paper, but her coffee tasted better with it. And she used the sports section to line the compost bucket. "Maybe it was smoking a little." She pointed at the caramel-colored waffle. "Want it? It probably tastes OK."

"Will I get a refund for part of my rent if I eat it and survive?"

"Ooh, you're asking for it."

"Actually, no. I'd rather not have it." He rubbed his jaw, scratched his beard. "Do you always get up this early, by the way?"

"Yes."

He nodded. Yawned. "Thought so." He turned, displaying his bare lower back under the gap between his pink T-shirt and black-and-white polka-dot pajama pants. Her gaze fixed on the low-slung waistband, willing it lower, just a little. He had a nice butt. Backpacking for months had done obvious miracles for the glutes.

But the man wore pink. And knitted. It hadn't occurred to her before that he might be gay, but maybe she was being obtuse, blinded by her own problems and, she had to admit, appreciation of his perfect, well-muscled gluteus maximus.

"I have a favor to ask," she said, surprising herself.

He turned in the doorway. "Fine, I'll eat it if you really can't bear to throw it—"

"No, this is a big favor."

Eyebrow lifted, he eyed the waffle warily. "Bigger than eating that?"

"Much."

He shrugged. "You can ask. Can't guarantee anything."

"For this I *will* give you a refund on some of the rent. Say…" Her desperation went to war with her frugality. She had to make it tempting. "A month's worth."

"That's really not necessary—"

"Will you come with me to a family party?" she asked.

"Yours or mine?"

She smiled briefly. Either sounded pretty bad. "Mine."

"This has something to do with your sister?"

"Yes."

"Do we have to fly? I'd rather not fly," he said.

"God, no. It's just up in Sonoma County." But she hadn't received an invitation yet, had she? With Ian's millions, they could throw a party anywhere in the world. "At least I think so. Probably. My mom and her husband and kids live in Rohnert Park."

"Practically neighbors with my family," he said with a smile.

"Not quite. They have a three-bedroom split-level from the seventies on a quarter acre."

"Some of my grandfather's place was built in the seventies," he said. "And there are multiple levels."

This time she saw the iron light turn green, and she removed the waffle and set it on a plate with a generous helping of cream cheese and fresh strawberries. She added a fork and held it out to him. "Will you do it?"

He shrugged. "Sure. You don't have to give me any rent money back. I'm not that kind of boy."

"Maybe I should tell you all about my family and the, uh, happy couple before you decide."

He sawed a corner off the waffle and made a face. "No, no. Ignorance is bliss. I'd rather be oblivious and just have a good time."

"I told my mother you're my boyfriend," she said. "You or whomever I can get to go with me. She told me…" Jane decided not to elaborate. He didn't need to know her mother would rather she didn't show up at all if she didn't have a date.

Holding his plate in the doorway, chewing his food, Grant

watched her for a moment until he realized she wasn't going to say more. "Will we kiss a lot?" he asked, his mouth still full.

Oh God. What was she getting into? She knew he was joking, but…

"Depends," she said. "Are you gay?"

"You only kiss gay guys?"

She smiled, overwhelmed by the ridiculousness of it all. "I was just wondering."

"But you said 'depends.' Like it influenced how we would behave."

"I'm just— I'm sorry— This is crazy. The truth is, the groom and father-to-be is somebody I dated in high school, and everybody is afraid I'm going to be weird about it. If I have a man on my arm, they can relax and not watch me, wondering if—or hoping, let's be honest—I'll start weeping into my Champagne."

"If I'm straight, do you still want me as your date?"

"Yes."

"*Phew*. I'd love to come."

"Really?" she asked.

"I'm a writer on a deadline. I'm happy to have an excuse to blow it off for a day. I'll be doing you a favor, right?"

She sighed. "Afraid so. I don't have a stable of potential mates waiting by. And you met my latest ex. Imagine how he'd react if I invited him."

"I only met him once, and I think *I'd* have a reaction if you invited him." He jabbed his fork into a strawberry. "Good waffle. I accept all bribes in this format, just so you know."

"I'll remember that."

"When's the shindig?" he asked. "I hope you don't expect me to dress up. You've already seen me at my most formal."

"Don't know when it is yet, but I'm guessing next month, which would give my mother time to plan things but not too much time for her to wait for something she really wants," she said. "And it won't be formal. I'll probably wear a dress, but…"

"Why will you wear a dress?"

Jane bit her lip. She always wore a dress around Ian. Kind of a promise she'd made to herself long ago. "August up there is pretty hot. We'll probably be outside."

"Right," he said. "I've got a new pair of cargo shorts I can wear."

"You're really going to do this for me?"

"Free food, no Whitmans, are you kidding?"

"If you change your mind, could you let me know in time to make other arrangements?" she asked.

"I'm not going anywhere, Jane. I don't have a life. This is it."

She shook her head. "I can't imagine."

With a smile, he handed her the empty plate, not a crumb left on its slick surface. "Maybe you should try."

9

Grant came back from his morning hike in the regional park up the street—a huge network of trails through redwood and oak, ravines and hills—to find Troy walking out of Jane's house.

An odd, irrational wave of irritation spiked through him. What was he doing here?

Grant waited at the bottom of the driveway, arms crossed, as his brother approached. The extra seconds gave him time to realize it had to be about Jane's job at Whitman. His first crazy thought had been that Troy was here to question his decision to be Jane's date at a family event, a decision he was questioning himself.

Under any other circumstances, he wouldn't have had second thoughts. Why not enjoy the company of an attractive woman for a few hours with people he'd never see again? He spent more time alone than he should, even more than he preferred. As long as it wasn't a corporate thing, like the one at his grandfather's house over the weekend, he never refused a party. Other people were interesting, and it was good for him to socialize. So much time alone in the wilderness eroded his social skills.

But Jane wasn't just anybody. He'd pushed the Whitman connection out of his mind to justify enjoying the convenient living and working quarters and, maybe, her company.

"Good or bad news for Jane?" Grant asked Troy, who was wearing a corporate getup that made him look to his older brother as if he were a little boy dressed up like a grown-up for Halloween: black suit, gray tie, shiny shoes with no tread. It was a wonder he could make it up and down the minor slope of Jane's driveway without falling on his ass.

"Neither," Troy said. "Grandfather has been in bed all day. Rachelle said he had a rough night and needed to sleep."

"Did you talk to him yesterday?"

"I talked to Nicole, Jane's manager. I think I know why he fired her." Troy cracked his knuckles, a nervous habit he'd had since childhood. "It's a mess. A client wanted Jane to inaccurately portray several of his lucrative assets on certain official federal, state, and local documents, and she refused."

"Somebody wanted Jane to cook the books?"

"When she wouldn't, the client took his business elsewhere," Troy said. "Recently that client told Grandfather it was because of Jane."

Grant felt uneasy. His grandfather was a difficult man but surely an honest one.

"I'm sure the prick lied about the details," Troy continued. "When Grandfather's feeling up to it, I'll tell him everything I know."

"Why would Grandfather believe this guy?"

"Frank Bostock just happens to be the son of Bob Bostock, who died a few years ago. Bob was Whitman's first client back in the seventies." Troy paused, raising an eyebrow. "He was

Whitman's first client because he was Grandfather's best friend."

As soon as Troy had said Bostock, Grant had understood the problem. He remembered Bob Bostock. They'd met. His picture was next to his grandmother's in the living room. "I can see why this might be awkward."

"Given Grandfather's poor health, I thought it was better to wait until he's stronger before I tell him the son of his best friend grew up to be a lying, thieving dickwad."

"Yes," Grant said reluctantly. "I have to agree."

"I came by to tell Jane she could come into the office today since Grandfather won't be coming in any day this week, but she refused. Formal guarantee or nothing." Troy cracked his knuckles again. "She's absolutely right. If only he'd just retire. He still has the final word over too many things."

"You need to tell him that," Grant said.

"I can't tell him now. He's sick in bed."

"When he's feeling better."

Troy flexed his fingers and made a fist. "I'm not sure he'll ever be feeling well enough for that conversation."

"You can't fire Jane if the client pressured her to do something illegal. She could sue for unlawful termination. Or something." Grant didn't know squat about the law, but he wanted Troy to be on Jane's side.

"And now you're living in her house. The lawyers will love that little complication."

"It was entirely my idea. I didn't realize—"

"You knew I was in a bad spot already. Why did you make it worse?"

"I was trying to help her in a way you couldn't. To reduce some of the financial pressure on her. Buy everyone some time."

Troy shoved his hands in his pockets and looked over at

his car with a sigh. "Yeah, I know. I might even be glad you did. If I can't save her job, she'll land on her feet. Probably make more money somewhere else. People like her always do well."

"People like what?"

"You know. Tough, driven, type A workaholic, born for corporate life," Troy said. "Dad would've hated her."

"That's a shitty thing to say."

Troy looked at him in surprise. After a moment he said, "Yeah, it was. I shouldn't have said it. Jane's all right."

Grant swallowed, uncomfortably aware his pulse was elevated. Had he almost gotten into a fight with his brother over a woman he'd met the day before yesterday?

He thought of the way she had acted after backing up into his old Rover, how she kept trying to force him to accept her insurance information or money. "It can't be easy, trying to be perfect all the time," Grant said.

But his brother thought he was talking about him. "It isn't," Troy said, smiling. "Maybe I should chuck it all and join a band. Mom could tour with me. She's been talking about traveling. Ben and Justin are too busy to go. Something about having jobs."

"You should do it," Grant said. "Then Grandfather would be forced to admit you're running the show."

"When it falls apart without me?"

"Would it?"

"Yes," Troy said. "I couldn't do that. Jane's not the only employee I have to look out for."

Grant glanced at the house. He would rather be talking to her than Troy, as charming as his brother was generally agreed to be. But he wouldn't be talking to her if he did as she asked and stayed in his room, which is where he should be anyway because his word count for the day was way too low.

"I should get back to work," Grant said.

"Me too. Listen, forget what I said. I appreciate it that you're trying to help. It'll work out."

"I'm sure it will," Grant said. "If the bank forecloses on the house, I'll lend her a tent."

"You can take her on your next wilderness trip," Troy said, then burst out laughing. "Can you imagine? Jane?"

"Sure, why not?"

Troy continued to chuckle. "You just met her. You don't know what she's like."

Grant felt his pulse rising again. "What is she like?"

"The type to use hand sanitizer after she shakes hands with anyone." Troy shook his head. "No, before and after. And casual Fridays? Nope. No such thing."

"Being fastidious at work doesn't mean she wouldn't enjoy a change."

Troy's laughter died, his eyes widening with alarm. "Grant, you're not— This is awkward enough— Don't even think about—"

"Relax," Grant said, telling himself the same thing. "You know me, I like to get everyone out of their cars and cubicles for a walk in the woods."

Troy nodded but looked uneasy. "I should let you get back to that new book so you can do just that."

"Right. Thanks."

"How's it going, by the way? How many pages have you written since you got here?"

"Goodbye, Troy."

Troy laughed, patted him on the shoulder, and jogged to his hybrid Lexus, waving one last time before he got in and drove away.

Reluctantly, Grant turned and went back into the house. It would've been much easier if Jane had her job reinstated and could go away and spend her time there. He was finding her presence to be distracting.

Before going inside, he made a silent vow to stay away from her. For his sake and hers.

---

THE WEEK DRAGGED on without any formal resolution of Jane's job situation, but Troy called her personally every day and assured her he was working on it. He confirmed her suspicions that Mr. Whitman blamed her for losing the Bostock account but assured her he would explain to his grandfather what had happened.

She already knew what he didn't say: Mr. Whitman might not believe it. The Bostocks had been tight with the Whitmans.

"I'll have something actionable for you on Friday," he said on Wednesday afternoon. And then on Thursday, he asked if they could talk at four on Friday afternoon. Friday arrived, and he called at four-oh-six. And twenty seconds.

"Have you spoken to Mr. Whitman?" she asked as she picked up a sponge and began scrubbing the grime off the burners on her late grandmother's stove. Sentimental memories of Grammy's peanut butter cookies and turkey stuffing (not served together, thankfully) kept her from replacing the stove with a model from the current millennium.

"I haven't had a chance," Troy said slowly.

She closed her eyes and reminded herself how unpleasant it would be to start over at another job, possibly adding years to her path to partner.

Troy continued before she could reply with the calm professionalism she was proud of. "He's been ill. Rachelle—his caregiver—wants to get him to the hospital, but he's well enough to yell— Anyway, there hasn't been a good time."

Jane's irritation lessened. "I'm sorry, Troy. That's got to be hard on all of you."

"I hate to do this, but could you wait another week? I've talked to Nicole about redistributing your client workload a little so you won't be swamped when you get back. Assuming, you know…"

Great. By the time she went back, if ever, nobody would need her anymore. "Do I have a choice?"

Troy didn't reply.

"I like working at Whitman, Troy." Jane threw the abrasive sponge into the sink. "Enough to wait a little longer."

She heard Troy exhale on the other line. "That's great, Jane. I won't forget this."

His lasting gratitude was exactly what she was counting on. But perhaps she should formalize it a little. "Nicole has always given me excellent annual reviews."

"I know that. I was just reading them yesterday, actually."

"I've brought a lot of business to the firm, I get along with all kinds of people, I'm a power user with the new software, and I've always been flexible about travel," she continued.

Troy waited a second before he said, "Yes?"

"I'm overdue for a raise."

"All right," he said. "I'll see what I can do."

"And I'd really like to work parallel with Nicole instead of subordinate to her."

"A promotion?"

"Senior manager." Jane took a deep, silent breath.

"Again, I'll see what I can do."

She smiled. "Thank you, Troy. I do hope your grandfather is feeling better soon."

He hesitated again. "Thank you. I'll be in touch."

Jane hung up and hoped she hadn't sounded insincere about his grandfather. If he died, she'd be back at work the next day.

But she would never wish somebody dead for a job or anything else.

"Damn it," she muttered, scowling at her phone. Did he think she would be happy at the idea of his grandfather kicking the bucket?

She picked up the cleaning spray and squirted the burner again.

Should she call him back? What could she say that wouldn't sound insincere?

Similar thoughts spun around obsessively in her mind for the next hour until every burner and oven rack was sparkling and her hands were painfully raw with light chemical burns.

When she heard Grant walking in the hallway, she fake-casually stepped out to join him. Shadow bolted out from the living room at the back of the house and headed directly to Grant, purr-barking and rubbing his legs.

"Oh, hi," she said. Then she noticed he was headed for the front door, an overnight bag swinging on his shoulder. "Going out?"

He bent over and stroked Shadow's back. "Going to drag my grandfather to the hospital. Literally, if necessary. My mother shouldn't have to do it."

"I'm so sorry," she said. "Best wishes to you and everyone."

"It's his bronchitis. He started smoking as a baby, as far as I can tell, and since that was, like, two hundred years ago, that's a lot of damage."

"He still smokes?"

Smiling at Shadow, he straightened. "No, but he did for a long time." He reached for the door handle. "This would've been a lot easier if he'd gone to the doctor during regular hours like a normal person. But he held on until five on a Friday, so now it'll be an emergency room thing with all the delays and my mom— He's not *her* father and wasn't nice to her when Dad was alive, so she's basically a saint. I don't want her to have to go, so. Anyway. I might be back tonight, might not."

"You don't have to… you know, keep me informed of your movements."

He frowned, looking away, and adjusted the strap holding the bag on his shoulder. "I know that. I just thought you'd like to know. Since there isn't a door yet and you like your privacy, which is completely understandable, and I'm in no way implying that it isn't."

"Thank you."

"And speaking of movements, I bought a plunger. For my bathroom." He flashed a quick smile, stepped outside, and shut the door quietly behind him.

Shaking her head, she went over to turn the dead bolt just as he was doing the same thing from the other side with the key. She waited a moment, listening for him to start up his car and drive away.

Shadow expressed disapproval of his departure by walking away with her head and tail in the air.

"It's not my fault," Jane told Shadow, who had obviously formed an unhealthy attachment.

Telling him he didn't have to inform her of his comings and goings had embarrassed him. Or maybe he'd just wanted to make a poop joke.

She unlocked the door and peered out at the driveway, just to make sure he'd left.

It was still warm, still sunny, the sky overhead a pale blue instead of the usual evening gray. Looking down at the bay, however, she could see that San Francisco was socked in under a blanket of thick fog and that it was creeping their way like a living thing. Within a few hours, Oakland and the entire east side of the bay would be swallowed by it.

Grant's SUV was creeping up to the stop sign at the end of the block, his turn signal blinking.

Nice guy. He didn't like his grandfather, but he fulfilled his responsibilities like the eldest in the family should do. She could relate to that, being the eldest of quite a plethora of siblings and half-siblings.

She wondered what his other brothers were like. What his mother was like. What his father had been like. Or even his grandmother, the wife of the man who was too stubborn to go to the doctor by himself.

It really wasn't healthy to wonder so much.

As she often did since she'd broken up with Andrew (and admittedly even while living with him), Jane fell asleep that night on the couch, streaming British TV with Shadow curled up on her stomach.

When the front door opened at the opposite end of the house, Jane bolted upright, making Shadow jump to the floor with an angry meow.

The room was dark around her except for the city lights pouring in from the wide windows overlooking the bay. She blinked, heart pounding, unable to remember at first where she was, what was happening.

After a moment, she picked up her tablet and checked the time. One fifty-eight. Remembering Grant had gone to the hospital with his grandfather, she got up, finger-combed her hair, and walked down the hall to…

To what? If she seemed eager for news, she might appear self-serving, just as she had with Troy. She paused outside his door, listening to the sound of him kicking off his shoes, throwing something on the floor, moving about.

And then opening the door. She gasped, embarrassed.

"Grant," she said. "Hi. I was just…" Being nosy, she realized. God, as soon as it was morning, she was calling Ian to rush that door.

He peered at her through the doorway, looking her up and down in surprise. "Were you waiting up for me?"

Should she have? She didn't want to lie, but she didn't want to admit she'd fallen asleep in her clothes. "Oh, I was just binge-watching a mystery series on Netflix. I had to find out who did it."

He didn't look as if he believed her. A gentle smile curved his lips. "Sure."

Her heart skipped. He really did have a nice face. Right there above his chest, which was also nice. Broad and strong-looking, encased in warm, manly fabrics like fleece and flannel. In her dream, she'd been giggling as she unfastened the buttons and licked the tufts of chest hair that—

Hold on. *In her dream?*

Delicious images and sensations came back to her in flickering, tempting waves.

Nononononono. No more sofa sleeping for her. If she couldn't fall asleep in her own bed, she'd try melatonin and yoga. Or just bungee cord herself to the headboard.

She slapped at the switch on the wall, illuminating the hallway with blinding, clarifying light. "How's your grandfather?" She crossed her arms over her chest, burrowing each hand into an armpit where it couldn't do any harm.

Grant shrugged. "They sent him home with antibiotics and an inhaler. They wanted to admit him, but Grandfather insisted that would be the beginning of the end, insulted the doctor, and threatened Justin with disinheritance."

Unfortunately, it was obvious Mr. Whitman had been in no state to discuss Jane's employment status. She would have to keep waiting.

"Justin?" she asked.

"Brother number three," he said.

"I've never seen him at Whitman."

"He's been there a few times but would've been quiet about it. He's an engineer. Doesn't really want the money but hates conflict." Grant frowned at her chest. "I hope you weren't waiting up for me. You look really tired."

Which would be more embarrassing—that she was or that she wasn't?

When in doubt, go with the truth. "I fell asleep on the couch."

"That doesn't sound like something you would do," he said.

She wasn't sure she liked the idea of him forming an opinion about what she was like after only knowing her a week. "Actually—"

"I'm sorry, it's none of my business."

"No, the truth is I fall asleep on the couch all the time." She shrugged. "I'm not as perfect as I look."

"Falling asleep on the couch doesn't mean you're not perfect."

She allowed her armpits to release her hands. They sank to her sides, where she shoved them into her pockets. "It doesn't?"

"Perfect people fall asleep on the couch all the time," he said. "So you're not off the hook that easily."

"I'm still perfect?"

"I'm afraid so," he said gravely.

She laughed at the ridiculousness of it but felt strangely disappointed, like she'd been let off the hook and then placed back on it. "Listen," she said, "you've had a rough night. Would you like a nightcap?"

"I know you mean a drink," he said, "but my first thought was of the wool beanie I wear when I'm camping."

"Let me guess. You knitted it yourself?" She could just imagine the crazy colors.

"Hell yeah I did. Want to see it?"

It was late. What was she doing? "Of course I want to see it, are you kidding?"

"Come into my boudoir and I'll show you. I'm pretty proud of it, as it happens." With a grin, he opened the door wide and strode away to a plastic footlocker near the wardrobe.

Jane bit her lip to stop herself from making a joke about etchings or how men lured women into their bedrooms for all kinds of things.

She glanced at the bed, surprised it was neatly made. He seemed to be enjoying the bedding she'd chosen. Of course, as a man who was happy with sleeping bags and thin foam pads over dirt, he couldn't be very picky.

He pulled out a wadded ball of orange yarn from the footlocker and unfurled it with a flick of his wrist. "My latest. What do you think?"

She had expected gaudy, but this was radioactive. "It's bright."

"I'm rather attached to my head."

"I know what you mean," she said.

"Which is why I'd rather it didn't get blown off my shoulders. It's good to wear orange during hunting season. Especially on the parts you'd like to keep."

"They shoot you when you're sleeping?"

"Ah, no. This is for walking around. I've got a few more. Hold on." He threw the orange hat to her as he turned and squatted down to the footlocker again. It bounced off her arm and fell on the bed. Her fingers brushed the soft comforter as she picked it up, triggering an impulse to lie down on the bed and curl up with a friend.

To sleep. Because she was tired. Very tired. The way you get overtired and your heart starts beating too fast.

She picked up the hat and, for absolutely no good reason, lifted it to her face and smelled it.

It smelled like him. Strongly.

She must've been exhausted, because her pulse took off in a frenzied sprint.

Curling her fingers around the wool, her fingernails slipping between the little holes, she lowered it to her side—casually, as if she had forgotten about it, when in reality she was fighting the impulse to smuggle it out of the room.

"What do you think of this one? Like the green better?" He waved another hat at her, this one in darker shades, and then pulled it over his head. It was lumpy, too tight on the left and bulging out on the right. A strand of olive-green yarn twisted down his cheek and stuck to his beard.

"Let me guess," she said, walking over to him. "A first attempt?"

His brow furrowed. "What are you trying to say, Jane? You don't like it?" Although he scowled, his eyes were playful.

She reached up and patted the lump over his right ear. "It's gorgeous." Then she tugged on the loose strand, pulling it away from his beard.

His hand flew up and captured hers. At first he was smiling, and she was too, but then something changed, electrifying the air, and both of them stilled. Her breath caught in her throat.

"Careful," he said softly, still holding her wrist. "It might unravel."

That it might. She opened her mouth to say something, but nothing came to her.

"Sorry," she said finally, barely more than a whisper.

She swayed on her feet, gazing up into his eyes, and told herself to pull her hand away.

His gaze dropped to her mouth. She could feel the heat of it on her lips. Her breath, which had stopped entirely a moment ago, now began to race in and out of her lungs in short bursts. Knowing he was watching and knowing it was an invitation but powerless to stop herself, she licked her lips.

And stepped closer. Her elbow brushed his chest, pressing a groove into the soft fabric.

He pulled her hand closer, bringing her with it. His fingers softened over her wrist and slipped along her forearm, trailing heat as they traveled.

Before he could kiss her first and take all the credit and all the blame, she went up on tiptoes, cupped her hands around his bearded jaw, and pulled his mouth down to hers.

This was her doing, not his, and she'd live with the consequences.

Later.

---

THE TRIP to the hospital had been awkward, painful, boring, and depressing, and his grandfather was furious with him for bringing him, as if it were his eldest grandson's fault he was aging and ailing, angry and afraid.

Later perhaps Grant would blame the difficult experience for why he couldn't resist taking just a moment to enjoy life a little, to remember the good things like silky female skin under his hands, soft female breath in his mouth, sounds of erotic female pleasure in his ears.

Jane kissed him firmly, her lips parted, and clamped her

hands on either side of his face as if a hole had opened up beneath her feet and she was afraid of falling into the abyss.

It certainly felt that way to him. He was kissing her the same way, not with tenderness or passion, but with hard, almost aggressive force.

It was as if she were saying, *I'm kissing you, damn it*, and he were replying, *Damn right, and I'm kissing you too.*

That kind of kiss doesn't last long. Not that he was an expert on that kind of kiss or would want to be. It was a little scary.

They broke away at the same moment, chests heaving, and glared at each other.

"Would you mind letting me go?" she asked, wiping her mouth with the back of her hand.

He realized he'd buried the fingers of his right hand in her hair. The thick curls wrapped around his knuckles, physical bindings that made it even harder to let go. She felt so good. With effort, he forced his fingers to relax and withdrew his hand.

"Listen, I'm sorry about that," she said.

He tried to catch his breath. "I'm not."

She paused. Frowned. "Really?"

Wasn't he? He should be. Maybe she wanted him to apologize. "No, you're right," he said. "I shouldn't have done that."

"*We* shouldn't have."

"It's late," he said. "You're under a lot of stress."

"And you were just at the hospital with your grandfather." She looked down, shaking her head as if disgusted with herself. "I took advantage."

He swallowed a laugh. She looked so serious. *Advantage? Of him?*

"Maybe we took advantage of each other," he said, not wanting to start an argument. He was still trying not to laugh at the idea of her stealing something from him that he'd been dying to give her for days.

He was going to relive that kiss for a long time.

"We don't really want to do this, obviously," she said. "But sometimes you can't help being a little curious. I'm sorry. As your landlord, I never should've come into your bedroom and put you in such an awkward position."

The only thing awkward about his position was that he was standing up several feet away from her instead of lying down with her in his arms. Why couldn't they just let nature take its course? They had chemistry, they were lonely. Especially him. How long had it been since he'd had sex?

As if he didn't know. He was just embarrassed to admit it, even to himself. Hiking alone in the wilderness wasn't known for its rich dating opportunities. The most exciting it had gotten over the past six months was exchanging a smile and hello with a cute woman who was also filtering her water at the creek, and that woman turned to wave at her cute boyfriend, a shirtless, muscular specimen with a rifle and a sharp knife. Talk about taking the romance out of the air.

He forced himself to look realistically at the situation. As adorable as Jane was, getting involved with her just because he needed a little company was like using a nuclear warhead to light a birthday cake.

There would be fallout.

"As much as I'd like to argue with you," he said, "you're probably right about this being impractical."

She laughed in a strained, pained kind of way. "Can you imagine what Troy would say?"

Troy would slice off his balls and feed them to the biggest koi in the pond outside Grandfather's bedroom. He laughed with about as much mirth as she had. "Too bad. I like you. I think we'd have fun."

She rolled her eyes as if *fun* were an absurd concept that had no commanding role in her life, then she moved to the door, where she paused. "Listen, I totally understand if you don't want to go to my sister's party—"

"No, we shouldn't let this ruin things. We're friends, we're housemates, we're going to that party. No big deal. It only becomes a big deal if we let it become a big deal. Deal?"

She gave him a genuine smile then. "Deal."

"Just let me know when and where, and I'm there."

"Thanks."

"No problem." She stepped into the hallway and shut the door behind her.

No problem they couldn't handle anyway.

11

First thing in the morning, Jane prepared for the day as she always did, even though it was Saturday. Fresh clothes, flat-ironed hair, expensive moisturizer, contoured eye shadow. And to keep herself from looking excessively dressed up, she put on sneakers. Nothing fancy, just cheap Keds, but they were as white as a movie star's teeth, having never been worn outside. She used a lint roller to remove the strands of Shadow's dark fur on the toes.

At nine, she called Ian. As she'd feared, her sister Billie answered. She hadn't wanted to talk to Billie yet, but it probably couldn't be helped. Of course she was happy for Billie. She was. But she wanted…

Damn it, she wanted…

"Hey, are you psychic or what?" Billie asked after she answered. "We were just talking about you."

In the background, Jane could hear Ian protesting gently.

"She knows it's only good things," Billie said, her voice slightly muffled. And then more loudly, "I know we're not really religious, but would you be the godmother for it?"

"You're still saying 'it,'" Jane said. But she felt a wave of love.

"It's going to love you," Billie said. "You always give excellent presents. I still have a sweater from ten years ago you gave me for Christmas."

"Is that all it—I mean, the baby—will need from me, you think? Presents?" Jane asked.

"You know we always liked the relatives who gave us good presents the best," Billie said. "I'm just being realistic here. For you, not for me. As the mother, I'll have to be tough."

Jane had to laugh. "You?"

"I'll have to be. All my spoiling will be through others. I can't have it walking all over me."

Jane couldn't imagine any other outcome. Billie was too sweet. "I'm sure Ian can help with discipline."

"Not if it's a girl. Can you imagine how spoiled it'll be?"

"When's the ultrasound so we can look forward to your using a gendered pronoun when discussing the…" At this point Jane was struck, for the first time, with the realization that she was going to be an aunt. Her sister was going to have a baby, and that baby would be her niece or nephew, a little being with tiny toes and sticky hands and cheeks like chubby silk pillows. And the thought made her throat tighten, making further speech impossible.

How could she have been such a selfish bitch? Billie was going to have a baby!

Nose starting to run, Jane reached for a tissue and said quickly, "Listen, how are you feeling? Are you tired? Throwing up? Anything like that?"

"Nothing," Billie said brightly. "I can't feel anything. Even when Ian is pounding—right, well, not even during intimate moments."

Jane blew her nose and didn't bother to move the phone

mic out of range of the blast. Hearing about Ian pounding into her sister was not a detail she relished. "Well, I'm glad to hear you don't have morning sickness yet. Hopefully that will last."

"You're such a downer."

"What? I said it was good."

"But it might not last," Billie said.

Jane opened the cabinet below the sink and threw away the tissue. The threat of her being a downer was exactly why her mother had demanded she bring a date to the party. "Listen, I have two things I wanted to talk about." Before Billie could jump in with suggestions and guesses, Jane went on. "First, I'm going to ask Ian if he's still willing to put in that door. Second—"

"Oh, I'm sure he is! Ian, you'll put in the door for Jane, right? She's asking."

Jane waited a beat, straining to decipher the mumble from Ian in the distance. All she could hear was a grunt.

"He'd love to do it!" Billie said. "Thanks for giving him the opportunity to enlarge his skill set."

"I thought he'd done this before," Jane said, suddenly having doubts. There was still time to hire somebody, although that would take money she'd rather pocket on the chance the job didn't get reinstated and would probably take longer too.

"Don't worry. Are you crazy? Of course he can do it," Billie said. "If not the first try, then the second. Third time, max. Isn't that right, honey bunny? You're very persistent." Then she yelped, sounding as if she were avoiding a projectile.

Jane was tiring of the conversation. The fitful sleep after the… *nightcap*… with Grant hadn't fulfilled her sleep requirements. "Tell him I really appreciate it. I'll pay for the permits and materials and tools and everything. No arguing."

"But why? He's got millions coming out of his ears." Billie

snorted. "That sounds like bugs or something. I don't mean it literally. I mean, the money is literally in the millions, especially this week—do you follow the markets? They were up— Oh, never mind, he's shaking his head. That was last week? This week they're down. Way down. Maybe you *should* pay for materials."

"I will."

Billie laughed. "Listen to me, I sound drunk. I just can't believe I'm going to have a baby."

"I'm so happy for you," Jane said.

"I know you are. Mom has no idea how lucky this kid is going to be to have you as an aunt. And right in the same city too."

"Did Mom suggest the baby wouldn't be lucky?" Jane asked, forgetting she didn't want to know what their mother might have said. "Never mind. Speaking of Mom, she says there's a party. Do you have a date yet?"

"It's the bridal shower, but we're going to throw in the baby thing for free and call it a party instead of a shower so people don't worry about bringing so many gifts. I'd feel bad having people buy stuff for us when we have more money than anybody. And this way everyone only has to come to one bash, which saves money too. Dad and his new and improved family from Seattle, Mom and the girls from here—it'll make it a lot easier for everyone."

"You'd think you'd planned it," Jane said.

Billie snorted. "Nobody else will. Anyway, the date is… Ian? What's the date for the thing?" After a pause, she said, "August tenth. Before school starts but long enough, hopefully, to see if the baby is, you know…"

"I know."

Billie turned serious. "Honestly, if I had the willpower, I would've kept it a secret for a while longer. Then I could have gone through the party four months pregnant and pretended I was just putting on weight. But I can't keep secrets from you. Never could."

Jane walked over to the window and looked out on the lemon tree, heavy with far more fruit than she could ever eat. Shadow sat below it in a patch of sunlight, watching the birds. "Thank you for telling me. I have a secret of my own."

"Ha! I was hoping you'd tell me! It's about your new guy, right?'

"You talked to Mom," Jane said.

Billie paused. "Email. She said you're bringing a date. I wondered if you'd lied to her to get her off your back."

Jane smiled. Billie was a lot sharper than she seemed sometimes. "In a manner of speaking. He's just a guy I met last week. He's renting the front room."

Jane didn't have to share all her secrets.

"How's he in bed? I hope you're using your queen, not the twin. Or did you put a bigger bed in there? Of course, you'd want to make it more appealing for Airbnb. Nobody uses twins any—"

"We're not sleeping together," Jane said firmly. And they wouldn't.

"Just sex?"

"Billie…"

She was laughing. "OK, OK, I get it. But how'd you get him to agree to go? Knock off a week's rent?"

"Thank you very much," Jane said.

"Oh, please. What would it take for *you* to go to some stranger's wedding and bridal shower?" Billie asked.

"He's just being nice. He's very nice." Too damn nice.

Billie paused. "Is he? How interesting."

"It's no big deal. I asked, he said sure. He's very easygoing." Jane could hear the defensive edge in her own voice. "And he… never mind." She was going to tell Billie about sort of losing her job and how Grant, as one of the family, might feel guilty about it, but she didn't want to get into it. Definitely didn't want to try to explain that one.

"What's his name?" Billie asked, far too curious.

"I forget."

Billie laughed. "Nice try, but I'll need to know for the invitation. Mom's doing it with ink out of a pen. You know, Caligula or whatever."

"Calligraphy."

"Right. So we need to know. What's his name?"

"Guest. First name 'and.' As in, 'Jane Garcia *and Guest.*'"

"Mom will get suspicious if you don't know his name," Billie said.

"I'll introduce him there. You'll be enough of a distraction until then," Jane said. "You'd think a woman with four children wouldn't be so excited about a baby."

"She lives for babies. And with it being Ian's kid, too, she and his mom are going crazy."

Billie and Jane's mother was longtime best friends with Ian's mother, both of them in the same town up in suburban Sonoma County where Jane had grown up.

The same town where she'd gone to high school with Ian and learned what passion *didn't* look like. If she'd ever had a kiss like that one last night, she would've known better.

"Tell Ian to email me about his schedule and the door," Jane said. "And give him my eternal gratitude."

"You've got mine," Billie said. "It'll get him out of the house. He's as bad as Mom. I hope you're ready to have him over there first thing tomorrow."

"That would be fantastic." Because her emotional barriers were obviously going to be inadequate.

---

GRANT WASN'T aware of the start of construction until the feel of shaking walls woke him from a deep sleep.

*Earthquake!* his nervous system insisted, flooding his body with adrenaline so he could run out of the house as if it were 1906.

He made it as far as the hallway before he realized the shaking was coming from a tall guy in cargo shorts with his fist raised to the wall outside Grant's bedroom.

"What the fuck?" Grant asked.

"Sorry, did I bother you?" the guy replied. "I'm Ian. Putting in the wall."

"On a Sunday?"

"Jane was in a hurry. Because of you, I guess."

"I guess." Grant leaned against the doorframe, waiting for his pulse to return to normal. He'd always hated earthquakes. It was embarrassing for a native Californian to react like an Iowan to a little geological activity, but…

He'd been asleep, damn it. Finally. After that kiss with Jane, he'd stayed up all of Friday night writing, which had been an interesting flood of creative energy he wasn't going to think about too deeply. He'd spent Saturday at the library, intending to research bird migration so readers would think he was a genius but wasting time on Twitter instead. Back at the house, he'd heard Jane moving around and found himself, as tired as he was, unable to sleep until after two, and then fitfully.

"Listen, I can come back later if this is a bad time," Ian said. "The door *is* for you, after all."

"Actually, it's for her." Grant nodded down the hall. "She likes her privacy."

Ian eyed him. "Do you blame her?"

"No," Grant said, telling himself Jane couldn't have told this guy anything. He was just the suspicious type. "Put in the wall. I'm not stopping you."

"It *is* noon."

"I don't care. Come back at three in the morning if you need to. It's Jane's house, not mine."

"Yeah," Ian said. He slipped his hands in his pockets and continued to watch Grant. "You know her long? You seem like, I don't know, like you two have gotten to know each other."

"What business is it of yours?"

Ian's eyebrows went up, but he didn't reply. Instead, he nodded, removing his hands from his pockets, and turned away as he cleared his throat. "I was just checking for studs."

Grant's mouth fell open until he realized the guy was talking about the wall. "Sure. Right. Like I said, no problem. Will you need to get into my room?"

"Don't think so. No."

"Then… as you were," Grant said.

"Thanks."

"Thank *you*." Now what the hell had Grant said that for? Something about this guy put his back up. With a manly snort, he returned to his room and shut the door, slightly more forcefully than necessary.

Since when did contractors interrogate people living in the house where they were working?

Grant rubbed the sleep out of his eyes. He must be a friend of Jane's, maybe even an ex. Definitely had a possessive vibe.

After pulling on clean jeans and a T-shirt, he went back out into the hallway to use the bathroom. There he saw the guy measuring the wall and tapping for studs again, tempting

Grant to pat his chest and suggest he look no further. Stud jokes never got old.

"I think you're putting it in the wrong place," Grant said, watching him.

"I'd also rather you had a separate entrance from the outside, for Jane's sake, but it's just not possible with the architecture of the house," Ian said.

"I don't need a separate entrance from the outside, but I do need to take a piss." Grant pointed over Ian's head at the door to the bathroom, located several paces past where he was working.

"Go ahead." Ian stepped aside and stretched out an arm.

Grant didn't feel like arguing with a man who seemed determined to be difficult, not when his bladder was full. Smiling, he walked past him, went into the bathroom to do the basics, and returned to the hallway more comfortable than he'd been a few minutes earlier, with minty fresh breath to boot.

Ian was still working in the wrong place. If he put the door between Grant's bedroom and the bathroom, Grant—and all future tenants—would be shit out of luck. So to speak. "Listen, maybe you don't want my advice," Grant began.

Ian looked up uncomprehendingly, and Grant saw he had bright green earbuds in his ears. He set down his measuring tape and pencil, took out one earbud, and said, obviously unhappy to be interrupted again, "Yes?"

"Are you putting the door right there?" Grant asked, in case he misunderstood what the man was up to.

"I'm trying to."

Grant smiled. Definitely an ex. He was a lot better than the stalker but not right for Jane. In spite of the tool belt, there was something slick and moneyed about him. His dark hair was cut and styled perfectly, no hair out of place. And his tools looked new, top quality. Even his pencil looked expensive—a mechanical model probably imported from Europe.

Not right for Jane. No wonder it hadn't worked out. She needed somebody less like she was, somebody more easygoing and less, ah…

Rich?

All right, maybe he was biased against successful guys. Being on the verge of financial ruin would do that to you.

"You're putting it between the bedroom and the bathroom," Grant said. "Isn't the point to give everyone some privacy?"

"Why don't you use the one— Hold on, isn't there…" Slack-jawed, Ian stared off in the direction of the front bedroom. "Damn it."

"Sorry."

"I was thinking there was a bathroom in there."

"Nope," Grant said.

"What was I thinking?" Ian slapped the wall with both hands and hung his head between his arms. "I know there isn't a bathroom in there. I tore the carpet out with my own hands. There's just a little closet."

"Yep," Grant said, suddenly curious about the carpet and the hands. "You help Jane a lot with the house?"

"Well, not much lately. She kicked me out." Ian continued to shake his head as he began moving his tools down the hallway.

"Did she have a reason?" Grant almost felt sorry for the guy, doing minor construction for a woman who didn't love him.

"She said it's because she likes her privacy, but it's really because I got engaged to her sister."

Grant's brain belatedly clicked into gear. "You're the brother-in-law."

"Not quite yet."

"I hear congratulations are in order," Grant said, realizing he'd badly misjudged the volunteer handyman. Post-traumatic stress from the faux earthquake, perhaps. "You guys are expecting?"

"She told you that?" Ian straightened, his tools forgotten, and leveled a hard look at Grant.

"I was around when she got the call."

"Interesting," Ian said.

"Is it?"

They regarded each other.

"I'd better get back to work," Ian said, not breaking his gaze.

"Let me know if you need a hand."

"I won't. We can't do anything until we have a permit. I'm just preparing the plans." Ian turned away. "But thanks."

"Sure." Grant returned to his room, wondering what he was missing.

He locked the door, grabbed a bag of trail mix, started the coffee maker, and took out his laptop to read the words he'd squeezed out in the middle of the night during one of his bouts of insomnia, pathetic and inadequate as they were.

Within five minutes, he knew it was hopeless. He could feel her down the hall, even with her oddly intense future brother-in-law lumbering around, banging studs between them.

That door was going to take weeks to get installed. The Oakland permit process wasn't as bad as Berkeley, but it wasn't going to be done overnight.

As much as he hated to get involved, he was going to have to get involved.

To make sure he didn't get involved in an entirely different way.

"Mark, nice to see you." Jane greeted her cousin at the door, embarrassed her mother had told her father—who had then told Mark's mother—about her home improvement project today.

"I'm here to offer my assistance," Mark Johnson said.

"That's sweet of you, but Ian's just measuring and planning today. For the city permits, all that."

Mark was actually her second cousin, and they hadn't spent much time together until recently, but their parents were aggressively working to change that. Even Jane's father, who lived in Seattle with his second wife and had skipped her high school graduation for work reasons and had forgotten two of her birthdays (seventeen and twenty-four), suddenly seemed eager to nourish the family ties.

It annoyed Jane. She liked her space and her time and her quiet. All were threatened by sociable relatives suddenly within a ten-minute drive.

And Mr. Nightcap in her front bedroom, a ten-second walk from her own.

She'd been so relieved to see him drive away earlier. So, so relieved. She was still feeling happy about it. So, so happy.

Standing in the doorway avoiding eye contact, her cousin Mark looked miserable himself. A somewhat famous computer geek who'd made a fortune in start-ups at a young age, he had limited social skills and, although happily married, seemed especially awkward around women.

"My mom thought you might want this door she bought at a salvage yard," Mark said. "I tried to just bring a picture, but she insisted I bring it over so you could see it in person."

Jane glanced past him at a large SUV parked behind her minivan in the driveway. "Look, Mark…," she began, dreading the inevitable rejection of her Aunt Trixie's junkyard door.

"I know, I know, but please look at it before you send me away. She'll know if I'm lying. She can always tell."

"I need an interior dividing door, not—"

"Let's take a look," Ian said. "Before we go to Home Depot."

Mark beamed at Ian. "That would be great. By the way, I'm supposed to tell you she loves the shelves you put in the kitchen closet."

"The pantry," a woman said, coming up behind him and wrapping her arms around his waist. "It's called a pantry."

"Hi, Rose," Ian said, smiling at Mark's wife. Jane had noticed that men always seemed to smile at Rose. She had long blond hair and a milkmaid complexion and had an effect on straight guys that Jane found surprising, given that her size was considerably larger than the conventional ideal. Jane had to admit she was a little jealous and wondered how she pulled it off.

"Nice to see you again, Rose," Jane said, waving for her to come in. They only lived a short drive away, and Ian and Mark had hit it off, which probably meant Jane would be seeing a lot more of them.

"I'm only here as Trixie's spy," Rose said. "She really wants you to see that door. If you don't actually walk to the car and look at it—with the hatch open, not just through the window —I'm not sure what. It involves punishing my husband, however."

Gazing adoringly at his wife, Mark's awkwardness faded away. "Punish me how?" he asked quietly, raising an eyebrow. "Will we be naked?"

"I apologize for him," Rose said to Jane, but her fair skin was flushed and she didn't look at all sorry. "Will you come see and get it over with? It is beautiful."

"How can a door be beautiful?" Mark asked.

"When it looks like this one, sweetie," Rose said, patting his abdomen.

"Can I come out and look at it also?" Ian asked.

"You better," Jane replied. "You're the handyman. Did you measure the, uh, whatever?"

"You mean the wall?" Ian asked.

"And whatever else, yes." Jane was feeling irritable with so many people crowded in her front hallway, her home. And none of them was—

No, she was glad Grant had left. She didn't know where or why, but he had, and she was grateful there was one less person she had to worry about. But she knew she would be glad when it was only him and the others were gone.

And there was a nice, thick door between them.

One by one, they filed out the door and down to the SUV, where Mark jogged ahead and flung open the hatch. Everyone yielded to Jane, who looked inside at a door that was indeed beautiful. A narrow oak door with ornate stained glass panels rested inside, reflecting the afternoon sun as it fought through the fog blanketing the hills.

Jane turned to Ian. "Will it fit?"

"Sure. Don't see why not."

"How will you get it to, you know, stick?" Jane asked.

"Lots and lots of glue," Ian said. "And tape."

Jane heard a snort, but everyone managed to keep a straight face.

"Then do it however you're going to do it," Jane said. "Please."

She and Ian got along as well as could be expected. He'd been a terrible boyfriend, scarring her for years because he'd had absolutely no sexual interest in her, and then, to make everything worse, last year he had somehow found that chemistry with her sister.

Not surprisingly, Ian and Jane didn't always enjoy each other's company. Her mother said it was very painful for everyone, and Jane should find a man for herself so Ian and Billie could truly enjoy themselves.

She turned to Mark and Rose, who looked surprised but happy. "You don't have to lie to her," Jane said. "I love it."

"Really?" Mark pinched his upper lip and rolled it between his fingers. "I had a whole story worked out. I had to brake really hard to stop from running over a dog, and the door bounced out the back and rolled down a cliff, and it was all terribly, horribly sad. But the dog was fine, thank God."

"That's a great story, honey," Rose said. "Except wouldn't the door slide forward and smack us in the heads?"

"At first, yes. Which is why I got confused and opened the hatch instead of the hazard lights." Mark rubbed the back of his head, flinching as if it had really been struck by planks of antique oak and glass.

"She'd want to know what kind of dog," Ian said.

"She'd get suspicious if I named a breed," Mark said. "I thought of that."

"Trixie's a huge dog person," Rose told Jane.

"I noticed," Jane said. She and Billie had gone to dinner at her house several times now, and there were at least three dogs running around.

"They're Chihuahuas, mostly," Mark said, "so she's actually a tiny-dog person."

"Well, no stories needed. Tell her thank you," Jane said. "And thanks, Mark, for offering to help."

"We won't be able to do a lot today," Ian said, "but we can get started on the permit. Help me get this out of the truck?"

The four of them carried the door up the steps, tripping over each other's feet, and into the house, setting it next to Grant's closed door.

Grant's door gave nothing away, no hint of what was inside. Would she regret installing a door with glass panels between the two parts of the house? The stained glass wasn't quite transparent, but not quite opaque, either. If the lighting was just so, a person could see shapes and movement on the other side.

She shook off her doubts. It was a lovely, unique piece of craftsmanship and would increase the value of her home. There wasn't any risk of her dancing around naked right next to it with the hall lights blazing; her privacy was secure.

Ian measured the door, sketched, took notes, and snapped pictures while Jane made everyone iced coffee and they hung around, watching Ian work.

"Nothing else I can do here," Ian said finally. "I'll have to draw up the plans at home."

"Thanks, Ian," Jane said. "Really."

"Well, we've fulfilled our mission," Rose said, squeezing

Jane's arm. "You don't need us to stick around for anything, do you? We're totally willing to stay if you—"

"No, not at all. Please, don't let me keep you," Jane said, adding a long ramble about how grateful and thankful she was to everyone for being there, for the door, for the company.

Rose gave her a knowing smile. "I'm married to a hermit," she whispered. "I recognize the signs. Don't worry, we won't start showing up unannounced all the time."

"But— I appreciate— I'm not—" Jane began, but Rose was already striding out the door.

Ian took off in his pickup, Rose and Mark in their SUV, leaving Jane standing in the hallway with only the antique door for company.

"I'm not a hermit," she told the emptiness.

And then sighed with relief to be alone.

She'd skipped lunch. What should she eat? Maybe a cheddar omelette or chicken-and-vegetable soup. Although it was July, the fog had never burned off, and the strong wind blowing off the bay felt as cold as Tahoe in February.

She heard a key in the front door, and then it swung open.

"Hi," Grant said.

Shadow, who had been hiding all day, appeared from nowhere and began rubbing against Grant's legs, making the bark-meows she did to express her annoyance with a long separation.

Jane, unfortunately, could relate to the impulse.

---

GRANT HAD WAITED until he saw the pickup and SUV drive away before starting up the Rover from where he'd parked down the street, then driving the rest of the way down the block to the house. He'd lurked another few minutes before going inside.

She liked her privacy, he liked his. By the time he was walking through the front door, he'd thought she would be safely tucked away on her side of the house.

A door was resting on its side in the hallway, and Jane was standing several feet away, staring at him, looking even prettier than usual: dark brown hair down around her shoulders, wide brown eyes unadorned by makeup, full lips slightly parted in surprise.

"Welcome… back," she said. Perhaps she'd almost said 'home.' "I hope you didn't have to leave because of the construction."

"I had something I needed to do," he said. And he'd done it, or hoped he had. They'd all find out tomorrow. "How'd it go with the door?"

"Early stages," she said. "Plans and permits."

He squatted down and ran his hand along the ornate door panel, obviously handcrafted, an antique. "Nice. Ian got you this?" The cat was jealous, so he petted her too.

"Please. He's helpful but not about to give me something beautiful." She came over and picked up the cat. "It's from my Aunt Trixie. She lives nearby."

"It is beautiful. Where'd she get it?"

"Mark said it was from a salvage yard."

"Who's Mark?" How many ex-boyfriends did she have?

Her tone sharpened. "Why?"

"No reason." He waved his hand dismissively, heading for his room. "Glad you have—"

He stopped himself from saying *so many men to help you.*

"So much help," he finished, opening his door.

"He's my cousin," she said behind him. "Trixie's son."

"Of course. Well, none of my business."

"No," she said, which annoyed him.

"I have to write," he said.

"Good luck with that."

And that annoyed him too. What was the matter with him?

## 13

The microwave was as clean as it was ever going to get.

Jane plugged it in—it was a countertop model from the previous century—and watched the 12:00 flash until she found her phone and the current time and figured out how to set the stupid thing.

It was twenty after ten on Monday morning, her second Monday morning without a job. Leisure wasn't her strong suit, and she was going to have to find something to do or she would end up hurling the microwave out the window, just to have something else to clean up.

The phone, still in her hand from checking the time, began chirping with a call from Whitman. Her body responded with a rush of stress hormones, and she had to take a calming breath before answering.

"This is Jane."

"Hey there. It's Troy Whitman."

Was it good news or bad? She couldn't tell by the tone of his voice. "Good morning," she said in a neutral tone.

"First of all, I want to apologize. Gr—that is, I realized I was dropping the ball on this in a bad way. And you were left hanging. Can you come in today?"

She still didn't know if it was going to be good or bad. "To work? Or to talk?" Like, say, about giving her a generous severance package, because she wasn't going quietly without at least what Lorraine had.

"Oh, to work. Sorry I wasn't clear. Fully reinstated. We look forward to having you." He paused. "If you're willing to come back, of course. But I hope you are."

She smiled and did a little dance on the kitchen floor before saying, her tone as cool as she could manage, "And the other things we discussed?"

"Not yet," he said. "I tried to make it happen this morning, but… not quite yet. You have my word I will do as much as I can, as soon as I can."

"Is Nicole part of the problem?"

"Oh, not at all," Troy said. "Which says a lot. If she can't muster up a nasty thing to say about you, you must be incredible."

"I am," Jane said.

Troy laughed, and then, after a moment, said in a serious voice, "Will we see you later today?"

She wanted to say "yes, of course," but she shouldn't throw away the moment. Mr. Whitman had been sick enough to go to the hospital on Friday night. Was this something Troy was doing behind his grandfather's back while he was indisposed, or was he officially retiring?

"Did your grandfather change his mind?" she asked.

"You don't have to worry. I've got your back. I've spoken to HR and Nicole. All right?"

He was asking her to trust him, but she couldn't afford to be trusting. "I just need to know a little more. Why today and not last week? We spoke at the end of the day Friday."

There was a long pause. "I had a little help realizing a few things over the weekend. It's time for me to step up. I will make sure everything is all right with my grandfather when he recovers." He cleared his throat and spoke more quickly. "So how about it? Should I tell Nicole you're coming?"

She wasn't tough enough to ignore the honesty and vulnerability she'd heard in his voice. "Yes, I can be there in about an hour. I just wanted to understand what I was coming back to."

"Sure, of course. No problem. Excellent." His charming self-confidence was back. "Thanks, Jane. Can't wait to see you in the office."

"You too, Troy." She was smiling as they ended the call. Back to work, thank God. No more scrubbing appliances and trying to ignore the sounds of the footsteps and breathing at the other end of the house. Every time she heard the water pipes running, she found herself wondering what he was doing, if he'd appear in the hallway, topless, a damp, skimpy towel slung low on his hips. She couldn't wait to get out of the house and be an independent, productive, moneymaking human again.

This eagerness kept her from analyzing Troy's words as closely as she might've done otherwise. She dressed, took the BART train across the bay to San Francisco, and walked up Montgomery Street to the Whitman offices with her thoughts on Nicole, the projects she'd had to abandon ten days earlier, her coworkers, the cream cheese sandwich she'd forgotten in her desk.

And then she was distracted by Troy himself, who called her to come by his office, where he shook her hand and offered her one of the peaches in the inky-black bowl on his desk.

"From the family orchard," he said. "My mom said they've got them coming out of their ears."

Most people were lucky to have a single tree. The Whitmans had multiple orchards. She took one to be polite and ran her thumb across its fuzzy skin. "Thank you."

"Great to have you back. Like I said, don't worry about a thing."

"All right." She smiled, but she didn't like the way he said it, as if he were still trying to convince himself. "I'm taking back my original clients," she said. "You'd handed them over to Charles, but it would be much better if I took them back."

"Obviously. Good call." He grinned. "Take another peach?"

"I'm good." She thanked him again before returning to her cubicle, peach in hand.

Her coworkers greeted her with a degree of enthusiasm somewhere between indifferent and oblivious. That was her fault, not theirs; except for Sydney, who was in a meeting all afternoon, she hadn't made friends with anyone. As the afternoon came to a close and she was sitting at her desk, going through her email as if nothing had happened, she wondered, for the first time, if she might be happier somewhere else.

*Don't be hasty,* she told herself. *A raise and a promotion is all you need.*

It was on the train ride home, barreling through the Transbay Tunnel under the sharks and container ships, when Troy's exact words came together in her mind and illuminated the likely scenario that had led to his abrupt show of managerial zeal this morning.

*I had a little help realizing a few things over the weekend,* he'd said.

Grant.

She hadn't been able to get a seat and was standing in an awkward few inches between a manspreading young guy on the disabled bench seat near the doors and a woman's pointy leather shoulder bag. The woman was tall, the bag had a short strap, and Jane was pissed.

Grant must have gone up to Marin on Sunday and talked to Troy.

About her, about her job.

It was profoundly irritating. Infuriating, really. If she hadn't been buried in commuter flesh inside a BART train, she would've uttered a string of vile curses to relieve the furious pressure building inside her.

How dare he? It was bad enough he talked to Troy and apparently told him to man up. But to then come back to her house and not tell her…

Was he there now, waiting for her to bounce through the door, giggling and relieved to have her little job back, the job she couldn't rescue all by her little self…

*Goddamn it. Godfuckingdamnit.*

"Sorry," the handbag woman said, twisting to one side.

Jane wondered how many of the curse words in her head she'd said out loud. "Thanks," she mumbled, almost embarrassed but not really.

She was the eldest of the six children her parents had in total between them (including with their current spouses), and she did not tolerate being treated like a child. She had been born first. She was responsible, she was capable, she was amazing. Help from a man she barely knew was not necessary. In fact, it was offensive. She was offended. He'd offended her.

The woman with the handbag shot her another uneasy glance and then pushed through an impossibly dense wad of bodies to her left to escape Jane's proximity.

Jane hoped Grant was equally respectful of Jane's wrath and power. Because just wait until she got home and told him where he could stick his paternalistic rich-boy privileged asswipe *help*.

Because Grant had been watching out his bedroom window for her, he saw Jane pull into the driveway at a reckless angle, jump out, and slam the door while she frowned at the house. At his bedroom window. At him.

She must've driven to the BART station and taken the train from there. Driving all the way to the city wouldn't be affordable, not with bridge tolls and parking fees. Troy had mentioned how he'd convinced Grandfather to subsidize employees' public transit costs. It had been Grant's idea, but Troy probably hadn't told him that.

He watched Jane march up to the house with a death glare on her face. In spite of himself, he smiled, more than a little turned on. It was the look she'd been wearing on the day they'd met, right after she'd been fired. He wished he could hear the patchwork of profanity coming out of her mouth. Her soft, red, sexy mouth.

He heard her slam the front door behind her, then knock on his.

"Grant, I want to talk to you."

There were a few ways he could play this. He could act dumb, pretending he hadn't spent an hour on Sunday coaching his baby brother to stand up not just for Jane but for himself. Troy would never tell Jane that Grant had convinced him that the rest of the company was slowly losing respect for Troy, respect that could never be regained.

"Standing up for Jane will do a lot to reassure the rest of the company that you're on their side," Grant had said. "Grandfather might get sick again. Even in the best of health, he's out of the office for extended periods. Good people will start leaving, fed up with a lack of leadership. The ones who do stay won't trust you."

"I don't want to hurt him," Troy had said.

"I know." Grant respected Troy's loyalty and affection for their grandfather. But Troy had always had too much heart for his own good and a need to please everyone that was impossible. "He knew this time was coming. You're the best one to tell him that time is now. He loves you. Trust him to trust you."

Several hours ago, Troy had sent Grant a quick message telling him that Jane was back at work.

"Grant!" She was banging on the door again.

Shadow had stolen one of his socks earlier, and after Grant had retrieved it, the cat had somehow found a way into his room. Now he worried she'd see the cat and think he'd stolen her.

He walked over slowly in his fluffy, sound-dampening wool socks and paused. It was tempting to play dumb, but she'd see right through him. And he kind of wanted the credit even if she was mad at him about it. It made him feel manly and powerful. Her cat-stealing knight in striped, hand-knitted knee-highs.

He opened the door. "I can explain."

Shadow bark-meowed at Jane.

"You should've told me," she said.

"I didn't want to get your hopes up. I didn't know if he was going to listen to me."

"So you admit it." She readjusted her fists on her hips, but he could see his answer had deflated her rage. "You talked to him about me."

"I had to. Not just for you, Troy, or even my grandfather. For me."

She frowned. "Why for you?"

"I was going to get dragged into it anyway if Troy didn't take charge. Grandfather wouldn't ever let go if he thought Troy wasn't strong enough to run the business he'd built."

Grant moved closer, unable to resist the pull between them. "My grandfather has never stopped pressuring me to live the kind of life he values. I think he's still hoping I'll go to spreadsheet school and take my rightful place at Whitman as his eldest grandson."

"You're saying you got my job reinstated to help *your* career, not mine?"

"I apologize," he said. "I'm a very selfish, horrible person."

Shaking her head, Jane turned and dropped her bag on the floor outside his door and then picked up Shadow. "It's not called spreadsheet school," she said, nuzzling the cat's neck.

"Sorry. Spreadsheet *University*."

Her lips twitched. "You still should've told me you talked to Troy. I always want the truth. How it affects my feelings is irrelevant."

He wasn't convinced she was as invincible as she wanted to think, but he nodded contritely. "I didn't expect him to take action so quickly. I didn't know if he'd be able to do anything that might hurt Grandfather. He loves that man, in spite of— Well, he's the favorite for a reason. He's the nicest of all of us."

Her eyes narrowed. "I'm not so sure about that," she said quietly.

"Oh, come on. I'm a selfish bastard. That's why I live in the wilderness where nobody can bother me. Me, myself, and I. Party of one. King of my domain."

She took off her pink sweater—oh God, she was wearing a clingy sleeveless thing underneath—and folded it neatly. "Well, Your Highness, soon your domain will have a door, and it will be a lot harder for me to bother you here." She held up Shadow. "Or my cat."

He would not stare at her breasts. He'd hiked miles through freezing rain, feasted on raw oats and muddy ramen, slept on sloping gravel; he could do anything. "You're never a bother, Jane."

During an awkward pause, he decided he probably shouldn't have said that.

"Right back at you, Your Majesty," she said finally, turning away.

He watched her disappear into the kitchen before taking a breath.

## 14

Over the next several weeks, Jane threw herself into her work, Ian installed the door, and life returned to normal. So far as she knew, Grant was working on his book, although she didn't see him very often anymore, only when they were both coming or going at the same time, which wasn't often. She followed a corporate schedule, up and out early, back late, and he— Well, she didn't know what he did. She hoped his writing was going well. Some evenings she paused in the hallway, watching for a glimpse of him through the colored glass panes of the new door, but usually she had the willpower to avert her gaze. Most of the time.

July became August, and the day for the Billie and Ian's engagement-bridal-baby party was only a week away. To her embarrassment, her mother, stepfather, father, and stepmother had chosen a corporate Mexican chain restaurant as the venue for the big event. Their daughter was marrying a millionaire, and they'd chosen to toast the couple at a Chevys Fresh Mex between a freeway overpass and a Toyota dealership.

"This is Sonoma, Mom," Jane had pleaded. She'd driven up in person to make her case. "There are all kinds of beautiful places up here for a party. Wineries, hotels, farms, anything." Her stepfather, Ken, was learning how to play the electric guitar. In the dining room, several yards away.

"That's awesome, dude!" her mother, Karen, shouted to her husband from the kitchen. She and Ken were one of those absurdly successful second marriages. If they'd ever argued, Jane had never seen it, and Ken had married her mother when she was in kindergarten. "What were you saying, Jane? It's great to see you, of course, but you look really tired. I got Billie some Epsom bath soaks as a nice little treat for her during all that's going on, but maybe I should've given it to you. I will. I'll go get it."

Jane caught her mom's wrist. "No, I'm fine. You know I don't like baths."

"Surely you've outgrown that by now?"

"Why would I outgrow a completely understandable dislike of sitting cold and naked in dirty water?"

Shaking her head, Karen sat back down and poured more coffee in Jane's cup. "So funny."

"What's funny?"

"You," Karen said. "Still the same person you were as a baby. I think that's funny. We think we, as parents, have all this power in how our children come out, but then reality hits. I'm so glad I had more babies after you."

Jane grabbed the tub of cream cheese from her mother's side of the table and jabbed her knife into it. Because Karen had been so young when Jane came along, their relationship was a little more casual than with her younger daughters. They liked the same music, borrowed each other's clothes, shared a hair stylist—and argued like sisters. Actually, Jane argued more with her mother than she did with Holly and Rachel, who, barely out of college, seemed too young and innocent to survive a good, energetic sharing of ideas.

"You're glad you had more kids because I turned out to be such a disappointment?" Jane asked, balancing a mountain of cream cheese on a single, tiny fish cracker. Her feelings weren't hurt; she just wanted her mother to think so and then apologize and agree to move the party to French Laundry or a Napa Valley winery. Anywhere other than *Chevys*. She was going to be bringing Grant Whitman, for God's sake. She kept remembering that estate in Marin with the suits of armor and orchards and private iron gate and...

"I do worry about you sometimes," Karen said. "You work so hard. I'm not sure it makes you happy."

Jane's mouth was filled with the cream cheese. She chewed while Ken struggled with a song that may have been Pearl Jam, then sipped her coffee. "I'm not either."

Karen nodded, folding a paper napkin into triangles. "What are you going to do about it?"

"I don't know." Jane shrugged. "At least I'm not a drug addict."

"That's a pretty low bar."

"Not at all. I hear about college friends who are alcoholics or have trouble with pain meds—"

"Yes, yes. I'm just saying you might want to aim a little higher than avoiding substance abuse."

"My whole life you've been telling me I'm too ambitious. Now you're saying I need to try harder?"

Karen had to shout over the electric guitar. "In some ways, yes."

This time Jane's feelings did suffer a glancing blow. "I'm always trying, Mom. Always. I wish you—" She cleared her throat, willing the bloom of emotion to die. "I wish you'd move the party. Ian's a multimillionaire. There's no shame in letting him pick up the tab."

"Of course there is. We are Billie's parents. We're throwing this party." The guitar came to abrupt halt. Karen lowered her voice but didn't soften her tone. "We're also going to help pay for the wedding, although Billie's giving us a hard time about that."

"OK, so you want to pay. So find a local, independent restaurant. There's got to be something cute and affordable that isn't a chain."

"Billie loves Chevys," Karen said. "And she says Ian's fine with it."

"Of course Ian's fine with it. He adores her. And wouldn't do anything to make you hate him."

"Hate Ian?" Karen laughed. "As if. Even you can't hate him."

Jane shoved a handful of crackers into her mouth and tried to figure out what Ken was trying to play now. He went to high school in the seventies, so it was only a matter of time before he attempted—

Yep, there it was. "Stairway to Heaven."

Her mom was right. It was impossible to hate Ian. He was a great guy and great for her sister. Her mind was on an entirely different man at the moment.

"What if I find a place I know she likes?" Jane asked, but she knew the battle was lost.

"I've already found a place she likes." Karen took Jane's napkin and began wiping infinitesimal crumbs off the table. She and Jane had more than a few things in common. "Why don't you tell me about this guy you're bringing to the party?"

Because so many reasons. "You'll meet him next week. Not much to say."

Karen shook her head, sighing, as if it were as bad, as hopeless, as she'd feared. "Why not?" she asked.

Oh, to hell with it. He'd helped her; she should just cut him loose and return the favor. "Confession, Mom. He's just a guy renting a bedroom in my house. We're not really dating. His brother is my boss at Whitman. He's writing a book about hiking and camping and living in the outdoors, which is where he prefers to reside."

"How interesting. What did you say his name was?"

"I didn't. I told you, we're not really dating."

"You're going to have to tell me his name sooner or later," her mother said.

Oh God. She was smiling.

*She doesn't believe me.*

## 15

When writing about his escapades in the outdoors, Grant often used a fictional point of view. It helped him let go of his ego and get the words on the page. Some bookstores shelved him in fiction, which he understood but didn't agree with. He wrote about the real world, what he'd seen, smelled, tasted; the way a blister felt when it popped: wet, sticky, hot; the annoyance of hearing the distant roar of a jet airplane when you just wanted one full day in your short life on this earth without ever hearing a machine.

When it had become clear that Jane was happy to throw herself back into her job, and happy to lock the door between his end of the house and hers, his writer's block had flattened him like that giant boulder in *Raiders of the Lost Ark*.

And so he decided to write from a different point of view for a while. It wasn't Grant taping up his blister and eating miner's lettuce, it was Jane.

Well, not Jane. Fictional Jane.

Fane.

He was going to have to come up with a better name, but Fane is what he'd been calling her. Luckily, he'd never been one of those writers who posted his daily pages on the internet. The only person who'd know whose eyes and ears and soul were interpreting the sequoias and slugs and pit toilets was him. Writing from Jane's—*Fane's*—point of view gave him the fresh, new, unspoiled perspective he needed to squeeze out one last book before he retired.

Because he'd known for a long time now that he didn't want to write creative nonfiction about the outdoors anymore. Not for a living, at least. He was as burnt out as an acre of drought-weakened Douglas fir, charred to stumps in an August wildfire.

His dream now was a cliché: those who can't do, teach. He already had his MFA—he'd gotten that after the first book—and had taught writing as a visiting professor at universities and community colleges up and down the West Coast. But before he returned to teaching for the long term, he was determined to fulfill his contract with the publisher and finish his final masterpiece.

Grant forced his hands back onto the keyboard.

*I didn't realize water could be so cold and not be frozen. I watch something small and creepy floating on the surface of the rapids and wonder what it is. A spider? I've always hated spi—*

Did Jane hate spiders? It seemed sexist to assume she was afraid of spiders. Truth was, it was Grant who was afraid of spiders. Anyone who had read his earlier books would know that. He'd once shrieked like a four-year-old when he'd found a spider in his underwear. Just because he was wearing them at the time didn't mean a man should cry like a baby.

But damn, that sucker had been huge.

A knock on the door interrupted his marathon of brilliance. He did a quick word-count check for the day.

Sixty-seven.

*Fuck me.*

"Grant? It's Jane."

Of course it was her. Who else would it be? A voice inside him suggested *Fane?* and he ducked his head, laughing to himself.

"Are you sleeping?" she asked.

He got up, walked to the door, and opened it. "Just trying to work."

"I'm sorry to bother you. I'll come back later." Her hair was pulled back tightly, sleek along her skull. He noticed her ears stuck out in a truly adorable way. Handles that would be good for holding on when he kissed her.

Fane was totally into outdoorsy guys.

"No, I was having trouble before you knocked," he said. "I'm psyched to have an excuse to take a break." He gestured for her and her head handles to come into the room.

"It's about that party of my sister's," she began.

"Day after tomorrow, right? Saturday at noon, the invitation said." He rubbed his stomach. "Looking forward to it. Love that salsa at Chevys."

She looked pained. "Not you too."

"More of a salsa fresca type, are you?" He went over to his mini fridge and popped it open. "Can I offer you a canned water? I'm fully loaded with a wide selection of flavored carbonated water in convenient twelve-ounce cans."

"Are you all right? You seem a little, I don't know, drunk or something."

"It's my book. I'm slowly going insane." He took out a lemon-flavored water and held it out to her. "Please, take it. It'll make me feel useful in the universe."

"Going that badly, is it?" Offering a quick smile, she accepted the can and popped it open.

"Worse."

"Then I have good news. You'll have all day Saturday to get caught up."

His spirits fell. He could actually feel them sink even lower than they'd been a few minutes ago. They were probably seeping out of his toes like blister ooze. "They canceled the wedding?"

"I told my mother you're not really my boyfriend."

"So she doesn't want me to come?"

Jane made an incredulous face. "You don't want to come."

"Oh yes I do. I told you. Love that sals—"

"Stop. You can't be serious."

"I am. I think they put sugar in it. If I ever find myself really shoveling something in and I can't stop, I know there's sugar. But it's not just the salsa, it's the chips." He kissed his fingertips. "So light and crispy."

"I can't believe this. Listen, if you want to eat there, you can go anytime. No reason to suffer through a family party with a bunch of strangers."

"I want to go, Jane," he said.

"You can't."

"Please let me go to the party, Jane." He put his hand over his heart. "Please."

"But why?"

"Look at me. You need to ask?"

She frowned. "I don't see how an awkward social gathering is going to help you with your book."

"You don't understand the creative process."

"Sounds like you don't either," she said.

"Ouch, Jane."

Her face twitched with a suppressed smile. "Sorry. I only have good thoughts for you and your book."

"I'm going stir-crazy. Going out with people is just what I need."

"Don't you have friends?"

"Nope."

She lost her battle with the smile. "I doubt that. You've probably got tons of friends."

"Why do you say that?"

"Look at you. You're funny, you're…" She bit her lip.

"Handsome?"

"Yeah. So handsome."

"It's the beard. It hides my flaws."

"Is that so?" she asked.

"Very so. I'm actually hideous under all this fur." He rubbed his jaw, wondering what else he could do to keep her from leaving the room. "Say, I've got some excellent, ah, dried cherries. Want some?"

"Bad for my teeth."

"Right. I lost mine years ago so it's not a problem." He stretched his lips over his teeth to hide them and opened his mouth in a wide, toothless grimace. "Thee?"

"You need to get out."

With his lips still pulled over his teeth, he said, "Thaf whaf I wath felling you."

With a snort, she sat on the bed and held out her hand. "All right, give me the cherries."

*Yes.* He went and got them and a bag of chocolate-covered almonds and handed them to her.

"Here's the deal," she said. "My family is complicated. Mom and Dad had us really early and realized their mistake before Billie was three. They were trying to figure out how to afford getting divorced and sharing custody when my mom met Ken, my stepfather—he's a pharmacist by the way—when she was filling a prescription for a yeast inf— Well, anyway, you can see it's a fun family story. Right around the same time my dad, his name's Victor, got a job offer up in Seattle. High tech. Lots of money."

"And he went?"

"He went. Working there meant he could afford child support, and she wanted to be with Ken anyway."

"He still lives there, right?"

She skipped the cherries and went straight to the chocolate-covered almonds. Once she'd looked through the bag and chosen a good one, she said before popping it in her mouth, "He got remarried too a few years later. Also much happier the second time around. They have two kids, a boy and a girl, still teenagers, I think."

"You think?"

She held up her finger as she chewed and swallowed. "They're nineteen or twenty. We don't see each other as often as, well, as often as you might think. My dad was happy to start over. We saw him mostly when he came here." She gestured around her at the house. "This was his parents' house."

Grant had been so close to his father he still got choked up talking about him. So he didn't talk about him. "Is he going to bother to come down for the party?"

"You make him sound like he doesn't care."

"Does he?"

Jane shrugged, shook the bag of almonds, peering inside again for a while before pulling out a small one this time. "In his own way. I think it's impossible to love people you don't see as much as people you live with. Even your own children."

The admission made Grant glad he'd given her the chocolate. "That's got to be hard."

"It is what it is." She shrugged again. "I've got a big family that loves me. Siblings right and left. A decent stepfather. I even like my stepmom. I really can't complain."

Grant thought it might hurt anyway. "I like having a big family too," he said. Although when he thought about family, he was remembering his childhood with his father, when two adults and four boys lived in a twelve-hundred-square-foot bungalow, there was never enough money, and the front yard flooded whenever it rained for too many days in a row, usually in January. Golf-ball-sized snails would be left behind when the water finally drained away, and the boys would collect them in a bucket and dump them on each other's heads.

"But to answer your question," Jane went on, "yes, he's coming to the party. They all are, I think. Which is why I can't believe my mother insists on throwing it at a chain restaurant. They're coming all that way for that? Ian can afford... anything! He could rent an entire villa and winery for a week."

"But he's too cheap?" Grant remembered the guy and his expensive pencils, wondering if he were the type to keep all the good stuff for himself.

"No, my mother won't let him. Insists on being the hosts because they're the parents of the bride. It's medieval. What next, a hope chest? A dowry? Give me a break!"

"I'd be the same way," he said. When she turned her rage-scowl on him, he cleared his throat. "That is, if I were a dad and my daughter was marrying some rich guy. Who cares how much money he has? I still have the right to be the one welcoming him to the family. Rich people don't get to be the boss of everything just because they have the most money."

Openmouthed, Jane stared at him, long enough to make him uncomfortable. He turned to find some other refreshment to offer her as a distraction.

"You're right," she said. "You're totally right." She stood up and came over to him, the bags of cherries and almonds in her hands.

"I shouldn't lecture you. I've got issues."

She smiled, creating small, adorable creases in the corners of her eyes, and handed him the bags. "No, it's good. I needed to hear it. The funny thing is—" She stopped herself.

"Yes?"

It seemed to take her a moment to decide if she wanted to answer. "I think I was embarrassed because you were coming. Having just been to your family place in Marin, I—"

He tried not to laugh, but he couldn't help himself. "Me? You wanted to impress Grizzly Adams?"

"I know, right? What was I thinking?"

"And then I went on and on about the chips," he said.

"It just made it worse. I felt like you were patronizing us."

"Do you have any idea how different my growing up was from that place of my grandfather's?"

She shook her head. "Troy mentioned you guys living there after your father died."

"Troy and my brothers. With my mother. Not me. I'd already left home."

"I didn't realize that."

"You know why they moved in with him?" Grant didn't like to talk about this, but in the face of her embarrassment about the restaurant, he felt he owed her. "Because she didn't have enough money to support the family on her own after he was gone. My dad never took my grandfather's money, even if he'd offered it, which I doubt. Dad was a junior high school teacher. Mom's family didn't have any money, and she'd left school at sixteen. When we were kids, she started painting—art, not houses—and selling her work at farmer's markets. There was enough for us when he was alive, but... I was in college, and Troy was about to go, and Ben and Justin were still in high school but had to eat and all that."

"I didn't realize," she said.

"So now that you know I'm just a poor nobody, will you

let me come to the party? Now that you know I can't afford food."

She pointed at the almonds and cherries. "Nice try. You got those at Whole Foods. You can't be hurting that badly."

"Dumpster diving."

"So you're not actually Grizzly Adams the guy, you're Grizzly the bear?" She threw her head back and laughed, exposing her soft, smooth throat, demonstrating what she might look like in bed if she felt really, really good.

The sight—and the thought—knocked the breath out of him.

"Well, then, all right," she said, recovering her composure with a deep breath, her eyes twinkling. "You can come to the party and eat as many chips as you like." With that declaration, she patted him on the arm and walked out of the room.

He could only smile and nod like an idiot.

## 16

*A* day after Jane had accepted the indignity of the suburban chain restaurant for Billie and Ian's party, her mother called her with an emergency, eleventh-hour change of venue. After another boring yet stressful day at the office, Jane had gone out for a walk, finding herself heading toward the huge regional park up the hill from her house. Acres of redwoods, oak, picnic tables, miles of trails—it had never appealed to her except as a selling point on her planned Airbnb listing. But it was a beautiful day, and the call of nature —not the bathroom kind, the stop-and-smell-the-roses kind —was too sweet to resist.

"Abel and Francesca are flying in and out the same day and asked if there was any way they could avoid the drive north," her mother said.

Abel and Francesca were her dad's new kids, her youngest half-siblings. "It would be an unnecessary hassle just for—" She was going to insult the restaurant again but said instead, "For a few hours."

"They were flying into Oakland, so we decided to have it there."

Jane was halfway up a steep dirt trail through redwood trees that were beautiful but apparently liked growing on a twenty-degree angle. She was drenched in sweat and panting like a dog. "Have it where?"

"In Oakland. Ken and I don't mind having an excuse to drive down. We love spending time in Berkeley now and then. We're going to splurge and stay at the Claremont. I'm getting a spa—"

Jane slapped a hand over her pounding heart. "You're having the party at *my* house?"

"Of course not!" Karen said, laughing. "I wouldn't do that to you, honey. The Johnsons have neighboring houses together, not too far from you."

"You invited the Johnson cousins?"

"Of course. I invited all the Johnsons, are you kidding? Billie would never forgive me if I didn't make sure your Aunt Trixie was there. She and your father haven't seen each other since your grandmother's funeral."

Trixie was Jane's father's first cousin, but they called her an aunt.

Everyone in the family had met at the house, which her grandmother had left to Jane and Billie, and seen what a mess it was. It had taken months to make it livable—while they were living in it. Ian, increasingly smitten with Billie, had helped out with the renovation.

"That was so upsetting," Karen said. "To see how she'd been living… all those cats… and that *carpet*…" Her voice shuddered.

"I know. Believe me. On a really hot day, you can still smell a hint of the cat pee."

"But just think," her mom continued, "if the house hadn't been in such bad shape, Billie and Ian wouldn't have had the chance to realize they were made for each other."

Jane made a skeptical sound. "They would've found a chance sooner or later. Sooner, I think."

"But they'd been friends for years, practically since you dated him back in high school."

Her mother wasn't afraid of bringing up the past. "Mom, they'd been in love with each other for years," Jane said. "They would've figured it out eventually, even without the cat-pee carpet."

There was a moment of silence. "You know, Jane, I think you might actually be glad they figured it out."

Why couldn't her mother believe she wished them well? "Of course I'm glad. I love Billie. Ian's perfect for her. They're crazy good together." Jane tripped over a root jutting into the path, which triggered her temper. "And how can you say that? 'Might actually be glad.' They're having a baby, Mom. Together. I can't wait to see what it looks like."

"Please don't say 'it,'" Karen said.

"Sorry. Billie's fault." Jane wiped the sweat off her brow. The cooling shade from the redwoods was behind her. Now she walked on the bare ridge overlooking the bay, exposed to the sun. San Francisco looked small compared to the rest of the sprawling Bay Area, just a hazy peninsula with a few tall buildings at one end. "Anything else changed about the party other than the place?" Mark and Rose's house would be a lot easier to get to, but poor Grant wouldn't get his favorite tortilla chips.

Thinking about Grant made her smile involuntarily. He was so damn cute. Dumpster diving at Whole Foods.

Oh Christ. She was thinking about him again.

"Nothing changed. You're still bringing your roommate?"

"Housemate. And yes."

"Can't wait to meet him," Karen said.

Jane rolled her eyes up to the summer sky. "Look, Mom, I

have to go. I'm about to walk back down into the trees where there isn't any coverage."

"Send me a selfie," Karen said. "I need proof you're really hiking."

"It's not hiking. It's walking."

Karen laughed softly. "Right. Like I said, can't wait to meet him."

"I've walked *before*," Jane began, but her mother said goodbye and hung up.

She *walked* back down the trail into the woods and then out the park entrance at the end of her street. A dozen cars were illegally parked along the road, and she nodded hello to two women getting out of their car for their after-work run.

Other people went to a lot of trouble to come to this park. She should take more advantage of how close it was to her.

For her walks.

Just as she was taking out her key to unlock her front door, Grant pulled into the driveway, every window in his old SUV rolled down, Top 40 blaring over the radio.

She lingered in the doorway, patting Shadow until he joined her. "Were you just enjoying the vocal acrobatics of the young and talented Taylor Swift?" she asked.

"I can't help but notice the hint of sarcasm in your voice," he said, bending down to pick up the pile of junk mail on the floor inside the door. He handed her a pair of flyers from local real estate agents who hoped she wanted to sell. There were never enough houses on the market for the demand.

"I'm just surprised, that's all," she said. "I would've pegged you as more of an alternative rock type of guy. Or very old school."

He gave her a proud smile. "I'm very complex. I have complex tastes."

"Huh," she said, stepping ahead of him. She was careful to

take off her shoes before they could track clumps of trail dust into the house.

"It just so happens my taste matches perfectly with the only radio station my Rover is currently able to play," he added.

"Ha," she said. "Right again."

He didn't say anything, just stared at her for a moment, long enough for her to notice he'd gotten a haircut. Even his beard was trimmed, more stylistically than she'd ever seen him wear it before, with sharp edges along his cheek and jaw. Her gaze lingered on the curve of his upper lip. It was almost as full as his bottom one. If he were a woman, he'd look great in lipstick. If he were a man, which he was, he'd look great right now. With or without lipstick.

Christ. Not again.

"Looking forward to Chevys," he said.

She grasped at reality with both hands. "Right, my mom just told me. I'm so sorry, but the party has been moved." She gestured vaguely over her shoulder. "Some cousins of ours have offered to have it at their house. Houses, actually. They have two, right next door to each other. Here in Oakland."

"Then forget it," he said.

"What?"

He didn't crack a smile for over three full seconds. "Just kidding. Same time?"

She told her heart to get out of her throat and back into her chest where it belonged. What was the matter with her? Yes, she found him attractive, but that doesn't mean she should have a cardiac incident when she thought he might back out on a nondate with her.

At least she was able to keep her face as serious as he had. "Yes. Same time."

———

"Thanks, man," Grant said to the Lyft driver, opening the door and glancing up at the Johnson house. Houses. He'd climbed into the front seat because it seemed rude to hide out in the back as if the driver had a disease, even when he was with a date.

Jane could pretend all she liked, but this was a date. He hadn't smelled this good since he'd gone out with a cosmetologist last year. They'd only dated for about two months, but when they decided to end it, he had more scented products in his toiletries bag than in the sum total of his lifetime to date. The packaging was all carefully, overtly masculine, in charcoal gray, hunter green, and matte black, with product names like "Blade" and "Steele." He wasn't sure what body part "Steele" was for, although he was tempted to rub it on his dick and see what happened.

That wasn't something he needed any help with today, however. Jane had surprised him fifteen minutes ago by appearing in a ruby-red, skin-tight dress with a slit up to her earlobe—at least that had been his first impression. He'd had to avert his eyes and had almost asked her to change into the bland cardigan and classy trousers she usually wore to work. How could he drive with that curvy leg stretched out next to him? But then she'd informed him they were doing a ride share to get to the party—"no parking up in Trixie's neighborhood, and this way we can drink as much as we want"—and he hadn't been able to think of another excuse to get her to cover up. Weather wouldn't persuade her; it was in the eighties, not a cloud in the sky, and she had a floppy straw hat for the sun.

She climbed out next to him and adjusted her hat. She almost struck him in the nose with her elbow, but that may have been because he was standing too close to her. Bee to honey. She smelled even better than he did.

"I guess I don't need to ask if we're in the right place," he said. The narrow street was already socked in with parked cars, their right wheels planted in the shoulder.

"You look nice, by the way," she said vaguely, frowning up at the two-story house.

"Thanks." Since she wasn't even looking at him, he checked his fly and tugged down his Fite Fitness T-shirt, which he'd worn in honor of the Johnson family, who owned the fitnesswear company headquartered in San Francisco. He was also wearing cargo pants. If she hadn't insisted he should dress as himself, whom she probably continued to secretly believe had the initials G.A., he would've dug out the business clothes he wore in New York when hobnobbing with publishing people. He'd been relieved by her insistence because most of his things were in a storage unit in San Rafael. When he was done with the book and knew where he'd end up next, he'd find a real apartment somewhere and live like an adult.

"Oh, look at the dog," she said.

A cheerful, three-legged black Lab was making his way down the driveway to them, his dark brown eyes begging for attention. Jane shoved her gift bag into Grant's hands and hurried over to the dog.

Her dress was even sexier from the back. Well, of course it was. She had a killer a—

"Jane!" Billie appeared on the front porch, a martini glass in her hand. After a vigorous wave that spilled the drink on the geraniums, she hopped down the steps to meet them. She wore a peach sundress and a floppy straw hat similar to Jane's. "You made it!"

"Brutal jet lag, but we'll manage," Jane said. "I assume that's not a real martini?"

"Pomegranate-infused mineral water," Billie said with a grin. She stepped over a low hedge of lavender—she wore orange Chaco sandals with thick hiking soles, footwear he owned himself—and came straight at him with a wide-eyed smile. "You're the fake boyfriend, right?"

"Not anymore," Jane said.

Billie's eyes got wider. "Not fake anymore?"

Grant thought of the kiss. That hadn't been fake. He swallowed a smirk.

"Not anything," Jane said. "I told Mom he's just a nice guy I barely know."

"Yeah, right." Billie turned to him and held up her declawed martini. "Can I get you a real drink, nice guy? Grant, right?"

"Yup. I'm Grant. Don't put yourself out. I'm sure we can find something for ourselves inside."

"Actually, the drink table is in the backyard," Billie said. "April's the bartender. She's another cousin. They're thick on the ground around here. That's her dog, Stool."

Grant looked down at the black dog, who had planted his tail on Grant's best Keen oxfords and now gazed up at him adoringly. As soon as he had his own place, he was getting a dog. Maybe seven. He squatted down and cupped Stool's face between his hands, scratching his cheeks. "Good name, buddy."

"It's because he eats his own poop," Billie said cheerfully, sipping her martini. "In addition to the three-leg thing."

Grant quickly put some distance between his mouth and the dog's flapping tongue. "Seriously, buddy? You eat shit?" He glanced up at Billie. "Pardon my language."

Billie smiled. "No problem. I thought you should know. You looked like you were going in for a kiss."

"Tempting, but I'll have to pass," Grant said, patting

Stool's velvety head as he rose. He turned to Jane. "Want to go find that drink table?"

"Dad and Sylvia are over at the other house, talking to Mark," Billie said. "The twins are over there too. They flew up from San Diego."

Grant noticed Jane didn't seem remotely tempted to greet her father and his other family. "Let's go find that drink table," she said. "Do we have to go through the house, or do we walk around?"

As Billie pointed toward the yard between the houses, she was called back into the house by a group of people Grant didn't know. He and Jane walked down the hill into a flat strip of lawn in the back. Beyond the trees stretched a view of the bay, almost white from reflected sunlight.

"I should find Trixie and say hello," Jane said, "but I'm kind of thirsty."

"That special kind of thirsty," Grant said.

"You know it." Jane waved at a few middle-aged women on the other side of the yard, then jabbed her thumb at Grant. The women's eyes all turned to him, raking him from head to toe and saying something to each other. They were too far to hear what they said, but Grant could lip-read *nice*.

"They think I'm nice," he told Jane, waving at the women. Then he put his arm around her waist and smiled down at her.

"What are you doing?"

"You want them to think I'm your date, right?" he asked.

"I don't care what they think."

He kept his arm where it was. "Who are they?"

"My mother, Ian's mother, and some lady whose name I can't remember. She may have been my teacher in second grade." She freed himself from his arm.

"Which one is your mother?"

"You're kidding, right?"

He was. The woman in the middle looked just like Jane, except a little older, with silver hair. She also wore a violet sweater and long, floral skirt instead of a sexy red dress. She wore a floppy hat, though. "Do people ask if you're sisters?" he asked.

"All the time. She loves it."

"Do you?"

Jane adjusted her hat, tilting the brim to hide her eyes. "It bothered me when I was younger. It made me feel like I wasn't really…" She paused. "Both of my parents had a second family. Sometimes… I was grown up for my age anyway, and the babies came along… I don't know."

He stepped around her to see past the hat. "Did you maybe feel like you weren't as much her kid as the others were?"

She faced him. "I've always been hyperaware of being the oldest. Sometimes I'd like to… not be hyperaware."

"I'm the oldest," he said. "It can suck. With great power comes great responsibility and whatnot."

Her lips curved. "Oh yeah? Like running the family business?"

"With great responsibility comes great flaking." He puffed up his chest. "For those strong enough to manage it."

She laughed. "I wish *I* were strong enough. I'd love to just dump everything and take off for a year or two, be a flake like you."

Like a hot poker through a campfire marshmallow, her words slid through his ribs and pierced his left ventricle. But he was an expert at hiding his feelings, especially the negative ones, and he smiled at her very funny joke. "Let's find the booze."

"Let's. Trixie has a thing for wine, but I like the hard stuff."

Sounded good to him. Flakes loved drinking too much.

At the card table near the back door of the house, a young woman wearing a lime-green Fite Fitness baseball cap was tending bar. The sleeves of her denim shirt were pushed up, revealing several tattoos on each forearm. "What can I get you, Jane Garcia?"

"Hi, April," Jane said. "I wasn't sure you'd remember me. We've only met a couple times."

"Of course I remember you. Mom made trading cards. She had pictures of you, Billie, your mom, dad, everyone." April grinned and held her hand out to Grant. "Hi, I'm one of the Johnson cousins. You must be the invited man meat."

"That I am," Grant said, grinning back at her.

"I'll make your drink first," April said, "and make my honey jealous. He's in the house, hiding with Mark. They're pretending to set up the video slideshow Mom made, but I don't think it takes two hours to attach her laptop to the TV. Introverts make terrible party hosts."

"You guys are super nice to host my sister's party here," Jane said.

"Aw, don't sweat it," April said. "I love parties. Mom and Liam and Bev do too. What can I get you, dude?"

Grant tapped a bottle. "A little of this with a twist of lime?"

April picked up the vodka. "Soda?"

He nodded.

"Same for me," Jane said. "Minus the soda. Extra vodka."

"My kind of woman." April made the drinks and handed them over. "Mothership approaching at eleven o'clock," she muttered.

"Yours?" Grant asked.

April pointed at Jane. "Hers."

## 17

"Shit," Jane said, lifting her drink.

"Too late for evasive maneuvers?" Grant mumbled to April.

April smiled at someone over his shoulder and nodded.

"Hey there, Jane, I thought you might come over and say hello to Mrs. Kilpatrick," a woman said behind them. She *sounded* a lot like Jane, too.

Jane turned. "I was just about to."

After sharing a meaningful eyebrow wiggle with April, Grant also turned around. Up close, Jane's mother didn't look as much like her. Her eyes were very different, a pale blue instead of brown, her skin was lighter, and she was much taller. But the bone structure and figure and expression were eerily similar.

"Hi," he said. "I'm Grant. The invited man meat."

Behind him, he heard April snicker.

"Sorry," he added, genuinely regretting his joke. She was Jane's mother, after all, and the party's hostess. He held out his hand. "It's a pleasure to meet you, Mrs.—" He realized he didn't know her surname.

She clasped his hand. "Karen Morrison. I heard April calling you man meat earlier, so I know you got it from her."

"I've always been a bad influence," April agreed.

"Jane tells me you're renting out a room at the house?" Karen asked.

Grant's mind went blank. To his surprise, he was nervous. "Yes." That was as good as he could come up with.

"Writing a book, isn't that right?" Karen continued.

He nodded. "That's what I do." When no more words came to him, he lifted his drink to his lips.

Jane jumped in. "He's an award-winning writer of creative nonfiction about the outdoors, California wilderness areas in particular but the West more broadly." Her hand landed on his shoulder. "The *Chronicle* put his first book on their ten-best list that year."

Slowly he turned his head to look at her. "How did you know that?"

Jane squeezed his shoulder. "He's too modest to tell people that. I found it online."

Before he could cop a feel, Jane removed her hand, stepped to one side, and gestured at the makeshift bar. "Do you have something to drink, Mom?"

Karen winked at him—yes, he was quite sure that was a wink—and then helped herself to a bottle of mineral water. "April, please let me know the second you're sick of doing this. Jane has more than enough experience mixing drinks."

"What's that supposed to mean?" Jane asked, but her tone was mild, as if she and her mother bickered out of habit, not passion. "I guess my secret's out. April, you might as well know I lead a wild, irresponsible lifestyle."

"I can relate," April said. "Before I met Zack, I crashed on my brother's couch and slept with strangers. You?"

Jane helped herself to another lime from an orange bowl

on the table and squirted it into her drink. "That actually sounds fun, except my brother is a college student. I don't think he has a couch."

"You want to sleep with strangers?" Karen asked.

Jane brought her glass to her lips and drained it, which couldn't have been healthy. She coughed a little and then said, "Sometimes, yes. Sometimes it crosses my mind."

Grant stopped himself from asking if he counted as a stranger. He feared not.

"You should go ahead and do it then," Karen said. "Whoever you find couldn't be any worse than Andrew."

"Thanks." Jane reached out for the vodka bottle. "Mind if I pour, April?"

"Help yourself. Don't expect a tip though."

Karen put her hand on Jane's shoulder. "I'm sorry, honey. I was just so shocked to see him here."

"See who?" Jane tipped the bottle over her cup.

"I suppose you felt like you had to invite him since you were together so long. Were you hoping he'd give Billie and Ian a nice gift? I never thought of him as the generous type—"

Jane stared at her mother. "Andrew is here?"

"You haven't seen him?"

"Of course not. I never want to see him." Jane's head swiveled as she searched the crowd on the lawn. "What does he think he's doing?"

Grant looked around too but saw no sign of the guy.

"Don't get upset," Karen said. "Billie must've invited him. She doesn't carry a grudge like you do."

"Of course she doesn't! She never lived with him."

"Don't let her know you're angry," Karen said. "This party means a lot to her. It's her happiness that matters, not yours."

Grant curled his toes into the grass, hoping to dig a hole

and disappear. The urge to defend Jane from her own mother was overpowering.

"In general or just today?" Jane asked.

"Jane, I love you very much, but if you make your sister cry at her combination wedding and baby shower in front of all these people, I'll cut you out of my will."

The use of money to manipulate family behavior was too much for Grant, who opened his mouth, struggling to find a polite way to tell Karen to shove her will up her ass.

Luckily, Jane spoke first. "Don't worry, Mom. The only person who's going to cry is Andrew." She took another sip of her drink.

"It's not that I'm not angry at her for your sake," Karen said. "How about I talk to her about it later?"

"This has nothing to do with Billie," Jane said. "She'd never invite him without telling me. She never liked Andrew."

"*You* never liked Andrew," Karen said.

Jane put her arm through Grant's and squeezed. "Grant and I will go have a little talk with him."

"Good idea," Karen said. "Show him you've moved on."

"I need a trading card for this guy," April said. "I'll spit in his beer."

Jane saluted her with her empty cup. "Thank you, but hopefully that won't be necessary." Still clutching Grant's arm, she turned away from the drink table. "You up for this?"

He drained his cup. "I have never been so ready." He put his hand over her soft arm, aware his heart was beating too fast.

"Here's the thing about Andrew," Jane said as they walked across the lawn, scanning the crowd. "He's socially obtuse, so subtle cues won't work with him."

"I noticed that."

"When he cheated on me and I started packing my bags,

he didn't do anything because he thought I was just going on another business trip."

"What did he do when you told him?"

"I never did," she said. "I have no idea how long it took him to figure out I wasn't coming back."

He laughed. "I almost feel sorry for the guy."

"You should. I made all his meals. He could've starved to death."

"Guess he figured out how to dial takeout," Grant said, pointing at the lanky figure in the driveway next door. Andrew wore khakis and a plaid camp shirt, looking more respectable than he had at the house when Grant had first met him. As soon as Andrew saw Jane, he stepped over the shrubs lining the driveway and strode toward them, shooting Grant one hostile look before fixing his gaze on Jane.

"I'll hold him down if you want to slap him around a little," Grant muttered.

"That would just encourage him."

Andrew was short of breath when he reached them, sweat beading on his high forehead. His soul patch was tiny and off center, as if his razor had slipped that morning and he hadn't been willing to shave it all off.

"You shouldn't be here, Andrew," Jane said.

"I was invited."

"Who invited you?" Jane asked.

"Your sister."

"Which one?"

"Billie," Andrew said, pointing at the house. "I got an email."

"You did not get an—" Jane cut herself off. She cleared her throat. "That email wasn't meant for you."

"Are you guys dating?" Andrew asked.

"None of your business," Jane said. "Go home."

"Why would Billie invite me if she didn't want me here?" Andrew asked. "Why would Billie invite me if *you* didn't want me here?"

"It was a mistake. I'm guessing you were part of an email group from before we broke up. Billie has been sending out emails about the party all week. You must've been included by mistake."

"You didn't ask her to send it, like, as a hint? You don't want to see me again?"

"I didn't and I don't," Jane said.

Andrew made a disgusted sound that seemed forceful enough to blow off the soul patch. "You know, I almost bought a present."

"Almost," Grant said. What kind of mental crisis had led Jane to live with this snail?

"You should leave now," Jane said.

Andrew looked at Grant. "Are you staying?"

"Yes," Grant said.

"All right, I can take a hint." Andrew took out his phone, turned, and walked away, typing into the screen.

Grant's muscles loosened. He'd expected more of a fight.

"Don't say it," Jane said.

"What a catch."

"I told you not to say it."

"I thought you meant I couldn't say he was a prick," Grant said.

"I did, but you did anyway, just indirectly, with sarcasm."

"He really is a prick. Why—" No, he didn't really want to know the gory details. "Never mind."

"Made me come every time," she said anyway.

He groaned. "I said never mind."

"Every. Time."

"I really don't want to know. I just had a drink on an empty stomach."

"The thought of my orgasms makes you sick?"

Grant remembered she'd had more to drink than he had. Her cheeks were flushed, her eyes bright.

He moved his hand up her arm and over her shoulder to the back of her neck and then down her spine. With his palm in the small of her back, he pulled her closer. "The thought of him with you makes me sick."

She leaned into him. Exposed by the low cut of her dress, compressed against his arm, her full breasts plumped together like scoops of caramel ice cream. "I admit it," she said. "I have terrible taste."

"I don't." He bent his head, aiming for her rosy lips.

18

Jane didn't know why she hadn't expected Grant to actually kiss her, given she'd mentioned orgasms and then rubbed her boobs on him, but she hadn't. A little smirk and an eye twinkle, max. A raised eyebrow and a veiled sexual allusion. A knowing chuckle.

Instead, without any suggestion that this was hilarious or ironic, he lowered his head and kept lowering, and then he was there, lips on her lips, face tilting to one side, tongue sliding between her teeth and entering her mouth.

*Holy mother of oh my god Jesus f—*

She went up in flames. *Whoosh.* Like tissue paper soaked in lighter fluid and dropped in a grass fire. Every moment today had been agony, having to keep her hands off his sporty, firm, cargo-pant butt when they were arm in arm. Her mother's jabs and Andrew's obtuse stalking had barely pierced the lust bubble she'd been encased in. Why should she care what was going on out there? In here, with her needs, her hot, growing needs, she had the energy to think only of Grant.

But now the bubble had burst. He'd broken it and climbed inside, and now he was licking the inside of her mouth. Oh yeah. He had muscular thighs, either from genetics or from all that mountain meandering (she didn't care which), and now one of those thighs was between her own legs, pushing them apart. She wanted to ride him, push him against the side of the house and rub and slide and take.

And then he pushed her away. "Jesus," he said.

Face burning with booze, lust, and shame, Jane recoiled. "You started it."

He nodded, cupping his hand over his mouth.

"I couldn't help but respond," she continued.

He held up a hand. "It's OK. My fault."

But it wasn't. In a court of law, she'd go down with him. Meaning incarceration, not fellatio.

"I need another drink," she said, tripping over a clump of yellow daylilies. "Want one?"

"Hell yes."

Hands at their sides, two feet between them, they headed back the way they came.

"Jane!"

It was her father. She considered ignoring him—he sounded as if he were far enough away to pretend—but maybe her father's sobering influence was just what she needed. "Hold up," she said to Grant. "It's my dad."

They waited for him to stride down the driveway. Victor Garcia was an absurdly successful tech executive in Seattle, never satisfied with his career or accomplishments, always striving and planning and thinking. For as long as she could remember, Victor had given up on his receding hairline, choosing to shave it off entirely. He usually wore black, although today, perhaps in honor of the happy occasion, he wore charcoal gray.

"Hi, Dad." She felt Grant move closer to her. She wasn't sure how she felt about that.

Victor smiled but stopped a couple of paces short of moving in for a hug. "How are you doing? You're going to be an aunt, can you believe it? And me a grandfather."

"I know. Hard to believe."

He kept smiling. Shoved his hands in his pockets, looked over her shoulder. "Hell of a view up here. Is that Alcatraz?"

"I think so," she said. Under normal circumstances, it was hard to have good conversations with her father, but right after the flaming, crazy kiss with Grant, she could barely speak in sentences. Nobody had ever kissed her like that before. Or maybe it was no man had done so little to bring about so much of a response in her. Adrenaline still pumped through her veins, preparing her body for fight or flight.

And Jane wasn't sure which it was going to be.

She wrestled her emotions into submission. "This is Grant, a friend of mine renting out a room in my house," she said. "Grant, this is Victor Garcia, my father."

They exchanged pleasantries and shook hands.

"Well, I saw you walking by and thought I'd say hi," Victor said. "Do you know where Billie is?"

"I'm not sure. I saw her when we arrived, but that was a while ago."

He nodded, smiling some more, and then gestured at the backyard. "I'd better go see where she is, give my regards."

"Sure," Jane said. "See you later."

As he walked away, Victor reached out and squeezed her shoulder. "Definitely."

When he was out of earshot, Grant said, "For a man with grown kids, your dad sure looks a lot like Vin Diesel."

"He'd love to hear you say that. I'm thinking he must take supplements."

Grant patted his chest. "Impressive. I want to be like that when I grow up."

"On steroids?"

"Really?"

She felt bad he'd believed her. "No, I'm sure he's not on steroids. He and my stepmother are health nuts. I'm just bitter because he's better looking than I am."

"Like hell he is," Grant said.

More adrenaline pumped into her bloodstream. Were fight and flight really her only choices?

"Do you want to meet the rest of my family?" she asked.

"At the moment, no." He looked down at her, moved closer.

They stood on a strip of lawn halfway between the front and backyard. She heard barking inside the house—the high-pitched yapping of several small dogs. Somebody turned up the stereo. A group of people on the elevated deck next door, overlooking where they stood on the lawn, were laughing and shouting at each other.

She didn't know how to be with him and have it work. What did she know about relationships? People? Men? She didn't inspire romance. And she did have terrible taste. Look at Andrew. Why would this turn out any better?

"You really should meet my sister Holly," she said, taking a step away from him. "She's into hiking." She began walking toward the music.

"That's not all I'm into," he said behind her.

ane walked up the steps into a screened-in porch facing the backyard. Stereo speakers were balanced on cardboard boxes, propped against the screens, aiming the music outside. The current tune was a Lily Allen single with the dirty bits bleeped out.

"Odd choice for a baby shower," Grant said.

"April made the playlist."

"I like it. Do you think your parents will mind?"

They walked up another step or two into the kitchen, which was busy with a trio of caterers moving around platters under foil. Food that smelled a lot like a popular Tex-Mex chain restaurant.

"They aren't easily offended," she said, dodging a woman lifting a tortilla warmer out of the microwave as they hurried through the kitchen. "In fact, there's my stepfather, playing along."

Ken sat at the dining room table with a guitar, acoustic this time, with a glass of iced tea and Aunt Trixie at his side.

"Jane!" Trixie jumped up and embraced her. "Don't you look sexy!"

That was the risk of interacting with Trixie; you never knew what she was going to say. "Thanks, you too."

Trixie held out her arms and twirled as if she were wearing a glamorous gown instead of a sleeveless, plaid shirt and lime-green capris. Her white hair was cut short, and she wore large silver hoops in her ears. "Hugo keeps me spicy," she said. Widowed years ago, she'd recently married Hugo, a local vet. She patted Ken's shoulder. "I'm sure you do the same for Jane's mother."

Ken strummed a chord. "She doesn't need my help." He glanced up at Jane and Grant. "Hey, kiddo. Going somewhere?"

"Right here, Ken." Jane leaned down and kissed him on the forehead. "You know me, I like any excuse to dress up."

"Girls," he said, returning to his music.

Jane glanced at Grant and started to move into the next room. There was no reason to form bonds between him and people he'd never see again. Just because she'd kissed him once or twice (twice) didn't mean they were going to get married and have babies and hang out with her family at future baby and wedding showers that might even be hers.

It would be pointless.

"Hi, I'm Grant." He offered Trixie a hand. "The man meat."

"Oh! You've met April." Trixie took his hand between two of hers and squeezed. "How's the door?"

"The— Oh, that was from you, wasn't it? It's fine. Beautiful."

"I hadn't met you yet when I picked it out," Trixie said, "or I might have found something less opaque." She laughed.

Jane was torn between embarrassment and pride. Nobody had ever flirted with Andrew.

Ken slapped his hand over the guitar strings and looked at Grant. "You're the one living with Jane."

"Renting the front room," Grant said.

Ken got to his feet and held out his hand. "Sorry I didn't greet you properly. I didn't realize who you were."

"My tenant?" Jane asked. What was the matter with these people? She'd told them he wasn't her boyfriend. Maybe that had been a mistake. Maybe they should start making out right here and they'd know there was nothing to get excited about.

There was nothing to get excited about. Even though Grant looked better in a pair of cargo pants than any man legally should. The trimmed beard gave him a movie-star quality too, although she looked forward to it growing out to the wild-hermit vibe he'd had when they'd met.

She looked forward to it? God. No. She would have to admire him through the colorful panes of the antique door that would forever separate their lives, for the better.

Until he moved out in a few months and then she'd never see him anywhere.

"Ian told me about you," Ken continued. "It's great to meet you. Come up to the house some weekend soon. We barbecue most Sundays in the summer."

"Thanks, sounds great," Grant said. "I'll bring a tri-tip. Unless you're vegetarian, in which case I'll bring a tri-tip but plan on eating it raw."

"After all that time in the wilderness," Trixie said, "you must be dying for hot food. In a few minutes they'll be serving lunch. Bet you don't get many enchiladas in the woods."

"Only reconstituted with filtered stream water," Grant said. "Somehow it's not quite the same."

"I'm sure Jane will get used to it," Trixie said, smiling at both of them before disappearing into the kitchen.

"Christ," Jane muttered.

"It's not bad with Tabasco," he said. "They make those teeny-weeny bottles that are really cute."

Ken was grinning at both of them, so Jane strode into the next room. It was a conspiracy.

Billie and Ian sat on a couch under the front windows, opening a present with their half sisters Holly and Rachel, both in their early twenties. Holly looked like Ken, tall with brown curly hair and glasses. Rachel was more like Karen, fair-skinned and full-figured. They both had beautiful voices, and the two were working on putting together a podcast about artisanal cheese in Sonoma County. Which was why they still spent a lot of time at home, since the profits hadn't materialized yet.

Unlike everyone else, Holly and Rachel took no particular interest in Grant. They greeted him politely, hugged Billie and Ian, and then ran off to join the rest of the party.

"Free food and alcohol," Billie said. "They're not stupid. It might run out before they've had as much as they can cram in."

"Grant, nice to see you again." Ian rose and held out his hand.

"It is?" Grant asked, taking it.

"Yeah, of course. Thanks for coming to this thing. Don't feel like you guys have to stay. Just grab some fajitas and take off if you want. Billie and I would if we could."

"I wouldn't," Billie said, "but that's because everyone is giving me stuff." She held up a yellow baby blanket wrapped with a white satin bow, which Jane had bought in a Rockridge boutique for an absurd sum of money.

"I meant to give you that in person," Jane said. "How'd you get it? Where—"

"You guys must've dropped it in the driveway," Billie said.

"Luckily, it had my name on it." She hugged the blanket to her cheek.

"I'm sending the wedding gift separately," Jane said.

"You don't have to give us anything." Ian took the blanket from Billie, handling it with as much gentleness and appreciation as she had.

"Sure I do." Jane kissed Billie, waved at Ian, and had the overwhelming desire to find a dark room and take a nap. Too many emotions were swirling around. She didn't like feeling so much. It led to trouble.

"You know, Jane, maybe we could take off after we eat," Grant said, rubbing his temple. "I'm not feeling great."

What? Jane gave him a narrow-eyed warning glare.

"That's too bad," Ian said—with a grin. "Headache?"

Grant pointed at him. "Yes. That's it exactly. I have a headache."

"You don't have a headache," Jane said.

"Take a platter of fajitas with you," Ian said. "I had them send extra."

"Chips too?" Grant asked.

"Oh, yeah." Ian slapped him on the shoulder. "Grab a bag. Whatever you want."

Jane snapped. Everyone around her was so happy about Jane getting some with the cute hiker guy when she wasn't actually getting some, and why should they be so happy, anyway? It was insulting, as if they were relieved, as if they'd thought without Grant she would've been flirting with Ian, reminding him of the good old days, which were definitely not good because she'd then had to sleep with every guy in college to convince herself she was attractive, because he hadn't.

Maybe they thought no man would.

Maybe she needed to go out for some air before she made a scene and ended up on Facebook.

Maybe now.

She leaned over and kissed Billie on the top of her head. "You're beautiful and I love you. Congratulations to you both." Then she turned and walked out the front door, down the steps, and thought about looking for the three-legged dog that liked to eat his own poop.

When she didn't find him, which for some stupid reason made her want to cry, she kept walking until she was in the road with the parked cars and a pair of cyclists. She kept going, and at the corner, she got out her phone and requested a ride, even though she didn't know where she was going.

GRANT FOLLOWED Jane out the door, not surprised to see her march down the driveway and keep going. He hung back, giving her space, but he wanted to catch her and apologize. He'd embarrassed her in a stressful situation. Not cool of him. All day he'd been trying to figure out how to turn flirting into reality, and he'd probably ruined what little chance he had with his lame attempt at humor.

Although he hadn't been joking. He'd wanted to take her home, as much for her sake as for his. The party had been making her miserable.

At the end of the driveway, he took out his phone and hailed a ride. The app asked if he'd like to share with another person and save a few pennies. Why yes, yes he would.

Funny thing: the car, a crimson Mazda hatchback, picked him up first.

He and the driver confirmed who they were to each other, and they continued down the road. When they reached the corner, where Jane stood with her arms wrapped around herself, he hoped he wasn't making a mistake.

Because of the tinted rear windows, she didn't see him until she opened the door.

"Hi," Grant said.

She swore. And then didn't get in. "How?"

"You didn't specify single rider," Grant said.

Stepping back, she began to close the door. "I will next time."

"Wait," Grant said, reaching for his own door.

"Dude, don't be a stalker," the driver said. He was about ninety-two years old and had more hair than Grant. He raised his voice to address Jane. "Would you like me to call the police?"

Grant froze in his seat. "I'm not a stalker."

"No, never mind, we're going to the same place." She got in and slammed the door.

"You sure?" the driver asked.

"He lives at my house," Jane said. "If he's a stalker, I chose poorly. But what else is new?"

The driver put the car in gear and began driving.

Jane took off her hat and smacked it against the back of the seat in front of her. "I don't need your help."

"I know," Grant said.

"The only thing I need is enough money to live alone where I won't be bothered by people who think I can't be happy alone."

"Money doesn't solve as many problems as you might think," Grant said.

"Solves a lot of them though," the driver called out.

"Thank you," Jane said. She leaned forward. "You have a very nice car."

The driver flashed a peace sign. "The womenfolk like it."

She leaned back in the seat and looked out the window. "I should've gone to the party by myself."

This wasn't how Grant had hoped the day would unfold. He wasn't sure where he'd gone wrong.

"If I'd gone alone," she continued, "nobody would've gotten the wrong idea."

"I'm sorry if I made things worse for you."

She rolled her soft hat into a tube, smoothed it out, rolled it again.

He looked outside for a good spot to stop the car. "There's still time. I'll get out right here, and you can go back."

"No, I'm going home." She pulled the hat over her head again, not realizing she'd put it on inside out. The tag unfurled in front like a dog's tongue.

"Mind if I come with you?" he asked quietly.

She turned her head, met his gaze. The inside-out brim hung down, blocking one eye. "You know what bugged me the most?"

The urge to readjust the hat was too strong to overcome. He reached up and unblocked the view of both her beautiful eyes. "What?"

They looked at each other. She turned back to the window. "That they're so relieved."

Grant let out an exaggerated snort. "That's not it."

"Excuse me?"

"I think you're forgetting who it is they were so happy to see you with. This isn't about you. It's about me."

"It that so?" She gave him an incredulous—yet amused—look.

"Exactly. I'm a famous author. They were caught up in the fame glow." He stroked his chest. "I've seen it before."

"Have you?"

"Oh yes. Serious people become giddy, so amazed to be in the presence of a genuine celebrity."

She bit her lip, trying not to smile. The hat had fallen back over her eye. "I hadn't thought of that."

"I could tell. I'm glad I could set you straight."

The driver had gone up to Skyline to make the short trip to Jane's house, and they were almost there. They didn't speak through the hairpin turns and vertigo-inducing drop-offs into the eucalyptus groves.

At the house, the driver wished them well, flashing another peace sign as he pulled out.

Jane got to the door first, hat still perched inside out on her head, the tag rustling in the breeze off the bay. "Thanks," she said. "I'm sorry you didn't get any food."

"Luckily, there are thirty-seven Chevys Fresh Mex locations throughout the United States, mostly in Northern California." He reached over her head and held the door for her. "I won't have to wait long."

"You had that memorized?"

"Since yesterday when I looked it up on Wikipedia," he said.

They went inside, took off their shoes, and paused in the small chamber between the four doors—the front door, the bathroom door, his bedroom door, and the Trixie door, as he called it.

He didn't make any move toward his own. He hoped she couldn't see the sweat breaking out on his upper lip.

"It's just that they're happy for me, but they shouldn't be," she said.

"Why not?"

"They think I'm having a some kind of undefined, irresponsible fling with a random guy renting a room in my house," she said.

"Really?" he said. "How bizarre."

"No, no, you don't get it. They think I'm having a great time. They think I'm finally enjoying myself."

He took her purse out of her hands and set it on the hall table. "Aren't you?"

The afternoon light shone through the stained glass behind her, giving her a rose-gold aura. Her lipstick had worn off, but her natural lips were even more beautiful.

"No," she said, and her low voice made every hair on his body stand on end.

"Let's work on that," he said, ripping the hat off her head.

2 0

---

ane had never thought she was capable of being swept away. For one, she was strong, heavy, and had enjoyed three years of self-defense training. And secondly, she just wasn't the type. Being intelligent, rational, and disciplined had gotten her far in life. She hated the pressure to giggle and blush and pretend to be an idiot to attract romance-minded males. College was different—everyone slept with whomever, and personality (or anything else) hadn't been an issue. But in the adult world, she'd struggled to find men who looked at her that way.

The way that Grant was looking at her right now, as he pushed the sleeve of her dress off her shoulder and began caressing her collarbone with a fingertip.

"What are you doing?" She didn't mean it rhetorically. She seriously wondered what he was going to do. Another kiss that went nowhere? Some heavy petting in the hallway? True love?

Her mind shied away from that. This wasn't about love. They liked each other, which was nice, but right now this burning, sweaty madness engulfing them was about sex.

He bent down and kissed her throat—just off center where she could feel her pulse racing. "What do you want?" he asked.

"I don't know, but we can't do it here." She tipped her head to one side to expose more of her neck, just like a maiden with a vampire.

Christ. She couldn't think in those terms. Or was it kind of kinky and she should just go with it? No, not her thing. The idea that he had razor-sharp canines that were about to pierce her skin and she was going to start spurting blood like a horror movie—

Total turnoff.

"Jane?" He cupped her cheek and turned her face to his. "Are you OK?"

One problem with a well-developed brain was it tended to keep churning along even when it was supposed to take a hike.

"Keep doing that," she said roughly, pushing his face back to her neck.

Her brain would have to get in the back seat and stop trying to drive everything. From a distance, it could notice the intense pleasure tingling through her body when his lips were sucking and moving around over one of her favorite erogenous zones. But her brain was not in the driver's seat. It was a quiet, impartial observer. Strapped in like a nonverbal, powerless infant who had absolutely no say in where Daddy was driving his Rover.

Oh Christ, was he Daddy? That was so gross. Her brain simply couldn't sit passively by while she made disgusting analogies.

She was the driver, he was the hot hitchhiker, and the baby was actually a laptop she'd shut down and stowed in her briefcase in the trunk.

"My place or yours?" he asked, sliding his hand down her

arm and capturing her fingers in his. He had big hands, rough and strong.

"Are we really doing this?"

"Yes," he said.

"Just checking. I didn't want to jump to the wrong conclusions. Maybe you thought we were going to kiss and order piz—"

His mouth came down over hers, snuffing out her babbling. Appreciating the assistance, she wrapped her arms around his neck and opened her mouth to deepen the kiss. As she licked the inside of his mouth, brushing her chin across his bearded chin, the laptop-in-the-trunk that was her brain seemed to get further and further away, like it wasn't even in the same car. Not even on the same road.

"My place," she said, panting. The antechamber was high in temperature and low in oxygen. She felt around her hips for her keys—not wearing pants, this was a dress, right, and her keys were in her purse which was over there—

Hands shaking, she fumbled with the clasp on her purse and got the door key into the lock while Grant came up behind her and found her breasts. Found wasn't quite right. He didn't seem to be confused about where they were; his hands landed directly on top of them without hesitation.

She tilted her head back on his shoulder and licked his bearded jaw, unable to continue the journey without a small pit stop. More car analogies. Only now they were on a raceway. Going very fast. Very dangerous. People could get hurt.

"Jane," he moaned, running his hand down her abdomen, her upper thighs, back up again.

Motivated to continue, she pulled out of his reach and pushed open the stained glass door to her side of the house. From the open window in the kitchen came cool air and birdsong, reminding her it was only midafternoon. Hands fumbling with each other's clothes, they tripped over each other's feet getting to the end of the hallway. To her bedroom.

"This is just for fun," she said, reaching behind her back for the zipper. "I'm going to have fun. We're going to have fun. Sex is fun."

"Christ, you've got great tits," he said, sliding his hand under her gaping dress and bra.

"Tit" was not her favorite word. "Thanks, but I've never liked—"

He interrupted her vocabulary lecture with skilled stimulation of her ti— her nipple, gently rolling it between his fingers until it was hard as the protective metal case of a laptop locked in the trunk of a car, far, far away from here, utterly forgotten.

His other arm caught her around the waist and pulled her to him, his mouth crushing against hers, his tongue pushing between her teeth and sliding over hers in a wet, hot dance.

They were still in a hallway. And he was still wearing pants.

She flattened her palms against his chest and dove into the pleasure of kissing him. She caught up handfuls of his shirt in her fists to pull him lower where she could reach more of his face. She wanted to slow down and savor his warm body and the hard curve of his jaw and then unbutton his shirt carefully, controlled and controlling.

But she was too excited and wanted too much right away to go slowly and carefully. There was no illusion of control.

"My bedroom"—she said between kisses—"over there." Their faces were pressed together, the house around them a blur.

"There?" He seemed to gesture to the family room, which her grandmother had filled with hoarded objects going back decades. It was empty now of everything but her desk and a sofa.

No bed.

Shaking her head, blindly unbuttoning his shirt, she tugged him around the corner to her bedroom. "Here." She shoved the shirt over his shoulders and smiled. "Ah."

"Your turn." He spun her around, unzipped her dress all the way down, and pushed the fabric over her hips. She kicked out of it, realizing only then that she wasn't wearing a sexy designer thong but a well-worn pair of Spanx, in beige, with a blueberry-sized hole on her left butt cheek. Well, it had been blueberry-sized that morning. With all the groping about, it had probably expanded to a plum, maybe even a peach or a single-serving watermelon.

But even without a hole, the control-top, thigh-length underpants, in beige, were not in any way the sexy undergarments she would've worn had she allowed herself to imagine this moment.

"Don't look," she said.

"Excuse me?" he asked, looking.

She put her hands over his eyes. "Wait."

"How long?"

"Just a second." She backed up into her room. "Don't open your eyes."

"No guarantees."

"Then turn around." Her dresser was behind the door, and although she didn't have a lot of sexy underwear, she had something better than what she was wearing.

The black hipsters were low cut, but they were cotton and a little faded. How about the red thong? God no, last thing she wanted was something that reminded her of Andrew. He'd bought that for Valentine's Day last year, and they were much too large, which made her wonder if he'd seriously estimated her body would fit in a 3X. He'd always been an ass man; maybe the large panties were aspirational. That dentist sure had back...

"Jane, what are you doing?"

She peeled off the Spanx and stood there in just her bra, staring into her dresser drawer. "Just a second." The pink floral panties were feminine and happy. The yellow boy shorts flattered her olive skin—

"Jane." He stood behind her and set his hands on her shoulders. He slid them down her back to her waist.

A shiver tickled over her. "Yes?"

"I hope you aren't looking for something to wear before I make wild, hot love to you."

"Only my underwear," she said.

"Do you think that's a critical garment right now?" He swept her hair to one side and kissed the nape of her neck.

"Think?" she whispered.

She could feel him smile against her neck. His beard was both rough and soft, depending on which way he was moving over her skin. Her muscles spasmed, both tickled and aroused.

He reached around and moved his hand between her legs. This was what she'd wanted for a long time. God, she'd needed this.

Groaning, she let her head fall back on his shoulder.

"I like your choice in underwear," he mumbled, sliding a fingertip between her folds.

She moaned something that would've sounded like "thanks" if she'd been able to form any consonants.

"This, however"—he unclasped her bra—"has to go."

She uttered some unintelligible agreement. The pleasant sensations between her legs were more important than talking.

But the angle was limiting if they stayed on their feet. Blinking her eyes open, she appraised the distance to the bed. Not far. God bless small houses. They could practically fall over into it.

"Let's go," she said. "Bed."

"Idea. Good," he said.

"Shut up and get naked."

He laughed, which she didn't like. She wasn't kidding around.

To help him get serious, she turned, lifted her hands over her head, and shimmied the way she'd learned in a belly dancing class a few years ago—just one of those things she'd wanted to learn, and so she had.

Done seriously, belly dancing was beautiful, luscious, a glory of the feminine. And under the circumstances, erotic.

"Oh my God," he said, reaching for her.

She pushed away his hands and continued to dance. "You're still not naked."

Nodding slowly, he took care of that problem quickly and then stood before her, arms at his sides, gazing at her body, then her face, no hint of mockery remaining. "You're a goddess."

She shimmied over to him, slid her hands over his shoulders, and offered a haughty smile. "Thank you."

"Really, Jane." He caught her by the waist and pulled her against him. "I'm going to worship you."

He was big. Hard. Warm. And she was tired of dancing on her feet. The bed was only a step away, and it didn't take much force to guide him over to it.

She swept back the duvet; he snowplowed the pillows onto the floor.

Then she sat on the edge and told herself she had no reason whatsoever to think about Andrew right now or ever again. The image of him sleeping with his dentist—and her dentist—had haunted her for months, but the nightmare was over. A sexy, handsome stranger with broad shoulders and a sly grin was going to worship her like a goddess.

Oh yeah. Grant was going to be one hell of an antidote.

He leaned down and kissed her on the lips, as light as a breath, and then set his hands on her shoulders and guided her onto her back. She started to wiggle up the mattress, but he caught her knees and held her at the edge, her feet on the floor.

And then he dropped to his knees.

She waited a moment, not entirely prepared for this. Modern grooming was a lot more demanding than it had been for previous generations. She didn't go full-porn hairless, but when she was dating Andrew, she'd trimmed and shaved here and there. Was Grant expecting her to be smooth as Barbie? Shaggy as Smokey?

He dropped kisses on her knees, then the inner slopes of her thighs, right and left. His hair and beard were rough against her skin, ticklish, delicious. Irresistible. She fixed her gaze on the ceiling and let her knees fall open, prepared for the exclamation of disgust or his immediate departure to the salvage yard for a scythe.

If he was disgusted, he didn't say so. And she certainly wasn't going to complain about anything, certainly not the confidence with which he navigated the area and definitely not, as the seconds turned into long, luxurious minutes, his endurance.

Oh God. She clutched fistfuls of sheet in her hands, and then as the pressure built, she tunneled her fingers through his hair. Just to give her some sense of guiding the spiraling rocket ship as it exploded in space.

She cried out—it was impossible to keep quiet during *that*—and released his scalp, letting her arms flop into the bed.

"Oh my God," she gasped.

He dropped kisses on her lower belly, giving little pats as he rose higher. While she recovered her breath, he put on a condom and then settled with his head near her breasts, fingering her lightly between her legs.

"Do whatever you want to me," she said. "I'm too happy to argue."

He pushed up on his arms and climbed on top of her. "I just might take you up on that."

Hearing the tension in his voice and feeling the sweat on his skin, she realized what a strain he was under, waiting for the finale.

And so was she, she realized.

She dug her heels into the bed, lifting her hips, brushing against him. When he groaned, she slid her hands around to his back, which was slippery with sweat, and invited him in.

He looked up at her, and they shared a moment of wordless understanding.

And then he filled her, slowly, and they waited a moment to adjust to each other.

"Jane," he groaned, drawing back, pushing in. Again.

The sense that what they were doing was just clean fun shattered. Raw need took over. He thrust into her, burying himself deeper. She took him, dug her nails into his back, squeezed him harder.

Wild and wordless, they clutched one another, threw themselves at each other, invaded and taken and free.

He came and she followed him over.

It was perfect.

Jane was smiling in her sleep.

Propped on an elbow, Grant watched her blissful face turned toward him on the pillow. Her hand was on his chest, fingers slightly curled, and one of her legs rested over his.

Any minute now she'd wake up and that smile would disappear. Regret would come into her eyes, and she'd push him away, telling him it was fun, but...

He knew it was coming. He'd known when she'd opened the glass door to invite him into her side of the house that it was a one-time offer. The world of corporate accounting and Jane didn't have room for Grant in the long term or even the middle term, and he was fine with it. Sad, disappointed, lonely, annoyed—a little. But life was life. You couldn't overcome a riptide; you had to play dead, then swim sideways. Otherwise you'd be swept away.

She was so beautiful. He was definitely a fan of her face. An excellent face, not so perfect it was boring but— No, he was wrong. It was perfect. A softly curved oval shape with full lips, velvety skin, a beauty mark on her slightly dimpled left cheek, the thick, dark eyebrows arching like graceful caterpillars on her round forehead…

Maybe not caterpillars. Much tastier than that. He bent over and lightly kissed one, enjoying their delicate softness under his lips.

He drew back before he got too aggressive and woke her. Holding her skin to skin, now that his desire was momentarily satisfied, was deeply relaxing. They fit together well, her round, smooth body with his angular, hairy one, and he wanted to lie here, holding her for much longer than he was going to be able to.

How would she say it? What words would she use to tell him to leave?

His stomach growled. Making love wasn't climbing Mt. Shasta, but it burned a few calories, and he was hungry.

He looked over to the window, where Shadow sat on the sill, a motionless black silhouette.

His stomach growled again.

Jane's smile, which he continued to gaze upon, widened. "Should we go out to Chevys?" she asked as she opened her eyes.

And then she leaned forward and kissed him.

When he didn't kiss her back, just stared at her at close range, she asked, "What?" Only then did her smile begin to falter.

"Are you sure you wouldn't rather get Chinese?" he asked.

"Like our first date," she said and kissed him again. "How romantic of you."

What was happening? He caught her behind the head and crushed his mouth against hers, with tongue, just to make sure.

She returned his kiss for a long time.

"Mm," she said finally, lifting her arms over her head in a

deep stretch as her legs fell open. "Do we have to leave the house?"

What house? He licked the nipple closest to him and then sucked it into his mouth, celebrating how tight and puckered it became under his tongue.

She began to laugh. "You need to eat. Your stomach is louder than the garbage truck going by."

"It's Saturday," he said, moving on to Breast Number Two. "There isn't a garbage truck."

"I was speaking metaphorically." She drew his face up to hers. "You're a writer. You should know about those."

This time he did hear his stomach, and yes, it was loud. "Delivery?"

"Whatever you want." She smiled, flashing both rows of her teeth. He'd never seen her smile like that before.

"I want you," he said.

That was becoming painfully clear.

"You can have me." She twisted around in the bed, giving him a prime view of her ass, and began searching the bedside table for something. "My tablet should be here somewhere."

"Video?"

She laughed. "Dream on. I've kept my boobs off the internet this long, I'm not about to blow it. So to speak." She peeked over her shoulder, shot a seductive glance at his dick, and winked. "How about pizza? Fast and easy."

"Like me," he said.

"Not too fast." She rolled back to him, tablet in hand, and kissed his shoulder. Two seconds later she was biting his nipple. "Just right."

Warning bells were chiming, but he didn't know what they were warning him about. They'd had hot sex, she was happy and wanted more. What was the problem?

He set a hand on her cheek. "Jane."

"Mm." She looked up. "What?"

Or was *he* the problem?

Now she pushed up on her arms and frowned. "*What?*"

He thought too much. Here was this smart, beautiful woman who turned him on—and was naked at this very moment—and he was wasting time thinking too much.

"I'm very particular about my pizzas," he said. She could interpret his seriousness as a joke.

"Me too," she said. "If I tell you my favorite topping, you'll be horrified."

"Pineapple."

"No. Worse."

"Worse than pineapple?" he asked.

"Way. Nobody puts this on their pizza except for me. It isn't even up for debate."

He grinned. She had hidden depths of fun. "Do I want to know?"

"I don't know. I usually hide it from people until we've known each other longer."

He gestured at their naked bodies. "This kind of accelerates the calendar, don't you think?"

"I think you're right. But you might never want to have sex with me again after you find out."

The implication of her saying that was wonderfully promising.

"What, is it like placenta or semen or another bodily fluid? Because that's what it would take to turn me off." He stroked her breast. "And even then, I'd just make sure we got separate orders."

"Semen and placentas. Yum."

"High protein," he said.

She fell on top of him, full straddle, and kissed his neck. "It's not that bad. I'm going to trust you with my secret."

Ridiculously, he shivered in anticipation. "I'm ready."

Stroking his chest hair, she moved her lips closer to his ear. He slid his hand up and down her spine, waiting for her to stop giggling.

"Promise you won't make fun of me?" she asked.

When he didn't answer, she pinched his nose.

"Ouch," he said. "Fine. I promise."

She inched closer, her lips against his outer ear. "Cream cheese. I put cream cheese. On. My. Pizza." And then she lifted herself over him, laughing, and patted him on the shoulder. "Have I driven you away for good?"

In the summer evening light, her eyes were warm brown flecked with gold.

"No," he said, his heart pounding. Or maybe it was the warning bells. "I'm still here."

———

THEY DID it again while they waited for the pizza. Grant had stopped expecting Jane to kick him out of bed—today, anyway. By the time they were composting the pizza box, the sun was finally setting and he wondered where he would sleep. If he got her back into bed again now, he'd probably end up spending the night there. Then he'd have to face her regretful but firm rejection in the morning, when he was as weak and helpless as a hibernating bat.

But could he resist the temptation of being with her again?

"Listen, Grant," she said as she opened the compost bin. It was a large rolling container outside the kitchen door. He'd followed her outside to offer help she didn't want or need.

"Yes?"

"I'd like to sleep separately tonight," she said. "It's been a long day, and honestly, I'm exhausted. If we get in bed together again… I don't think we'll sleep as well as if we were in separate beds."

"Sure. I didn't expect to move in."

That was a dumb thing to say, given that he lived in her house.

She frowned. "Right. OK. I was just—" Her phone rang, and she took it out of her pocket. "Hold on, it's Billie. She should hate me."

"Why?"

"Because I took off like that." Jane held up her finger and walked away with the phone at her ear, talking quietly. She disappeared into the house.

Grant turned away from the door and looked at the bay through a gap in the neighbor's acacia trees. The sunset was a uniform orange glow, muffled by fog. For miles in every direction were people, cars, houses, office buildings, freeways, stores, parking lots. He felt the familiar itch to get in the Rover and get out of the dense Bay Area, sleep under stars that weren't hidden by the incessant urban glow.

Jane would hate camping. He sighed, imagining her despair when he handed her the little shovel and rationed square of biodegradable toilet paper for poop.

He didn't begrudge her taste in comforts. He knew he was an outlier.

"Grant?" Jane stuck her head out the door. She still had the phone in her hand, but at her side. "Quick question. Kind of urgent."

"Sure, what?"

"Can I tell Billie?"

"Tell her—oh, about us."

She lowered her voice. "I wanted to make sure it was OK with you. You know, because of Troy."

"Is your sister going to tell Troy?"

"No, but she'll tell Ian. And probably my mother but only because our mom will ask point-blank and Billie's a terrible liar."

Grant wondered why she wanted to tell Billie, if it meant it was serious or all a big joke. After leaving the party, it probably was just a convenient explanation that made everyone feel good.

It had certainly made him feel good.

"Sure, whatever." He kissed her on the lips, just because he could. They curved in a smile.

"Thanks," she whispered, pulling away. She lifted the phone to her ear. "Yes."

Grant could hear a squeal piercing out of the phone from several feet away.

Jane ran her hand through her hair. "That's all I'm going to say about it, so relax. Are you— Sure, go ahead. Of course. Give him my sisterly love." She hung up.

"She sounded happy," Grant said.

"She did." A relaxed, happy smile spread over Jane's face. "I can't tell you what a relief it is to have Billie in a good place."

"Was she in some kind of trouble before?"

"Not really trouble but not really happy, either. Bad boyfriend, bad job, bad apartment. I was worried she was never going to get it together." Jane opened the door to the kitchen. "Are you coming in, or did you need more outdoor time?"

He couldn't tell if she was kidding. "I'm coming in."

They went inside, Jane locked the door, flicked off the kitchen lights, and hesitated by the counter. "I could make us coffee."

"No, I'm fine. I think I might see if I can get a little writing done."

"Really? You're not too tired?" she asked.

He stroked her cheek. "Good kind of tired."

"Listen, about the separate beds. I promised my mom and Trixie I'd help clean up after the party first thing tomorrow, so I really need to sleep."

"It's good." He kissed her forehead. "It's all good."

She put her hand on his chest, a faint smile on her lips, and turned away.

But then she spun around, gave him a quick kiss on the lips, grinned, waved, and strode away. Her short black robe clung to every curve as she left the kitchen, reminding him of what he would be missing tonight.

He waited a moment before going to his own room, where he immediately sat down with his laptop and began to write.

The words came easily.

Many hours later, when the first light of dawn was arousing the songbirds, he'd written seven chapters. He backed it up, emailed himself a copy, closed the laptop, and fell into bed. At this rate, he'd be done with the book before September.

It turned out Fane was quite an inspiration.

Sunday morning around nine, Jane tapped on Grant's door. There was no response.

Would it be rude or reasonable to open the door herself? They had spent hours together in the most intimate circumstances, and this was her house.

But in the end, she decided privacy was even more important under those circumstances. She knocked again a little louder.

This time there was a creak of bedsprings and floorboards, and the door opened to reveal Grant, bleary-eyed and tousle-haired and sexy-everywhere.

He'd obviously been sound asleep a second ago.

"I'm sorry, Grant. I didn't mean to wake you."

He squinted at her. "No, no, it's totally fine. Come in." As he opened the door, he tripped over his own feet. "I'll make us coffee."

"No, I can't stay. But thanks. I wanted to tell you I have to go out. To Trixie's. My little sisters and I are helping clean up from the party."

"Nice. OK." He yawned.

"Are you all right?" She glanced at the recliner he'd put in the corner, where his laptop rested. "Were you up late?"

He smiled. "I was indeed."

"How late?"

"Late enough."

"Good for you." She reached out and squeezed his arm. There had been lots of squeezing yesterday, but now it was awkward.

"I can come with you to help." He scanned the floor. "Let me get my shoes."

"No, you need to sleep." She stepped back into the hallway. Having him there with her little sisters and Trixie would raise too many questions—or answer ones they'd had yesterday. "You earned it."

He grinned. Then yawned. "I must be getting old. I used to be able to pull all-nighters without falling apart like this."

"Go back to bed. I've got to get going. I'm late." She waved and pulled the door shut between them.

She hadn't known what to expect—a quickie? A speech about friendship?— But that interaction had clarified nothing. Now it would be even more awkward when she returned this afternoon.

The door flew open.

"Hey," he said.

She turned, her heart skipping. When she saw his face, she smiled. "Hey."

He came out into the hallway, pulled her into his arms, and kissed her. She leaned into him, her heart singing, and returned the kiss. His breath was minty fresh, almost too much so.

After a second kiss, he lifted his face away from hers. "I would've done that earlier, but my mouth was nasty. I just chugged some Scope."

Since he didn't have a sink in his bedroom, she was afraid he really had swallowed it—either that or spit it out into the potted plants. "I could tell."

"Sure you don't want me to come?"

She nodded. "Easier if you don't."

"Got it." He grimaced, stifling a yawn.

"Go to bed, seriously." She noticed Shadow had slipped past her into his room again. "First I'll get my cat out—"

He kissed her one more time. "Leave her. She's good company."

"I'll leave the middle door open so she can use the litter box. Close it if she's bothering you."

"Will do. Have fun." He opened the front door for her and shut it behind her.

As she walked down the steps to her van, she glanced back and waved at the window, although she wasn't sure he was watching.

And as she drove to Trixie's house, she listened to a pop playlist that normally she would've hated but today seemed to capture her stupid, happy mood.

Her sister Rachel's car was in the driveway when she arrived, so she parked on the shoulder, a treacherous maneuver in the minivan, but she was feeling lucky.

She gathered the carrot cake she'd made for Trixie (with cream cheese frosting, of course) and walked up to the house. Before she could knock, the door opened and her sister Holly appeared carrying a zucchini as large as her arm.

"Never mind, Jane," Holly said. "Aunt Trixie doesn't need our help. She said we could go if we took some of these." She held up the massive vegetable.

Rachel stepped out of the house next to Holly, also holding a zucchini. "I told her Mom would make bread out of them. I hope it's true. Think she'll do it?"

In Jane's eyes, Holly and Rachel acted like teenagers. When she was that age, she had already worked two years at a Big Four accounting firm and was studying every spare minute for the CPA exam.

They produced an intermittent podcast about cheese.

"Not so fast," Jane said, holding out her arms to herd them back into the house. "Trixie was just being nice. We said we'd clean. We'll clean."

Trixie appeared in the doorway. "Morning, Jane! Aren't you looking refreshed!"

"You do look kind of happy," Rachel said, frowning. "What happened?"

Behind Rachel, Trixie winked.

Jane felt her face get warm. "Just got a full night's sleep, that's all. Now I'm ready to get to work. And so are Holly and Rachel."

"Oh, no," Trixie said. "You don't need to do that. It was just a little party, and nobody broke anything. It *would* be helpful if you took a few zukes. Honestly, it would be helpful if you took *one*. I never learn. One day they're small as my little toe, the next day they're bigger than Zeus."

A small, funny-looking dog with a protruding tongue stood up and put his paws on Jane's shin.

"This is Zeus?" Jane asked.

"That is Zeus." Trixie leaned down and petted the funny dog. "Hugo wanted to put him in a cone for licking his paw too much, but he knows I'll take it off when he's not looking. Hugo, I mean. Being a vet makes him tough. He doesn't seem to feel guilty about poor Zeus being miserable when he can't lick himself."

Jane glanced at Holly and Rachel, who were playing around with the zucchini, pretending to fence and beat each other with them.

Were they fourth graders? Honestly.

"We'll take the squash, but we'll also clean," Jane said. "We won't take no for an answer."

"*We* will," Holly said.

Rachel, pretending to be impaled with the zucchini by holding it under her armpit, writhed in mock agony. "There's nothing to clean up, Jane," she said in the strained tones of a dying soldier. "Chill."

Usually being told to chill by one of her little sisters would rankle, but today Jane was too happy to let anyone get to her. "I think Trixie is just being her usual nice self."

"Aren't you sweet?" Trixie reached out and put her hand on Jane's arm. "Come on in and see for yourself. Let your sisters take off and get into whatever trouble they've got planned for that zucchini."

Holly and Rachel laughed and stabbed each other with the squash again.

"Are you guys drunk?" Jane asked.

They laughed harder.

"Sugar rush," Trixie said. "I gave them cake."

"And ice cream," Holly said.

"And really strong coffee," Rachel added. "I think we could fly home."

Jane's sisters began walking down the steps to the driveway.

"No way we're going home," Holly said. "We're going to IKEA first. I need a MALM. Or maybe a YORG."

"What's a YORG?" Rachel asked.

"No idea. I made it up," Holly said, turning. "Thanks again, Aunt Trixie."

Rachel echoed her, and the two walked the rest of the way to their mom's hand-me-down Prius that waited for them in the driveway.

"Come on in, Jane." Trixie pulled her inside and closed the door. Zeus was ahead of them, panting and dancing with three other little dogs.

A little girl, still a toddler, marched into the room, playing a plastic saxophone. Jane recognized her cousin Liam's daughter, Merry. They lived next door.

"Our prodigy," Trixie said. "I babysit on Sunday mornings. And whenever I can steal her."

Merry, Jane noticed, could already play "Twinkle, Twinkle Little Star."

"Hi, Merry," Jane said. "You're really good at that."

Merry smiled around the red plastic mouthpiece but didn't stop playing.

Jane looked around and had to admit the house showed no sign of a party the day before. Trixie's husband Hugo was sitting in the living room in a modified Lotus pose on a yoga mat and cushions. Very modified. He wasn't bent much more deeply than he would be were he sitting on a barstool. She wondered how he would get off the floor.

"Hello, Jane," he said, waving. "Don't let her give you any vegetables."

Jane held out the box of carrot cake she'd brought. "It's all right. I made you two something, so we're even."

"Don't say I didn't warn you." He brought his hands together and closed his eyes.

"I've always wanted to try yoga," Jane said.

"Can't be any worse at it than I am," Hugo said.

"I know you won't leave until I prove you're not needed, so come along and see the backyard." Trixie took the box of carrot cake. "Cream cheese frosting, my favorite."

"Yes, me too," Jane said. "Sometimes I skip the cake."

The backyard was indeed clean and tidy. No red plastic

cups littering the grass, no crumpled napkins, no furniture needing to be put away.

"Zack and April cleaned it up last night," Trixie said. "There was no stopping them."

"Really? April doesn't seem the cleaning type. Sorry, I don't mean—"

"No, you're right, she's a slob. And Zack is a neat freak, so it's a blast to watch them together. Their romance is still young, and they pretend it doesn't bother them." Trixie was eating a piece of Jane's carrot cake with her fingers. "Young love," she mumbled with a smile.

"Well, tell them thank you from us," Jane said. Now what was she going to do today? If Grant needed to sleep, she didn't want to hang around the house feeling… feeling… whatever she'd be feeling. Lonely? Frustrated? Impatient?

Or maybe relieved? They had no idea what they were doing, after all. Were they going to leave the door unlocked now? Well, of course they would.

Right?

"Young love," Trixie said again, her eyes on Jane. She popped another square of carrot cake into her mouth.

"Well, I guess I'll be going."

"I'm sorry I didn't call and tell you and your sisters to save yourself the trip," Trixie said. "Honestly, I forgot. But I'm happy I got to see you again."

Merry flung open the back door to the kitchen and blasted her saxophone hard enough to overwhelm the plastic instrument's abilities. The only music was a faint, breathy whistle.

Zeus, still at Jane's heels, began to howl. Merry laughed, sucked in another breath, and blew again. The other dogs inside the house began to squeal as well.

Jane smiled at her, admiring the little girl's spirit. Her eyes were sharp, too, as if she had countless thoughts and opinions she was keeping to herself. Not a wishy-washy type, this one. Jane had imagined having a daughter like her, maybe more than one. And if she had a son, he'd be the type to appreciate a woman with brains and guts because he'd be her kid and she'd teach him. A dad who knitted his own socks would be a good role model—

Her smile fell. Grant would be a good father. A great one. But the parents had to be compatible in the long term, and the two of them would be lucky to last until the end of his lease.

Jane made her goodbyes, too softhearted to refuse a pair of round zucchinis as big as grapefruit, and returned to her mini-van. She set them in the back and helped herself to a bottle of water from the case she kept there. Her home away from home.

Speaking of which, it was too early to go to the one where Grant was. She had to do something.

Her talk with Billie last night had only covered a quick question about Jane—*yes, we did it*—but hadn't covered Billie. Not Ian, the party, her pregnancy, the wedding plans, family gossip, or school plans (Billie was taking classes at the junior college, preparing to transfer to one of the UC or CSU campuses). Just because Jane hadn't been herself lately with personal issues didn't mean she could neglect her closest sister when she was going through bigger stresses of her own.

Gazing out the windshield at the white morning haze that made the sky hurt to look at, she called Billie. She'd invite her out to that boutique in Rockridge to fawn over overpriced but gorgeous baby gear from Europe. And then a mani-pedi and whatever Billie wanted for lunch—she'd mentioned how hungry she was all the time. They could get gourmet ice cream on College and see a movie. When was the last time they'd hung out together like friends? Too long ago.

Billie's voice came over the receiver, but it was a recorded message, the old one she'd had for years.

"Just checking in," Jane said. "Text me."

But then she remembered Billie had said she and Ian were having dim sum with their dad and stepmother in San Francisco today. Just the four of them, welcoming Ian into the family.

Well, Jane didn't mind being excluded from that. In fact, she'd rather see a friend than family after that party yesterday. Sydney from work lived in Oakland. Maybe she was free. Jane called her.

"Yoga in half an hour and I need it big time," Sydney said. "We could get together after that if you can wait."

"I've been thinking about starting yoga," Jane said. "Where's your class? Is it a club, or can I drop in?"

"You aren't going to like yoga."

"What do you mean? I've done yoga before."

"When?" Sydney asked.

"A long time ago. Are beginners welcome at this place you go to?"

"Sure. I'm not very good either," Sydney said. "You really want to do this?"

"Yes." Jane put on her seat belt. She always kept an extra gym bag in the van. "I'll buy us coffee afterward."

"I'm off caffeine. Let's make it a smoothie."

"Deal," Jane said. "Where do I meet you? Do they have mats, or should I buy one on my way there? Any other equipment I need?"

"You can borrow a mat at the studio," Sydney said. "But listen, girl. I hope this isn't about fitting into your skinny jeans, because I've been doing this for three months now and I'm still the same big, beautiful woman I've always been."

"Nothing like that," Jane said. "What's the address?"

Grant drove up the driveway of his grandfather's estate and parked next to the landscaper's pickup in the back. Grinning at the memory of Jane shoving twenties at him, he walked over a stone path to his mother's cottage. She'd called him, worried about Grandfather again. His physical health had improved, but he was more irritable than ever, shouting at repairmen, the cable TV news, her.

Grant had been unable to sleep after the quick kiss with Jane, regretting he'd been too sluggish to pull her into bed for more before she'd driven away. Driving to Marin had given him an excuse to get out of the house. Otherwise, he'd be pining away, waiting for Jane to return. Yeah, he was in bad shape.

His mother, Brandi, was cleaning her brushes in her art room when he arrived. She painted with acrylics on small canvases because they hadn't had room for large oil paintings when he was a kid, and she'd developed a name for herself in small works. Although she had access now to a massive estate and could have canvases as big as a garage door and industrial ventilation for the chemical fumes, she continued to work in acrylic-based miniature.

"He's really upset about something," she declared, not looking up, "but he won't talk to me about it."

Grant picked up one of the wet brushes she'd just cleaned and painted on his wrist the way he'd done as a child, enjoying the feel of cold, silky bristles on his skin. "Did he mention the Bostocks?"

"Bob Bostock? He died more than a year ago."

"His son took over. Not a good guy, probably crooked. Troy had to tell Grandfather about it recently."

"This isn't about work."

"Bob Bostock was his best friend. Oldest client."

"This isn't about work," she repeated.

Grant knew it was hopeless to argue with his mom when she'd made up her mind about human interaction stuff. "You could just ask him."

"I did, but you know how he is." She took the brush away from him and set it on her drying rack. "I'm not family."

"Nice of him to let you live here for free then."

"I'm not blood." She stood and tilted her head back to look at him. Although only five feet, she never gave the impression of being a small woman. Without raising her voice, she could fill a room with quiet strength. "I'm not you."

"Me? We've never been close."

"And I think it bothers him. A lot."

"Why now, after all these years?"

She straightened his collar. "I think he misses your father."

The familiar grief pricked at him. "I know I do."

"You're so much like him."

"I try to be," Grant said.

She smiled. "I meant your grandfather."

"Thanks a lot." He picked up another brush.

"You know I'm right." She took the brush away. "Troy is too sweet to stand up to people."

"Oh yeah? He just stood up to Grandfather. Any day now, he'll actually retire."

"Troy did that only because you told him to do it."

"Dad stood up to Grandfather," Grant said.

"Not quite," she said, sighing. "Your father was the love of my life, but he wasn't always as tough as he should've been. He married me in secret and never came up here to have it out with his father man to man. It was easier to avoid him, make a living on his own, tell himself he was taking a stand—"

"That's not fair," Grant said. "He did take a stand. He never asked Grandfather for anything."

"And why not? When you came along, we didn't even have a place to live. Good thing my milk came in, because we wouldn't have been able to afford formula." She reached out and squeezed his shoulder. "I'm not criticizing him. I'm describing him. You must remember how he'd never argue about anything. I had to fight all the battles. Getting the landlord to return the security deposit, having it out with the neighbor who kept blocking our driveway with his RV, sending food back at restaurants when it wasn't what we ordered—"

"All right, all right," he said, turning away to study her latest painting. It was about the size of a piece of notebook paper, still in the early stages, mostly abstract shapes in shades of cobalt blue. "I'm a nice guy too."

She put two palms on his back. "I'm not saying you're not nice. You're wonderful. But if you fell in love with a woman your family didn't approve of, you wouldn't run off with her and hide. You'd stand and fight and make them love her as much as you did."

He couldn't tear his eyes away from the unfinished painting. "I had no idea." He cleared his throat. "That he… that you… I didn't realize."

"Don't worry. I'm fine now, other than missing your dad. Your grandfather wasn't such an ogre after all. In fact, he begged us to move in with him. Troy didn't want to switch schools, so Grandfather got him a driver to bring him out to Point Reyes every day until he graduated. He built me this cottage. He never said a bad word about your dad and insisted on paying for anything we wanted. Cars, travel, clothing, school, anything."

"He felt guilty."

"He felt love. And grief." Brandi patted him on the back and then hooked a hand on his arm and turned him around to face her. "You're the only one he couldn't reach."

"I didn't want his money."

"This isn't about money, and you know it," she said. "Go talk to him. Today. Now."

"Mom, I was up all night working, and—"

"Do it."

He had to laugh. "Are you sure I don't take after you? With the stubborn thing?"

"I'll know if you don't talk to him, so don't try to skip out of here without doing it."

"I'm not a kid anymore, lying about my homework."

"We all have some growing up to do," she said. "No matter how old we are."

"Even you?" Grant couldn't imagine his mother changing or needing to change. She was a rock. If she wanted him to do this, he'd do it. "I'll talk to him, but I don't guarantee it'll go well."

"To break the ice, ask him about his collection. I saw a truck deliver something new today."

Grant loved his mother, but even she couldn't get him to

talk to his grandfather about medieval armor and heraldry. "I'll think of something." He gave her a quick hug and left her to her painting, bracing himself for another awkward, pointless conversation with the family patriarch.

AN HOUR LATER, Jane was in the bathroom of a yoga studio near Lake Merritt, pulling on her leggings. Unable to find parking in the popular neighborhood, she'd had to park the minivan more than a half mile away.

But she was going to do yoga. For years now she'd been meaning to try this and here she was. Grinning, she walked across the bamboo floorboards to Sydney, who had spread out two mats side by side for them in the back.

The class was packed, mostly with women who were young and female and looked much more flexible than she was.

But she didn't care. When the class started and she immediately fell behind—the instructor called out poses by name and didn't explain what to actually do with her body —Jane just stretched and flailed and wobbled and did her best.

Child pose was very helpful. She was good at the pushups, bad at everything else. She thought of Hugo on his mat and cushions and kept going.

The corpse pose at the end was her least favorite. She hated doing nothing. She wanted to get her shoes on and put away the mat and grab Sydney and talk about work and maybe hint about Grant, but that would be dangerous because of Troy and the Whitman family and—

What was she going to do about Troy and the Whitmans and work if they found out about her and Grant?

What was going on with her and Grant?

"Will you relax?" Sydney whispered, lying on her back next to her. "I can hear you stressing."

"How long are we supposed to just lie here?"

"*Shh*," Sydney said.

Jane crossed her arms over her chest and frowned at the beamed ceiling.

"Arms at your sides," the instructor said, squatting down next to her and touching her shoulder. "Empty your mind."

"Why?" Jane asked. She'd never heard a good reason for that. The world had plenty of empty-headed people already.

"*Shh*," Sydney said.

Finally, they sat up and bowed to each other and people began talking and moving around. The torture was over.

They put away their mats and went out to the street.

"I knew you'd hate yoga," Sydney said.

"I loved everything until we had to play dead. Are there classes that skip that part?"

"No."

"Is it bad if I leave when it starts?"

"Yes."

Jane tugged down her underwear, which had crawled up practically to her shoulder blades during downward-facing dog. "I can get used to it, like going to the gynecologist."

"You owe me a smoothie." Sydney pointed to a place across the street. "And you're going to tell me what's up with you."

They jogged across the street, their gym bags smacking their hips. The fog hadn't cleared off yet, and the thick silver sky made it seem more like an afternoon in November than midday in late summer.

"So what's his name?" Sydney asked.

Jane stopped walking. "How…?"

"You're too happy for this to be about work, so it has to be a man." Sydney adjusted her sunglasses and continued walking down the sidewalk.

After pausing a moment to admire Sydney's insight, Jane said, "You'd make a great therapist."

"Thinking about it," Sydney said. "Might as well get paid for the work I do anyway."

"Seriously?"

Sydney opened the door to the smoothie shop. "Yes." Then she sighed. "No, not seriously. But I have been fantasizing about a coconut mango blast with chia seeds and wheatgrass since yesterday."

They ordered at the counter—Jane passed on the wheatgrass—and brought their number on a metal stand to the back patio, where they sat near a glowing heater.

"Oakland in summer," Sydney said, pulling on a sweatshirt.

The counter guy brought the smoothies.

When he was gone, Sydney asked, "Were you with a man yesterday?"

"Yes," Jane said. "But I can't tell you about it."

Sydney made a knowing face and sipped her smoothie. "You don't have to tell me. I can guess."

"You can?" Jane leaned back in her chair and smiled at her, impressed. She had told her about Grant moving in, but nothing—nothing—about any of the boiling sexual tension leading up to yesterday. But Sydney always seemed to know things anyway.

"Got to be work related for you not to tell me," Sydney said.

"Oh." Jane frowned at the frothy coconut milk in her glass. "Not necessarily."

"It's Troy, isn't it?"

"What? Oh my God, no. Ew. How could you think that? He's…"

"Sexy. Sweet. Smart."

"He's Troy Whitman," Jane said, laughing. "Not my type."

"How can he not be your type?"

"Is he your type?"

"Hell yes," Sydney said. "What's the matter with you?"

Jane leaned over the table. "You have a thing for Troy?"

Sydney regarded her. "You really didn't sleep with him?"

"No. I've never— No."

"I don't know why you're acting like it would be so bad to want to get to know him a little better," Sydney said. "Not that we should, but it's completely understandable for a red-blooded woman of the heterosexual persuasion to consider it."

"Frequently, it sounds like," Jane said.

Brown eyes twinkling, Sydney sipped her smoothie, smiling around the rim. "No law against it, is there?"

"I had no idea," Jane said.

"Now you do. Keep it to yourself."

"I will." Jane looked around as if their colleagues from across the bay were sitting on the smoothie café patio with them. "Not a word."

"Your turn."

"I can't," Jane said. "This isn't just… thinking. This really happened."

"And you're going to do it again, it looks like, so you might as well tell me because I'll find out soon enough, especially if it's some guy from work. Better to have me in your corner now, so I can help smooth things over for you when they go sour."

"You're optimistic," Jane said flatly.

"You're going to marry the man?"

Jane set her glass down on the rickety table, holding it so it wouldn't topple off. "Are you going to marry Troy?"

"I might if he asked."

Jane stared.

"See? Now you have to tell me," Sydney said. "I've bared my soul."

"Wow. I had no idea."

"Spit it out, Jane. I've got to get home and do my laundry."

Jane was still reeling at the discovery of Sydney being secretly in love, or even lust, with Troy Whitman.

"It was Grant," Jane said.

"The furry brother," Sydney said, nodding. "Of course. That Whitman magic strikes again."

"It had been building up for some time."

"And you didn't tell me anything about it," Sydney said.

"There wasn't anything to tell you, not really."

"Sounds like there was."

"Now there is," Jane said.

"And Troy doesn't know?"

"Of course not. Neither one of us wants him to know. That would be… bad."

"I suppose you're right. Especially after what happened on Friday," Sydney said.

"What happened on Friday?"

"I thought that was why you called me today," Sydney said. "I thought the yoga was a ruse. A different ruse. There were rumors flying around all afternoon."

"For God's sake, tell me."

"New guy coming in. Senior manager. Taking Nicole's spot."

"Where's she going? Please don't tell me she's—"

"Not partner. Deep breath. She's leaving."

"Where?"

"I don't know, but the rumor is she's moving to New York," Sydney said. "She's always wanted to join the big leagues."

THE IMPLICATIONS SANK IN. They were bringing in some guy from the outside to take Nicole's job—and not promoting either Jane or Sydney.

"Damn it," Jane said.

"I'm thinking about going into private accounting," Sydney said. "I'm tired of being passed over, you know? I know you know."

"I do know."

"I'm mad, and I'm cool with being mad for a little while," Sydney said, "but I'm not going to sit around and take it. If I can't find a better job soon, I'm going to go back to school."

"But… all that work to get your CPA, the years at Whitman. What would you—"

"I don't know, but it's got to be better than what I've got now. I need to respect myself even if they don't." Sydney took out her phone. "I'm really sorry, but I really do need to do my laundry. I've got nothing to wear tomorrow. Some of it needs to hang dry, you know? In this fog, it'll take forever." She stood up, holding her cup.

Jane didn't move. Her joy was gone. Now she kept imagining some man walking into the office and taking a job that she'd earned for herself.

Troy had said he would do what he could.

Either Troy couldn't do much, or Troy didn't care.

She slowly got to her feet. "Thanks for letting me come to your yoga class." Why hadn't Troy told her on Friday about the new guy?

"I really am sorry I didn't tell you earlier. I thought you knew." Sydney used her napkin to wipe off the table for the next people. On the way out, she'd drop a few bills in the tip jar. Her mom had worked as a waitress for years, inspiring Sydney to be the best kind of customer.

"But then why would you think I'd slept with Troy?" Jane lifted her bag over her shoulder. "Why would I sleep with him *after* he gave my job to some guy off the street?"

Sydney shrugged. "Because you'd decided you had nothing left to lose." They walked back into the café and out the front door to the street. "It's what I would do," she added, smiling.

2 4

<hr>

Grant sat in his Rover outside Jane's house, his head spinning. He'd ended up talking to his grandfather for over an hour.

A lot to think about.

Because she often put her minivan in the garage, he couldn't tell if Jane was home yet. As much as he wanted to see her—well, get her in bed—he was also wanting a hike to settle his mind.

An idea came to him. Smiling, he took out his phone.

*Are you home?* he texted.

Within a minute, she replied. *Yes why are you sitting outside?*

*You saw me?*

*Yes.*

*Come hike with me.* He added a tiny mountain emoji.

*Now?* she asked.

He got out of his truck, locked it, and set his favorite hat on his head before replying.

*Busy?* he asked.

She also didn't reply right away. And then finally,

*Coming.*

He debated sending another emoji, this one with sexual connotations. That O-face one, for instance. Or was he supposed to be screaming?

"Why didn't you come inside and ask me?" She stood on the front step wearing a hat, a pink visor that didn't cover her hair, and a parka he would've considered suitable for fieldwork in Antarctica.

His heart jumped to see her again. And other parts, which was why he hadn't gone in. He waited for her on the sidewalk, and when she reached him, he caught her up in his arms and kissed her the way he'd been imagining for hours.

She smelled like flower shampoo and tasted like…

"Cookies?" he asked, dragging his lips across her cheek to her temple, which knocked the visor off her head.

Rather breathless, she readjusted the hat, smiling at him, and held up her other hand. Resting on her palm was a brownish-orange rectangle in plastic wrap. "Carrot cake. I brought you a piece."

"I smelled it baking this morning." He didn't want cake, but he took it so he could put his arms around her again. She felt soft and warm. Especially in the parka. "Are you sure you're up for a hike?"

"Why?"

"I thought you might have a fever," he said. "Your coat is rated for ten below. It's pushing seventy."

"It's windy," she said. "And the sun isn't going to come out. I hate getting cold."

He smiled and kissed her again. "Fair enough." He pointed to the park at the top of the hill. "I'll put the cake in the truck for later, all right? Let's go."

They walked hand in hand without speaking. He had his own thoughts to occupy him, many of them about her, and she seemed distracted as well. When they'd walked for over ten minutes and still hadn't said a word, he began to get uneasy. Maybe he should've walked by himself and not inflicted his company on her when he was in a mood.

When they came upon the fork for his favorite trail, she pulled him back and pointed straight ahead. "Flat trails for me today," she said. "I seem to have hurt myself in yoga."

"I didn't know you did yoga."

"Neither did my hamstrings," she said.

He laughed. "I thought you were cleaning up after the party."

"It was already done when I got there," she said.

"That's nice."

"So then I called a friend and we went to yoga."

"Harder than you expected?"

"I liked the hard parts," she said. "I'll probably go again. If Sydney doesn't mind."

"Sydney's your friend?"

"From work," she said, giving him a look.

"Huh," he said, not knowing what she meant by that.

She slipped her hand out of his grasp, ostensibly to move a branch off the path, but he suspected it was personal.

"Did something happen at Whitman you want to tell me about?" He could hear the reluctance in his own voice as he asked the question.

"Not particularly," she said. "We shouldn't talk about Whitman."

He completely agreed, especially after talking to his grandfather. For the first time Grant could remember, he hadn't pressured him to work at the firm, even after extracting the humble details of his financial situation.

"You're a good writer," his grandfather had said. Scowling and gruff, but he'd said it. "Keep at it."

It had meant more to Grant to hear it than he'd imagined.

"You've read some of my stuff?" Grant had asked.

"Some? I've read all of it, dummy."

As moments went, it could've been better, but God knows it could've been worse.

Pretending Jane hadn't intended to drop his hand, Grant caught up with her and reclaimed it. Although he completely agreed they shouldn't talk about the firm, he was also completely incapable of suppressing his curiosity and not asking about it. "So, something didn't happen, or something did happen but you don't think we should talk about it?"

Her fingers tensed under his. "Let's just enjoy the walk."

He looked up into the redwoods, inhaled the sweet, earthy smell, and shook his head. "I can't. I need to know whatever it is."

"Even if it's about Troy?"

"I've noticed my relatives like to fire people on weekends," he said. "Was it Troy who shit-canned you this time?"

She tried to pull her hand free.

"Sorry," he said quickly, holding tighter. "Trying to lighten the mood."

"They gave my promotion to somebody else, some outside guy."

"What do you mean, 'your' promotion?"

"I admit it may have been Sydney's promotion. I wouldn't be upset if they'd given it to her."

"Sydney of yoga fame?"

"She's the one who told me what happened on Friday with the new guy."

He wished he hadn't pushed it. Now he didn't know what to say. Troy could've hired the man for all kinds of reasons, none of which Grant had anything to do with. "I'm sorry," he said. Lame.

She nodded and didn't reply. He relinquished her hand, and they continued walking. They came out of the trees into the open ridge heading north-south along the park. The sun was only a faint glow in the west behind the thickening cloud cover. The San Francisco skyline was buried under fog.

"Do you want me to talk to somebody?" he asked.

She stopped and turned. "What?"

"Just thought I'd ask." He kicked a fallen log next to the path. "I'm sorry. I just feel like I should be able to do something to help you."

He expected her to call him an idiot for suggesting anything so stupid. Instead, she put her arms around him and rested her cheek on his chest.

Surprised but pleased, he held her, enjoying the feel of her body pressing against his but wondering if he'd be driving back to Marin tonight to plead her case with his grandfather.

"You *do* want me to talk to somebody?" he asked finally.

She tightened her embrace and shook her head against his chest. "You are so sweet."

"I am?"

"You are." She looked up. "No, I don't want you to talk to anybody. I'll deal with this myself."

The hug was nice, and he didn't want it to end. "How about Sydney? Maybe I could talk to somebody for her."

Smiling, she cupped his face. "I can see why you didn't go into corporate finance. You're too nice."

"Now you're complaining?"

She laughed.

With an exaggerated sigh, he dropped his arms to his sides. "Too nice. Too handsome. Too sexy."

"Too tall." She stepped onto the fallen log, wrapped her arms around his neck, and kissed him.

They did that for several minutes. Under the parka, which

he quickly removed, she was wearing a stretchy tank top and skin-tight leggings that made each inch of her particularly soft and inviting. When his hand reached beneath the waistband of the leggings and slipped between her thighs, she squealed and toppled off the log.

Luckily in his direction.

"Let's go back to the house," she said.

"Too far." Arms around her waist, he pushed her against another tree, one that was still upright. "This works for me." This was a popular trail, especially on a Sunday afternoon, so he was kidding, of course. Mostly.

Almost.

She grabbed his wrist to stop its return journey into her underpants. "Jogger," she said, wriggling to one side.

Accepting the inevitable, he took her hand, helped her back into her coat, and escorted her back the way they'd come —in a much better mood than he'd been only moments ago.

If he wasn't careful, he was going to get in trouble with this woman.

And he'd never been careful about much of anything except filtering his drinking water, so this could get interesting.

25

The new guy was younger than either Sydney or Jane.

"But he has a penis," Sydney pointed out.

She and Jane were having lunch at their favorite Chinese restaurant. They'd ordered cocktails and didn't hurry to get back to the office after twenty minutes the way they usually did.

"It's not like it can add and subtract," Jane said.

"I know, right?" Sydney glanced over her shoulder and offered her a pork bun. "I don't have one myself, but computation is not a task they're known for."

They snorted into their drinks.

"Is he related to the Whitmans?" Sydney asked.

"I don't think so."

"Maybe you could ask your lumberjack."

Jane felt herself blush. "No."

"I updated my resume. I wish I had more clients in tech, because I'd really like to get into tech."

"Go for it," Jane said.

"I am." Sydney pushed away her plate of curried tofu and turned her attention to her margarita. (The restaurant had a full bar that ignored cultural boundaries.) They'd had the talented, flexible bartender serve them in iced-tea glasses so any passing coworkers wouldn't know they were having an early happy hour. "You should quit too."

"I can't," Jane said. "I don't have enough saved up to make a change right now."

"Saved up for what? Get another job first, then quit."

"I've got a lot invested in Whitman. I don't want to start over."

"You might come out ahead," Sydney said. "That's what I'm counting on. And unlike penises, I'm damn good at counting." She held up her glass in a toast.

Jane clinked her glass. "You sure are."

They smiled at each other.

"You know what your problem is?" Sydney continued. "You're too conservative."

"Just because I wouldn't get a tattoo with you last year—"

"Oh, that! How can you not have any tattoos? You're like my mom."

"I don't want one."

"But you *do* want one. You sure did last year when we saw the mermaid in that studio in Berkeley. You totally wanted that mermaid, Jane. On. Your. Body."

It was true, but Jane shook her head. "I'd regret it."

"So? What's life without regrets?"

"Happy," Jane said. "Restful."

"Boring."

Jane ate her pork bun. Her life hadn't been boring at all lately, so she didn't mind having this conversation with Sydney as much as she usually did.

Sydney raised an eyebrow. "Things must really be going well with your lumberjack. Normally you'd rip me a new one for saying that."

"I've found Zen."

"You've found something that isn't known for computation, if you know what I mean."

Jane laughed. "We should get back."

"Why?"

"To work."

"Oh, right," Sydney said with a sigh. "I suppose we should put on a show, anyway."

"Troy's wearing that purple shirt you make fun of."

"The one that brings out his eyes, you mean? His gorgeous green eyes?"

Jane dropped her chopsticks. "That's the one. You really don't think it's dorky after all?"

"He's got style. I like a man who's not afraid to show his feminine side."

"Especially when it's wrapped around big muscles, a significant pile of inherited wealth, and a charming personality," Jane said.

"Keep your eyes on your own paper."

Jane put down cash for both of their lunches, insisting it was her turn, and they returned to the office very full and a little drunk. Downtown San Francisco was in the low sixties, cold enough for a heavy sweater. If they went down the escalator at Market Street and got on a BART train traveling east, each mile would get hotter—Oakland in the seventies, Concord in the eighties, Livermore in the nineties, Tracy in the low hundreds. People who commuted in from the exurbs faced a daily struggle with their clothing choices. At that very moment, a shivering woman in a sleeveless peach sundress was jogging past them on the sidewalk holding a steaming cup from Starbucks.

Sydney opened the door to the Whitman building and waited for Jane to enter first.

But Jane was transfixed by the woman in the peach dress scurrying down the sidewalk. How far away did she live? Where did she work? Did she like her job, her life?

Was she happy?

"Jane?" Sydney asked.

Jane looked up at the skyscraper in front of her. How many hours had Jane spent in this building? How many late nights and weekends?

The sad thing was, she was capable of making a reasonable estimate. Using her calendar and work records, she would be able to come up with a grand total of hours, days, weeks—years—she had spent scrambling in the Whitman hamster wheel.

"If you're going to puke, we should get you inside to a bathroom ASAP," Sydney said, touching her arm.

"No, I'm fine," Jane said. She couldn't go in. She didn't know if it was sex with Grant or MSG from lunch or a sudden midlife crisis, but she couldn't make her legs propel her through the doorway. "Actually, no. I'm going home. Because I'm sick."

"Food poisoning? Or are we talking in euphemisms here, Jane?"

Annoyed corporate drones pushed past them to get inside. Sydney moved away from the doorway, joining Jane on the sidewalk.

"I'm not sure." Jane frowned at a pair of men in jeans and T-shirts striding by, eating their lunch out of wrappers as they talked and hurried into the building. One also had his phone out and was texting.

"I feel like I need to lie down," Jane said.

"It's my fault," Sydney said. "I ordered the margaritas."

"No, it's probably PMS or something."

"Maybe you're pregnant," Sydney said, laughing.

"No, it's too soon," Jane said. Although she could be if the condom hadn't worked. "Too soon to be sure, anyway."

Sydney stopped laughing and stared at her. "You're scaring me. You are way too casual about the idea of a baby. Maybe I should help you get home." She put a hand on Jane's forehead. "I don't feel a fever. Never can tell that way, though."

"It's nothing like that." Jane flashed a smile. "I haven't had enough sleep, I drank too much on an empty stomach, something like that. You'd better go in. We'll talk later."

After Jane promised a status report, Sydney finally went inside. Jane turned around and walked back to Market Street, where she took an escalator down to catch a BART train to Oakland.

When she got home, she walked through the front door and into Grant's room without putting down her purse. He slept face down on his bed, one arm slung over the edge of the mattress. His laptop was on the bed next to him, wedged at an angle between his hip and the wall. From her perch on the windowsill, Shadow watched over the man she loved, ignoring Jane completely.

She dropped her purse and stretched out next to Grant. "You didn't close your door," she whispered in his hair. He smelled like oregano, or was it cumin? Maybe he'd had tacos for lunch. She could only imagine what she smelled like. Margaritas and garlic probably.

He flung an arm out and pulled her into a sleepy embrace. "Mm," he said. "Is it seven already?"

"No. I came home early."

He opened his eyes. "You did?"

"I did."

"Is everything OK?"

"Fine," she said, and couldn't resist smiling. His hands were already unbuttoning her shirt.

He rolled on top of her and buried his face in the crook of her neck. "Glad to hear that." His tongue traced the curve of her ear. "So glad."

"I want to ask you something." She'd figured it out on the train, and now the idea was a growing bully in her mind, stomping around and dominating everything else.

"Yes, I will go down on you," he said, moving to do just that.

Straining even her vast stores of self-discipline, she stopped him. "Wait. Talk first."

"Talk during," he said, unfastening her pants.

She laughed—no, God help her, it was a giggle—and wriggled out of reach to sit up. "Please. I need you to listen. This is important."

Frowning, he brushed the hair off his forehead. "Bad important or good important?"

"Good, I hope."

He continued to look wary. "I hope so too."

Remembering Sydney's joke about being pregnant, she realized she should get to the point. "I had an idea," she said, lifting both fisted hands in a rah-rah gesture. "Let's go camping!"

His response came after an awkward delay. "Camping?"

"I got the idea after having lunch with my friend Sydney. I just froze up—literally and figuratively. Couldn't go inside. I realized I really, really need a vacation."

He nodded. "I agree."

"Something new. Something that gets me outside." She was surprised he didn't seem excited, but she had just woken him up. "It's so cold in the city this time of year. I've got weeks of vacation time saved up."

"Right," he said. "What about Shadow?"

"Billie and Ian will take him. They've done it before when I had to travel for work."

He scrubbed his face with his hands. "When were you thinking you'd like to go?"

"Now," she said. It was a quiet time of year, and she did have an absurd amount of vacation time, but she'd just taken off in the middle of a workday. When she'd taken vacations in the past, she'd informed everyone months in advance.

She couldn't wait months. As crazy as it was, she didn't think she could wait another day.

She'd tell them she was sick. Suddenly. Violently. Vomit, fever, pink eye—yes, pink eye was perfect. Nobody wanted her within miles of the office if she had pink eye.

With that plan established, she turned her attention back to Grant. "Are you able to get away? I thought you could bring your laptop along like you said you do sometimes. I completely understand you need to work."

"I could take a break," he said. "That's not a problem."

"Then what is?"

"It's peak season. This time of year, such short notice… it might be impossible to find anything available."

"Anything?" She turned in amazement. "In the entire state of California?"

"The places you'd be comfortable in are really popular. They can fill up a year in advance."

She raised an eyebrow. "You assume I need pampering."

"I assume you need a cot and a bathroom," he said, "and possibly four walls. Curry Village at Yosemite, for example, would be perfect, but we'd probably have to wait until October for a cabin, and then it might snow."

"I said camping," she said. "Not cabining. I expect a tent to be involved."

"OK." He rubbed his eyes. "Even tent sites can be hard to come by in August."

"Hard to come by in Yosemite, sure. But not in regular places." She poked him in the chest. "I'm starting to suspect you're not interested in coming with me."

He put his hand around her wrist, pulling her close for a kiss. "I don't want you to hate me."

"Why would I hate you?"

"Because you'll get uncomfortable. You'll be cold and hungry, and you won't be able to sleep."

"But it's my idea," she said. "Why would I blame you for anything?"

"You'll hate how happy and comfortable I am in the same circumstances, and you'll resent me and then blame me for giving you the idea in the first place to go out into the wonderful world of nature."

She could only stare at him.

"And you'll be afraid to go to the bathroom out in the open," he added.

She snorted. "The only thing I'm afraid of is giving in to the temptation to hit you right now."

He drew back a few inches. "Really?"

"Don't have such a low opinion of me."

"That's not it at all," he said. "Most women—I mean, most people—don't like roughing it. It's uncomfortable. The thrill wears off the first night you can't sleep."

"Maybe so. But I want to go anyway." She had to admit, she wasn't thrilled about the bathroom thing. "We'll just come home if things get really bad." But they'd be fine. If she truly dedicated herself to something, she could handle anything.

"We can go somewhere not too far from the freeway. When you get sick of ramen, we can drive out for a burger."

"You really think I'm a princess, don't you?"

He tackled her again, pinning her to the bed. "I don't. I really don't. You're brave and amazing."

"You think I'm going to bring an ironing board."

He laughed. "You can if you want to."

"Of course I don't want to."

"Great. I'm used to being wrinkled." He returned to his earlier task of unbuttoning her shirt. "My gear is in storage. I'll need at least a day to get it together. And you'll probably need a few things. How about we leave Friday?"

"But today's only Monday." She didn't want to waste her vacation sitting around at home, and she'd become obsessed with the idea of getting out of the Bay Area.

"Thursday?"

"Wednesday," she said. "That gives us all day tomorrow to get what we need. You're a pro at this, right? You can manage it."

He looked like he was going to argue, then nodded. "The food is usually the hardest part."

"Don't do anything special for me," she said. "I'll pack my own meals."

"No," he said quickly. "Let me do it."

"Why?"

He kissed her lightly on the cheek. "More efficient this way."

"Is there anything we can do tonight to get started?"

Sliding his hands under her back, he unfastened her bra. "Tomorrow's soon enough."

His lack of enthusiasm was disappointing, but she'd ignore his bad attitude.

Especially when he was kissing a path down her abdomen.

## 26

Just before six on Wednesday morning, Grant put the gas nozzle in the Rover and watched Jane through the rear side window. She was scrolling through her tablet, studying topo maps and reading a digital backpacking magazine. They'd be on the road all morning, heading north on I-5 to the Trinity Alps. Not as crowded as Yosemite or a state park and easier for a spontaneous trip.

He was filled with dread but managed to hide it. It wasn't the first time he'd taken a friend camping with him, and he'd learned to be cautious. Some people—most people—liked the idea of roughing it more than the reality. Even he didn't like spending more than two weeks at a time in the wilderness. His method of research for his books involved long stretches of car camping in places with amenities and reasonable access to supermarkets. He'd also rented rooms from Vancouver to Baja for months here and there, recuperating, writing, or preparing for his next jaunt.

He'd much rather rent a hut on a beach in Baja for this trip with Jane, and he knew she would, too, but was too proud to admit it. Maybe next time.

His honest fear was that there wouldn't be a next time. She was a city person, and the discomforts of the cold, hard ground, even under a Therm-a-Rest pad, would make her irritable on the first night. She was going to hate bathing with a damp microfiber washcloth out of a public sink. And her beloved cream cheese needed refrigeration, as did the organic cream she put in her coffee, refrigeration they didn't have. The ice packs would only last the day.

He felt as if he were chained to the tracks and the runaway locomotive was bearing down on him. Nothing to do now but wait for disaster to strike.

Jane rolled down the window. "Get a receipt for the gas," she said. "We'll tally the expenses later, and I'll pay you for my share."

"Don't worry about it."

She climbed out of the car and looked at the screen on the pump herself. "I do worry about it." She recorded the amount in her phone. "You're nice to do this. You shouldn't have to pay for it."

If she were his girlfriend, unambiguously so, he'd insist on paying. But what were they? They weren't even friends with benefits, but landlord and tenant with benefits. Boss's brother with benefits.

They couldn't get out from under the looming shadow of a financial transaction.

"How about you pay for lunch?" he suggested.

"It won't be enough. Just let me do this." They both got back into the car, and she leaned over to his side, offering a goofy smile. "Please?"

How could he resist? He kissed her, tasting her sweet, optimistic enthusiasm under the bitterness of her SPF-50 lip balm. "Whatever makes you happy."

"Receipts make me happy," she said. "It applies order to the universe."

He started the car, checking that the lights were on because the sun hadn't come up yet. In spite of his worries, he felt a familiar surge of excitement at the beginning of a new trip. "Why would you want to do that?"

"For the same reason you had a checklist for all the gear," she said. "It prevents disaster."

He hoped so.

They hit the road, caught up in the morning rush hour until they were north of the Bay Bridge and driving against the commute through Richmond, over the Carquinez Bridge into Vallejo and, finally, out of the Bay Area.

The sun rose, the traffic thinned, and Grant couldn't help but be happy. He felt good when he was with Jane even if he feared the good times wouldn't survive their current adventure. He pulled on his sunglasses and tried to live in the moment.

About two hours into the drive, Jane began playing DJ with his ancient car stereo, and Grant shared his remarkable inability to carry a tune.

"I'm impressed," she said.

"Very funny."

"I'm serious. I'd love to sing like that."

He wiped a drop of coffee off his lip. "I find that hard to believe. I've been told I'm tone deaf."

"Yes, that aspect is terrible," she said. "But you belt it out really well."

He smiled. "I'd think that's a negative under the circumstances."

"I think it's great." She adjusted the single station, another pop song, and cleared her throat. "I'm going to try it. Brace yourself. I know a few words to this one."

Perhaps it wasn't much of a compliment, but she was

much better than he was. He smiled at her so long he almost drove off the road. "Whoops. I'd better listen, not watch."

She tried to sing a high note. Her voice cracked, cracked again, and then she broke out laughing. "I bet it's easier to watch than listen."

He reached over and stroked her upper thigh, soft and full under her cargo shorts. Not releasing her, he took the next exit and pulled off onto the shoulder.

She looked around at the empty farmland. "What are you—"

He cupped the back of her head and drew her to him, his mouth greeting hers in an openmouthed kiss. He slid his tongue past her teeth and licked the inside of her mouth, ran his fingers through her hair and pushed deeper. He twisted in his seat to touch her cheek with his other hand, feel her soft skin, feel her give and take, feel her respond to him.

He couldn't get close enough.

"Wow," she gasped, turning her head away for a second. "I should sing more often."

He tried to pull her into his lap, but it just wasn't possible, even in a roomy SUV. "Let's find a motel."

"Good idea," she said. "No, wait. We've only been driving an hour."

"Two."

"Are we in the wilderness yet?"

"No, but we're in Yolo County," he said. People from other places thought it was a joke, but no. Yolo County, home of the unincorporated community of Yolo, was real.

She laughed and moved away. "We should keep going."

"The tent won't be nearly as comfortable as a bed."

"We have beds at home," she said. "Remember?"

He remembered. Last night in hers had been short (since they'd never talked about him doing otherwise, he continued to return to his own bed for actual sleeping) but hot. The way she said "home" made him uneasy, however. He paid to live there, and not for much longer.

With that chilling thought, he reclaimed the wheel and got back on the road. He still wanted her, but she was right; this wasn't a romantic getaway, it was a camping trip. The great sex would have to wait until they got back. If they were lucky. She might not realize it, but he did.

She took a turn driving, suggesting he work on his book. He pretended to write and then put it away. Just because he was saving his secret for later didn't mean he had to lie about it.

He'd finished his book two days ago. It was done. The torture on the rack was over. When the time was right, he'd tell her and they could celebrate with their bodies like nature intended. After they got home and had running water.

Around ten, they stopped in Redding for an early fast-food lunch, used the bathroom, and necked a little in the parking lot before heading west on 299. Typical for August, Redding was as hot as the surface of Venus. "Measurable only in Kelvin," he muttered as he turned up the AC. He was grateful they'd soon be driving into the mountain forest, escaping the sunbaked death pancake of the Central Valley.

They stopped by the ranger station in Weaverville for a wilderness permit and another bathroom break.

"Too much iced tea," Jane said.

He watched her disappear into the restroom, wondering if she'd insist they come back first thing in the morning after her first taste of roughing it. Day or night, he'd never seen her looking grubby, unwashed, or rumpled.

But maybe, even at the campsite, she'd find a way to keep clean and tidy. He'd have to up his game. Camping alone or with other guys had made him a bit lax in the outdoor-hygiene department.

She returned to the Rover looking as fresh and smooth as ever. He stole another kiss. Then another. If it weren't for the impending disaster, he would've felt happier than he could remember feeling for a long time. Ever.

Ever again?

It was early afternoon when they pulled off Highway 3 into the campground that would be their home away from home.

He paid for their campsite, drove past a row of well-equipped RVs with folding chairs out front, and parked at their little patch of dirt under the ponderosa pine and cedar.

"I feel like I'm the landlord now," he said, cutting the engine.

"How much do I owe you?"

He started to make a sexual joke before remembering her fetish for exact records. "The campsite is fourteen dollars a night."

"Is breakfast included?"

"Of course," he said. "The rangers come by with fresh-baked scones and homemade marmalade in a bear-proof picnic basket at eleven."

"You think I'm going to hate this, don't you?"

"Not at all," he said. "You'll love it as much as I do."

"I love a man who's a terrible liar."

They each froze. It was only a figure of speech, but the L-word hung between them like woodsmoke.

"Popular place, isn't it?" Jane got out of the Rover and walked to the fire ring. "There's a bag of marshmallows over here."

"I know what we're eating for dinner," he said.

"No, it's just the bag. The marshmallows have already been consumed."

"That's all right, I brought more." He joined her at the fire ring, plucked the plastic bag out of the ashes, and crumpled it in his fist.

"I'm surprised people litter like that."

"The bears are even worse," he said. "And don't even get me started on raccoons. Those dudes are pigs. So to speak."

"I thought people who came out camping were nature lovers."

"Most of them think they are, I suppose."

"Then why do they litter?"

He put an arm around her, nuzzling her hair. "Your innocence is sexy."

"My stupidity, you mean."

"Try not to let it bother you."

"My stupidity?" she asked, raising a mocking eyebrow.

"Humanity."

She sighed, looked up at the trees arching over their heads. "This isn't the kind of place you go, is it? I imagined you out in the true wilderness."

"We're right next to the wilderness," he said. "You have to start somewhere. This is a good launching point. I car camp in spots like this a lot so I can write. I don't bring my laptop backpacking. Not usually."

"We're not backpacking?" She scowled. "But we brought backpacks."

"Just for day hikes. Backpacking is when you live out of your pack for days or weeks at a time, far from the car."

"Let's do that," she said.

"We can't. I didn't plan for it."

"If I can be spontaneous—*me*—you can. Come on, Grant! Let's do this right."

He gestured at the little brown building in the middle of the loop of campsites. "There's a bathroom here you can use. Toilets you can sit on. No trowel needed."

"You're underestimating me. I was all psyched up to go in the woods."

"I know it *sounds* fun, but—"

She laughed and smacked him on the shoulder. "It sounds horrific. But I want to do it."

"Why?"

She met his gaze. With a brick-red bandana tied around her head, pulling back her hair, her eyes were enormous. Aside from the SPF lip balm, she didn't wear any makeup. She looked so pretty, so perfect, he forgot to take a breath.

"Because it's what *you* do," she said. "You know about me and my life. My family, my job. I wanted to know about you."

Something deep inside him snapped, sank, shifted.

"Me?" he asked.

She put her hand on his jaw, ran her fingertips over his beard. Her eyes were smiling. "You."

In a daze, he nodded slowly. At that moment, he'd jump off a cliff if she asked. "All right. We'll hike into the wilderness and find a spot to sleep off the trail."

"My hero," she said.

He hoped so.

---

THE CLIMB WAS HARDER than she'd expected, and her back was soaked with sweat under the heavy pack, but she was exhilarated by the taste of fresh air on her tongue and the soothing sounds of wind in the trees, a gurgling creek, and her own panting breath.

Grant walked behind her, and she felt the pressure to go

faster than she'd like, knowing he could book past her at twice the pace.

She stepped aside at a trail switchback and reached for her water bottle. "Why don't you go ahead of me?" Her voice betrayed the strain she was under.

"It's better I go last," he said. "Otherwise, I'd go too fast and wear you out."

"I'd be much happier if you went first," she said. "Really."

He adjusted his green cap, tugging the visor up to wipe his brow. She thought he was pretending to be sweating; she saw no sign of effort on his part.

"I'll try to keep it easy," he said. "Let me know if I'm going too fast."

"Will do." She put her bottle away and gestured at the trail. "Onward." She waited until he walked past her before sucking in a deep breath she hoped would reach the bottom of her lungs. Working out on the cardio machines at the gym should have given her better endurance. Maybe it was the heat. The gym was as cold as a meat locker.

"We can swim in the lake when we get there," he said.

"I didn't bring a suit."

"I usually just strip down to my underwear. It's like doing laundry and a bath all at once. Very practical."

Imagining that fun sight, she cheerfully dropped her gaze to his butt. There wasn't much to see under the huge backpack and the baggy cargo shorts, so she made do with his muscular calves, flexing out from thick wool socks. They were gray and boring.

"Did you knit those socks too?" she called out.

"No, I'd get blisters if I tried to wear mine. I'm not good enough to make them smooth. I bought these."

"Did you bring the ones you made?" she asked.

He slowed to look at her around his bulky pack. "Maybe," he said. "Why?"

"Just wondering."

He nodded. "They turn you on, don't they?"

She closed the distance between them and slipped her fingers over his hip belt, pulling him to her. "Wildly."

"You're teasing me."

"Never."

He smiled slowly. "I may have brought a bit of yarn with me." He slid a hand around her waist and lowered his voice. "I might even share."

Laughing, she pushed him away. "I can't wait."

He stared at her a moment, making her thumping heart thump a little faster, and then turned away to continue hiking. The creek running along the path next to them was louder now, gushing down through the trees and rocks. She wondered what the trees were but was afraid to ask and look stupid. Pine trees? Cedar? Whatever they were, they smelled good and cast lovely, cooling shade.

It was all lovely. Exhausting, but beautiful. Tension she hadn't known she was carrying began to soften and unwind. When they came out of the trees into a gold-green meadow where a waterfall tumbled over a bank of jagged rocks, she made a sound of pleasure.

Or she'd meant it to sound like pleasure. Grant turned around, looking concerned. "Are you all right?"

She sucked in a breath. "Great." Another breath. "Beautiful." She pointed at the waterfall, the wildflowers dotting the meadow, the pine-or-whatever-they-were trees, and white rocky peaks along the horizon, and the sapphire sky above.

"I've always loved Trinity," he said.

She indulged in another mouthful of water and then

marched past him to go first. Since he'd been here before, she should be first, like sitting in the first car of a roller coaster.

"I had no idea," she said. About the meadow, about the waterfall, about him.

About what it could be like. Whatever it was.

"It gets even better," he said.

She stepped over a gnarled root and glanced at him over her shoulder. "Really?"

"Just you wait," he said.

Grant stopped and said it was time to make a campsite —much earlier than Jane had expected. The sun had fallen below the mountains, but there was plenty of light to keep going for a while.

"Aren't we going to the lake?" she asked.

"No hurry." He peeled off his pack and set it against a tree. "I thought we should rest."

"You mean me."

"It's been a long day. We were up early." He lifted a water bottle to his lips and tilted his head back to drink. His shirt clung to his chest, his biceps bulged— It was even sexier than a diet soda commercial. He lowered the bottle. "Let's enjoy the moment."

He had a point. She was enjoying this moment already. Although there was that one thing she'd been putting off.

"Grant, I have to pee."

A look of dread passed over his face. "Right. Well, it's like I warned you, there's no toilet out here."

"Of course there's no toilet," she said. "I hardly expected you to pull a Porta-Potti out of your pack."

"I tried fitting it in, but it would've meant leaving all the food behind."

"Are there rules about where I should go?"

"Dropping trou on the trail is bad form, as you might guess," he said. "We can find a tree for you that can give you a little privacy. Let's walk up around that big one over there and see what—"

"You don't need to come," she said, smiling. "I've got this."

"If you, ah, have more than, you know, then I have the trowel and some paper."

"I'm fine." She had been psychologically bracing herself for peeing without her Charmin. "I'll be right back." She marched up the slight rise into the trees, telling herself about her countless ancestors who had thrived without toilet paper.

She found a secluded spot—although it felt like the financial district at lunchtime when she lowered her pants. As her bare bottom hovered over the leaves and dry soil, she prayed to the gods of sanitary waste disposal that she didn't soak her underwear. Imagining the odor tomorrow if she did, Jane reached down and opened herself up a little to give the stream unhindered access to the bare earth.

Oh God, what a relief. She wondered if you could have an orgasm from peeing. She'd been holding it for a while, knowing Grant would give her exactly the worried, dreading look he had just given her.

And then she was done. Victorious, she shook herself off, wiped her hand on a bunch of leaves, and yanked up her pants as she rose.

She looked down at the puddle she'd made and was forced to revise the perfect score she'd given herself moments ago.

She'd tinkled on her boots. Not a lot, but there were definitely splash marks on the dusty toe of her left foot.

Well, it wasn't as if she was about to have an important job interview. Grimacing, she raked her boot through some dry leaves, covering up her business and giving herself a shoeshine at the same time.

She adjusted her underwear and stopped herself from finger-combing her hair. Her hand needed to visit the stream first. In the meantime, she'd rub them again with pine needles and more of the leaves.

Refreshed—ha ha—she strode down the slope through the trees to where she'd left Grant, who was staring at his own feet, frowning as he gnawed on a strip of teriyaki turkey jerky.

She stopped and watched him from behind a few thin branches several yards away. Why did he look so miserable?

"Did you pee on your boots too?" she asked.

His head jerked up, and a big, unconvincing smile appeared on his face. "Hey there." He stood up, watching her closely. "Are you OK?"

"Other than the bears, sure."

"You saw a bear?"

She'd been kidding. "There really are bears around here?"

"They're usually shy here, so don't worry. It's not Yosemite."

Of course people talked about bears all the time, and she had friends who'd talked about seeing them on camping trips, but somehow she hadn't believed there were real bears just walking around loose.

"I'm an idiot," she said, shaking her head. If she'd thought about it consciously, she would've known she was being foolish. "What should I do if we see one?"

"Scream and flap your arms."

"Come on, I'm serious."

"So am I," he said. "We don't want them eating our food."

She still didn't believe him. "You think I'll freak out, and you just don't want me to feel bad about freaking out."

"No, I'm hungry," he said, "and I don't want some bear chowing down our packets of freeze-dried turkey tetrazzini." His face continued to hold the big smile, but his tone was sharp.

"Fine," she said, trying not to catch his bad mood. He said he was hungry, so they'd eat. "How do we cook it?"

"First we have to find a place to make camp. We'll want to find a place where other people have already put a tent down to leave less impact. I'll walk around and see if I find a good level spot for the tent."

"I'll help. How big a spot do we need?"

"You should stay here."

"Why?"

"I don't want to have to worry about you," he said.

"Then don't." She offered a smile that was as fake as his had been, then turned and marched up into the area of her sanitary repose.

She'd seen a secluded spot behind a rocky slope when she'd been doing her business. It wasn't a Marriott, but it had a remarkable mountain view to the east. If he kept being unpleasant, she'd come back here to have a handful of trail mix and wait for him to snap out of it.

She was just about to go find him when he found her.

"Over there," he said, pointing at her find.

"I was just thinking that," she said, pleased.

He gave her a patronizing smile that suggested he didn't believe her. "Great. Let's get our packs and set up the tent."

"Seriously, I was. I was just coming to get you and see what you thought."

"I think it's perfect," he said, patting her shoulder before he left her again.

Was she irrational to want to shove him down the hill? She jogged after him. "I noticed that it has a flat area that would be perfect for our tent," she said, "as well as being shielded from wind by those rocks."

He reached their packs and lifted hers first. "Why don't you rest while I set up camp?"

"Why are you carrying my bag?"

He strode past her with her pack on his back, his muscular calves flexing, and didn't answer her question.

"Grant," she said.

Without stopping, he raised a hand in a wave and kept going, soon disappearing behind the rocks.

All right, he was underestimating her. She'd told him she was a city person, and he was trying to be helpful.

But it was damn annoying.

She picked up his bag—Lord, it weighed twice what hers did, maybe more—and, weaving from side to side under the load, swearing under her breath, she staggered after him.

He appeared at the top of the slope, saw her carrying his bag, and lost his shit.

"What are you doing? That's too heavy for you." He ran down the hill, tripping over a gnarled branch, then a cluster of rocks, and came to a breathless stop in front of her. Tearing the bag off her shoulders, nearly knocking her down with it, he said, "I'm used to this kind of load. It's not a macho thing, it's just physics. If you twist an ankle or pull a muscle out here—"

She stopped him by putting her hand—yes, it was the pee one, because she was upset and hadn't thought to use the other in time—over his lips.

"Relax," she said. Nothing else, just that. And then held his gaze.

Her calm, firm interruption, or maybe it was the aroma of her fingertips, broke through to him. She saw his shoulders sag, his expression soften.

When she was convinced his fit was over, she dropped her hand.

They stared at each other.

"Sorry," he said.

"I'm starting to understand why you usually hike alone," she said.

He flinched. Nodded. "Sorry," he said again.

"Are you like this with other people? I can't be the first person you've taken backpacking."

"Let's get the tent set up," he said. "I'll feel better when you've—when we've got shelter for the night."

She frowned at the clear sky, their sweaty T-shirts. "This is hardly Donner Pass."

"Nights are cold. You'll see." He stepped away, his pack on his shoulder, and walked up the hill in big strides.

He thought she was a wimp. Or maybe he was like this with all women. An unhappy thought.

Picking up one of their water bottles still perched on a fallen log, she gave herself a moment to admire a clump of wildflowers in the growing shade from the mountains to the west. A cool breeze, much sharper than only a half hour ago, had picked up as the evening approached.

Maybe Grant was right and they should be cautious. He was the expert. If she were doing his taxes, he'd probably think she was excessively tense and controlling, because as the specialist, she knew just how much could go wrong.

Refreshed with those warm, charitable thoughts, Jane went to find him at the campsite. He'd already rolled out a blue tarp on the ground and was tugging rolls of nylon out of a small sack.

"Can I help?" she asked.

"I was thinking you could filter us some more water," he

said. "The creek is down that way, just follow the trail back to the trail and—"

"I can find it, thanks." Jane gathered the filter and empty bottles and left him to his homebuilding. Had he really thought she couldn't find the creek on her own? They'd been walking along it for two hours. At times they'd had to talk loudly to hear each other over the gurgling of the running water.

She climbed down to the rocky shore and took her time pumping water through the filter into the bottles. When they were all full, she balanced them between stones and leaned back against a boulder to watch a water bug dancing across the surface of a still pool behind a log. It was impossible to get upset here. Nature was a drug. Maybe that's why they called it "stoned."

Speaking of stones, she saw something moving behind the ones on the opposite side of the creek. An animal. Too big to be a squirrel. Too big to be a beaver. What other animals were there? Eagles. She'd heard about eagles, but obviously eagles didn't scramble around the shore, nor did they have brown, shaggy fur.

When its head appeared with its little round ears, Jane jumped to her feet, heart pounding in her chest, and did as she'd been told.

## 28

"Yah yah yah!" she screamed. And flapped her arms like an eagle, the kind that didn't walk around rocks because it was a bird and not a bear.

It was a bear, right there, a real bear. Oh my God.

"Yah yah yah!" she shouted again, but her breath was too shallow to allow much sound to come out. She was like her toddler cousin with the plastic saxophone. Weak whistling air was all she could manage. Just last month she'd watched that movie with Anthony Hopkins where everyone got mauled and eaten. They'd blasted the bear with shotguns at close range, and it just kind of looked at them and got pissed off before it tore their heads off with a clawed swat. *Bam.*

Grant came running down the trail. "What's the matter? Jesus, Jane, what happened?"

"B-b-bear."

"Where?"

She pointed. The beast was galloping along the shore toward them. If she hadn't just relieved herself, she would've wet her pants.

She sucked in a breath and screamed. There, that one had some power behind it.

"Jane!"

She screamed again. Then again. And waved her hands in the air.

Grant grabbed her shoulders. "Stop! For God's sake, calm down!"

He was yelling too, but at *her*.

How dare he? They were about to get mauled by a bear, and he was yelling at her. "I am perfectly calm! You *told* me to scream!"

"If the bear was near our stuff. But it's way over there, on the opposite side of the creek. Or it was." He squinted across the water. "I've never seen a bear run so fast. You scared the complete shit out of it." He rubbed his eyes. "And me. Jesus."

"You told me to do that." Her fear quickly and easily turned into anger. "If you didn't want me to scream, you shouldn't have told me to scream." She spun away from him and tromped over the rocks to the trail above. Her pulse was still racing with fright. And her hands wouldn't stop shaking.

Grant was at her heels, carrying the water bottles. "Sorry, Jane. You startled me. I thought you were really in danger."

"How would I know bears don't cross over water if they're really motivated? I've seen videos of them charging into rivers to eat salmon, why not—" She clenched her jaw shut. She would not show him how upset she was. It would only confirm his low opinion of her.

Head high, she climbed over rocks and branches to get to the trail and then kept going to find the campsite.

But the pile of rocks she thought was the one she'd seen earlier was actually a new pile of rocks, and the row of pine trees, or whatever trees they were, was a different row of pine trees. Or whatever they were.

She stood in a clearing with a view of Mt. Shasta gleaming in the rays of the setting sun and pinched her eyes shut to stop any tears from falling.

She would *not* cry. She'd been startled—and then insulted. They weren't wimpy tears, they were strong, fierce eye droplets.

Inhaling deeply, she brought her bandana down her forehead, surreptitiously wiping the fierce eye droplets in the same swipe.

There weren't grizzlies in California anymore. She was able to remember that now. Later, she might laugh about how panic had made her forgetful.

Maybe.

She heard Grant calling her name behind the slope to her left. If he thought she was going to shout and scream to draw attention to herself, he was mistaken. Let's see how good his tracking skills were. She wasn't in any hurry to rejoin his company.

Why was she getting so upset about his patronizing attitude? She should be used to it by now as a woman in corporate finance. And he was just some guy renting a room in her house. They had sexual chemistry, a casual friendship, mutual ties through Whitman. He was writing a book, soon to be moving on, and she was reevaluating her career. Both were adults. If she'd thought she could really care about Grant, she never would've let him move in, let alone slept with him.

The thought struck her like a bear's claw tearing Anthony Hopkins's face off.

Why wouldn't she have let him move in if she'd realized she could like him so much?

"Jane! There you are." Grant waved from the top of a large boulder, up the hill to her left. He'd taken off his hat, and the strengthening wind ruffled his hair. His sunglasses rested under his chin, hung from a colorful wool cord.

He knitted his own eyeglass holders.

"Here I am," she said, lost in thought. What would be wrong with liking him, or a man like him? What would be wrong with truly caring about someone?

Nothing should be wrong with it. She was out of her twenties and had always wanted a family. But did she? The thought of loving Grant or anyone made her want to run screaming down the mountain and ask the bear to go ahead and gobble her up like a chicken nugget dipped in honey mustard sauce.

She'd like to blame Andrew for her emotional disorder (infidelity had left deep wounds for anyone), but hadn't she dated Andrew precisely because he wasn't very lovable? Billie had joked about nobody liking Andrew, not even Jane.

Grant came up beside her, short of breath. "Were you lost?"

She looked at him. He was ridiculously good-looking, a rugged man's man who wore dirt and sweat the way an international fashion model wore Prada.

"Just admiring the view," she said.

"I've always liked looking at Mt. Shasta more than I liked hiking it." He stared off into the distance, a faint smile teasing his lips. "There's a McDonald's in Weed that has an awesome view. I always stop there when I'm passing through, especially if there's a good bit of snow at the top. Looks like a kid's drawing of a mountain, just a sharp triangle pointing at the sky. Much better than Mt. Tam, which disappears when you get too close. It blends into the Marin headlands. There's nothing in the Central Valley to compete with Shasta."

Jane was reminded of the internet meme about finding a man who looked at you the way he looked at something he really loved. Grant had that kind of expression on his face—open adoration that asked nothing in return.

Who could compete with that?

She shivered, a surge of exhaustion suddenly washing over her. "Did you finish setting up the tent?"

"Yeah, it's up. Are you as hungry as I am? It's a good idea to start cooking before the light fades. Easier to clean up and bear-proof the food."

"I'm hungry." In fact, she was shaking. Her nervous system hadn't fully recovered from the bear scare. It had rattled her more than she'd like to admit.

Grant paused, then kissed her on the lips. She responded without much enthusiasm, and he backed away, his brow furrowed, and led her through the rocks and trees. Eventually they reached the clearing with their tent and packs leaning against each other. The red nylon dome looked like a giant cherry gumdrop that had fallen from the sky. It certainly hadn't evolved from nature amid the granite and pine.

"I'll get the camp stove going," he said. "I usually avoid making campfires in the wilderness because it leaves more of a permanent mark, but somebody has already beaten us to it. Would you like a real fire?"

"It's more work, right?"

He nodded.

"Let's just use the stove then." Over the past two days, she'd daydreamed about necking in front of the campfire with her hiker boyfriend, but now that she was here, all she wanted to do was take off her boots. She was afraid a hot spot on her right pinkie toe was going to be a blister tomorrow.

And whenever she thought about having a hiker boyfriend, she felt another surge of fight or flight, as if the bear really were a grizzly and she were dipped in honey mustard.

"Anything I can do to help?" she asked. When he said no, she sat on the tarp in front of the tent, took off her boots, and unzipped their red gumdrop.

She climbed inside and wondered what the hell she was going to do about how she was feeling.

How she was going to stop feeling it.

While Grant busied himself with his camping gadgets, she zipped up the flap between them. It glowed almost as brightly as a stained glass door.

## 29

Grant stared at the ceiling of the tent, wallowing in regret.

He never should've brought her into the wilderness. Yosemite would've been plenty. They could've driven through, discovered there were no camping spots, and then gotten a hotel outside the park.

When she'd screamed at the bear, he'd dropped his pack and started running, in such a panic that he tripped and smacked his elbow into a slab of granite. For a moment he'd been in such agony, he'd worried he'd dislocated his shoulder. Even now it throbbed, and he had trouble clenching his fist. At least it wasn't his dominant hand.

Jane wasn't hurt, and that's all he cared about. My God, the way she'd screamed… It had been a B-grade horror movie scream. No bear deserved that kind of reaction.

He couldn't help but recognize how vast the gulf between them was. The bear, young from the size of him, had been as cute as a stuffed animal, but she'd gotten hysterical. He would've loved to take a picture of it for his website, but it was running too fast.

Running away from the terrifying human.

He turned toward Jane's profile. From the sound of her breathing, he knew she was asleep. They'd consumed bland noodles out of featherlight bowls, split a Snickers bar, brushed their teeth with bottled water, and returned to the tent.

If she'd been burning up with lust, she'd hidden it well.

He fell asleep thinking about her and woke up thinking about her.

It was still dark, too early to be awake, but he couldn't push himself back down into sleep. Jane was snoring, her head wedged against his shoulder. He smiled, suppressing the urge to wake her with a kiss or a grope. It was too cold to fool around now, and she needed to sleep. All that screaming probably wore her out.

That was unfair, and he felt guilty for thinking it. Smiling, he leaned over and kissed the top of her head, inhaling the scent of her. She smelled like fresh air and toothpaste. Brushing in the dark without a sink or mirror had its disadvantages.

With his head nuzzled against hers, he felt himself falling back into a contented sleep. He was used to being alone. He'd thought he'd preferred it, especially when he was hiking. But now he knew he'd never again wake before dawn in a tent and not miss having Jane at his side, snoring and smelling like Colgate.

A thud just outside the tent snapped him awake. The undeniable sounds of a large animal dragging something around got him out of his sleeping bag and scrambling out of the tent on his hands and knees.

Now *that* was a bear. Dawn was breaking, illuminating the dark animal huddled over the human's bag of goodies.

Jane's backpack.

He'd put their food in a bear-proof canister, but the animal must've smelled something in Jane's bag. The way he was knocking it around showed he thought it was something delectable. Unfortunately, she'd zipped and snapped the bag closed, so the bear was forced to try other methods of releasing his prize. Bears could tear open pickup trucks, so a little fabric, no matter how thick, waterproof, and double stitched, wasn't going to be an obstacle.

She'd just spent several hundred bucks on that bag, and this was only the second day of use. He jumped out of the tent and did as he'd told Jane—shouted and flapped his arms.

Unfortunately, he jerked his left arm at just the wrong angle, pulling the muscle he'd just injured. His pain gave his next shout a burst of extra enthusiasm and was perhaps higher pitched than his first yell. The bear lumbered back a few steps, but it had already torn open a hole in the side of the bag.

Grant shouted and clapped his hands, sending more stabbing pain up his arm, but the bear was too motivated now to stop. After scooping out clothes and other inedible gear, it grabbed the pack with both paws, pushed its snout deeper, and then came out with a rectangular green package in its mouth.

Having claimed the prize, the bear turned and sauntered off into the trees, his rounded hindquarters rolling from side to side like an old man on a Sunday stroll, with all the time in the world.

It all happened so fast, by the time Jane climbed out of the tent, the bear was gone.

"What's the matter? What's going on?" She got to her feet and crossed her arms over her chest, shivering in the frigid mountain air. "Are you all right?"

"Another bear," he said. "It got into your pack."

"You screamed," she said.

"I shouted to scare it away, or I tried to."

"That wasn't a shout. That was definitely a scream. You got mad at me yesterday when I made a noise like that."

"I didn't get mad," he said. "I was afraid you were hurt."

The look she gave him was as cold as the Denali summit at midnight in winter.

"If I made a funny sound, it was because I hurt my arm yesterday," he continued, "and I bumped it when I was trying to rescue your stuff."

"You never mentioned hurting your arm."

Oh God. This wasn't going well. "I didn't want to worry you."

She shot him another frosty glance, pushed her feet into flip-flops, and walked over to her mangled pack. Her belongings were scattered all over the ground, and when she picked up the bag, it cracked open like an oyster, with only the interior frame at the back holding it in one piece.

"You left a granola bar in your pack," he said.

She grimaced. "I didn't mean to."

"Black bears can be really aggressive when there's food around."

"Good thing you made so much noise then," she said, "or he might've done more damage."

Something about her tone made him uneasy. She didn't sound entirely sincere.

"We'll have to hike out," he said. "Put the stuff in the Rover, set up at the campground. We can go for day hikes from there."

"I'd like to go home."

Part of him would be relieved to go home to where she was comfortable, but he was afraid it might not be so comfortable for him. "Are you sure? It's downhill to the car, and we'd have energy to find another—"

"I'm sure." She dropped the carcass of her backpack and

began picking up her things, folding them into a neat pile that she placed on top of the torn fabric. "We can have breakfast in Redding. Save you the effort of getting out the camp stove again."

"I don't mind getting out the camp stove," he said. "I can make us coffee."

"I'll wait for the good coffee," she said. "You know me, I like things the way I like them. Kind of a princess, really. But you knew that about me. You had me figured out from the first day."

Things were turning rapidly from not very good to bad, definitely bad. "I apologized for raising my voice at you yesterday," he said, hearing too late the defensive tone in his voice.

She picked up a pair of lightweight synthetic pants and a yellow camp shirt and strode off behind the tent to get dressed.

She didn't want him to see her naked.

He cursed under his breath and considered, for the first time in his life, taking up archery and tracking a bear during hunting season.

How had things gone so wrong? No, he shouldn't be surprised. Of course they had. He'd known they would. Ignoring his instincts always got him into trouble.

And this trouble wasn't the kind he could fix at the sporting goods store.

They were home before noon.

Jane carried the remains of her backpack into the garage, leaving them in a pile next to the washing machine, and then went to her bathroom.

On the drive home, Grant had made a big deal about how much she'd enjoy taking a shower after her night in the wilderness, but now everything he said sounded patronizing, and she felt no pleasure as she shampooed her hair and cleaned the dirt out from under her fingernails.

Shadow was still at Billie's, but she'd retrieve her later, maybe tomorrow. She wasn't up to explaining to her happy little sister why she'd come home so early.

She got dressed for work. It was Thursday, and she'd taken unplanned leave since her lunch with Sydney on Monday. The madness that had swept over her then seemed long ago and far away, and she was eager to return to her office, explain her absence to her clients, and resume her journey up the corporate ladder.

"I've got some email I have to deal with," she told Grant on her way out the door.

Grant hadn't showered and stood in his doorway in the same T-shirt and cargo pants he'd put on in the tent that morning. "Don't you think we should—" He scratched his chin. "No. Never mind. We'll talk later."

"It's good we came back, actually. I've got a client who really needs to talk to me. And I forgot about a meeting."

"Sure. Of course." He shoved his hands in his pockets. "I'll take a look at your pack and see if it can be saved. I know a guy in Berkeley who repairs gear—"

"Don't bother. I think we both know I'll never use it again." She smiled to take the sting out of her words, then waved, nodded, waved again, and hurried out the door.

She went to the BART station, she waited on the platform, she got a train to San Francisco—but she didn't get off at the Montgomery Street station and go to work. A part of her intended to, the part that was lying to herself, but the rest of her, which included her actual body, stayed in her seat.

When she got to the end of the line, she stepped out on the platform, her mind as empty as it was supposed to be after that yoga class, and lingered there until another train came along. She walked onto it and sat down, and when that train also reached its end of the line, she stood up.

She was at San Francisco International Airport. An urge to take out her credit card and buy a ticket to Maui washed over her. A condo with a view of the beach and the whales. A guava cocktail.

Recently Billie had gone on a vacation to the South Pacific with Ian, and the pictures she'd shared at the time hadn't tempted Jane at all. But now Jane was struck by a desire to escape so intense that she had to turn away from the sign directing her to the terminal and put her hand over her eyes.

The Pittsburg train on the other side of the platform was about to return to the safe, familiar environs of the East Bay.

Nowhere near home but a prudent distance from any flights to Maui.

She was too young for a midlife crisis. This was more like a head cold. In Berkeley, she got off the train, walked to a vegetarian restaurant near the station, and had a huge bowl of sizzling rice soup. Then she had her nails done. And went to the library, picked up books whose covers she didn't bother to read, and then wandered back out to the street and the stairs down to her train home.

She couldn't put it off any longer.

The short ride put her to sleep. The shallow, uncomfortable, and interrupted sleep in the tent had caught up to her. Just in time, she heard the call for her station.

She'd made a decision, and it was time to act on it.

Whatever this was between them, she wasn't ready for it.

It was almost six when she walked in her front door, took off her shoes, and paused. She heard Grant get off his bed and come out of his room to meet her.

"We can't do this anymore," she told his chin, not quite able to meet his eyes.

He didn't look surprised, but he didn't look happy.

"I called you at work," he said. "You weren't there."

"You called my desk?"

"I called Troy."

That was exactly what she didn't want happening. "You shouldn't have done that."

He leaned against the wall. "Why'd you lie to me?"

"I meant to go." That part of her had anyway.

His gaze dropped over her black trousers and gray twinset. "You left your laptop here."

"You looked through my things?"

He pushed away from the wall and pointed at the bag resting next to her shoes. Her purple laptop bag.

That's who she was—a woman who had laptop bags in multiple colors to coordinate with her business outfits.

"Grant, face it. We're incompatible. It would never last."

"Does it matter if it lasts?" he asked.

And that was the question she'd been grappling with all night and all day on the train.

The answer was yes. It mattered more with him than it had ever mattered with anyone. If it didn't last, she'd—

"It matters," she said. "It's better for both of us if we end this now before it gets too complicated."

"Does it seem complicated to you?"

What did he mean by that? That she was making a big deal out of nothing?

Perhaps she was the only one who could get hurt, and he'd never considered his own danger because he wasn't in any. "Maybe it isn't complicated. Which is good, because we could never make it last. We both know that. We knew it the second we met."

"I'm not sure about that." He took a step forward. "I was glad you ran into me. I thought you were sexy."

She took a step backward. On the train, she'd prepared a speech, but now she couldn't recall a single word. "We have chemistry, obviously, which is great"—damn it—"but it's not enough."

"I think it could be," he said. "We should find out."

Taking another step away from him, pulse racing, she shook her head. "My parents had chemistry. It didn't work out."

"The fact that you're here talking to me says otherwise."

"They had me, they had Billie, and then they had new families that made them happier." Her voice was too loud, betraying too much.

"We just started getting to know each other," he said.

"Don't you think it's a little early to start worrying about divorce?"

His words stung. It didn't mean as much to him. She straightened, adjusted the bag on her shoulder, and gestured at his room. "If you decide to leave, which you have to agree would be easier for both of us, I'll refund your rent money."

"Only if I leave?"

Her face burned. "I'll refund it right now."

"Because I earned it, I guess."

She gritted her teeth. To think she'd been feeling guilty about telling him it was over. "Don't flatter yourself. I don't want to risk any legal trouble. You paid six months in advance. It's only fair."

He turned into his room and closed the door. She heard the lock turn.

Seriously? He was just going to walk away without another word?

Before she gave in to the temptation to knock on his door and—what?

There was nothing he could say that would make her feel better. She opened the stained glass door, locked it behind her, and went to her room to open her laptop and send her tenant a full and complete refund.

With interest.

## 31

Grant took two bags with him and left the rest behind. He couldn't pack up the TV and all his things quickly enough for his mood. Getting into the Rover and driving away from her and that house was all he cared about.

He drove too fast and got pulled over, which only made him angrier; he was too upset to smile and apologize to the cop, who seemed to enjoy giving him a ticket.

His tent and gear were still in the truck, which was convenient because he planned on using them that night at Point Reyes, about an hour's drive on the west coast of Marin County. He got as far as the Richmond Bridge, stuck in the tail end of the evening commute, when his mother called.

"He's asking for you," she said. "I think you should come."

"Hold on. I'm in the car. I'll have to call you back."

"Talk to me when you get here," she said. He glanced down and saw she'd hung up.

Swearing to himself, he set aside his phone. The last person he should talk to when he was snarling like a wounded badger was his grandfather. Being polite was difficult enough when he was his usual easygoing, cheerful self.

But his mother had made it sound serious. That last talk with his grandfather had shaken him. Just when they learned how to talk to each other, he could be gone. Much of the conversation had felt like a goodbye, a settling of accounts.

Already on the freeway headed that way, he reached the estate about half an hour after getting her call and went to see her first.

As soon as she opened the door, he asked, "Is he sick? Think he needs to get to the hospital again?"

"He's fine. Thanks for coming so fast." She pulled him into a hug and then quickly released him. "You've smelled better."

"Just got back from camping," he said. "Haven't had a chance to shower yet." Of course he could have when Jane went out, but he had a superstition about not showering after a hike until he'd written at least one complete page in his journal. He'd been in no mental state to do that after Jane had dressed for work and walked out right after they'd come home.

"You can use mine," she said. "Your grandfather is going to tease you. Although your beard looks nice. Did you trim it recently?"

He had. Since meeting Jane, grooming had become more of a priority. With that sobering thought, he said, "Grandfather will have to take me as I am."

"He's waiting for you in the garden under his tree."

Grant knew which tree she meant. Unless it was pouring, he sat there every day to read the paper. "If he's not sick, why the hurry?"

"Ask him," she said.

Irritated with her, Grandfather, the world—and Jane and himself—he left her before he said something rude.

As expected, his grandfather was reading the paper where

he always did, in one of the two patio chairs next to a small outdoor dining set. The old oak tree didn't like flowers planted underneath its wide, gnarled branches, so the only bright color was the blue fabric of the chair cushions.

"That was fast," Grandfather said.

"I was already on the road," Grant said. "Headed to the campground."

"Looks like you slept in the bushes last night already."

Grant shrugged. "You know me." He sat on the teak stool he'd brought with him from the patio.

"Not that you make it easy."

Grant didn't have the discipline to smile. "My mother says I get it from you."

Grandfather's eyebrows shot up, then he laughed. "She's not bad, your mother. You take care of her when I'm gone, or I'll come back and haunt you." He lifted his arms and pretended to float. "Woo, woooooo…"

His mother had said he was fine, but Grant was skeptical. "You wanted to talk to me about something?"

"I hear from Troy you've gotten yourself into a little trouble."

Three hours ago, Grant had been desperate enough to call Troy and ask if he'd seen Jane. Troy had drawn the obvious conclusion.

But for him to tell their grandfather…

Rage percolating, Grant gripped his thigh to keep his voice level. "He shouldn't have bothered you with gossip about my sordid love life."

"Love life? Is that what your new book is about?"

Grant stared, feeling the blood coming to his face. "He talked to you about my book. Right." Better than his love life, but not great. "Forget what I said about the love life thing."

"*Sordid* love life."

"Not really," he said. He leaned forward, elbows on his knees, and looked at his grandfather's feet.

Then looked more closely. They were Birkenstock Arizonas in natural. "Those aren't the ones," Grant began. "That was too long ago for them to be… Are those…?"

Grandfather held up his foot. "If you treat a shoe right, it can last damn near forever."

Grant had given him that pair of Birks after his first book hit the *New York Times*. Even now he wasn't sure what he'd meant by it—a peace gesture, a poke in the eye, he wasn't sure. It had been Christmas, and he'd been expected to join the family here in their new home, with gifts for everyone.

"You actually wear them?" Grant asked.

Looking away, Grandfather rubbed his lips. "I'm wearing them now."

"They've been sitting in a box for ten years, haven't they?"

"Be happy I didn't throw them out."

Grant laughed. "I am happy." At least about that.

"Tell me about the sordid love life."

Shaking his head, Grant got to his feet and began to pace under the canopy.

"Spit it out. I can tell you want to tell me."

"I don't," Grant said. "I really don't."

"What's her name?"

"I'd rather talk about the book."

"Sounds boring. If you don't want to write it, I probably don't want to hear about it."

Grant sank down onto the stool. His grandfather's comment probably would've upset him months ago, but not now. The book was shorter than he'd planned but interesting. Different. It might not sell, but he wasn't embarrassed to have his name printed on the cover. "It's not too bad, actually."

"Great. Tell me about the girl."

Grant had to smile. "She's smart. Conscientious. Beautiful." He didn't know how to describe how she always looked good, put together. "She's a very snappy dresser. She's unhappy at her job but just works harder to make it better. She puts her feelings last, her job and duties first."

"I like her already."

Grant looked at him, thinking about all the trouble his grandfather had caused without knowing it. If he hadn't fired Jane, Grant wouldn't have convinced her to rent him the room, and what had happened later wouldn't have happened at all.

It was a terrible thought, the worst he'd had in a long time. Ever.

He fixed his gaze on his own feet, also in Birks. Even though he felt like death, he wouldn't go back and do anything differently.

Except the bear thing. Both bears. If he could go back, he'd join her in screaming at the bear cub on the opposite side of the river and then encourage the bigger one at the campsite to help himself to her entire pack and his too. Right now they'd be making love on an air mattress, drunk on fresh air and rehydrated meat loaf stew.

"Her name's Jane," Grant said. "I'm pretty sure I'm in love with her."

## 32

"But you screwed up," his grandfather said.

Grant opened his mouth and began to explain that he'd known a backpacking trip was too dangerous at this stage in their relationship. But his grandfather never liked to hear excuses. "Yeah, I screwed up."

"If you hadn't, you'd look a lot better," Grandfather said. "You'd certainly smell better."

"I thought old people lost their sense of smell."

"They do," his grandfather said. "Which just proves how much you stink."

Grant smiled. "Mom said you'd make fun of me."

"Remember what I said about taking care of her."

"I'll remember," Grant said.

"Does she know about Jane?"

"No."

"Probably for the best," Grandfather said. "You know how nosy women can be."

They both nodded their heads.

"There's not much to tell her," Grant said. "Not now."

"Because you screwed up."

"Yes."

"Are you going to fix it?" his grandfather asked.

Grant remembered the smell of toothpaste in Jane's hair. "She'd never settle for me long term. I just got swept up in her midlife crisis."

Grandfather snorted in disgust. "Don't fall for that bull. It's all midlife until you're dead."

"What she wants is a guy like her, some suit working his way up the corporate ladder the way she is."

"She told you that?"

"Not in so many words."

"Not in any words, I bet," Grandfather said.

"Just today, when she kicked me out, she said we were incompatible."

"That's exactly what you're saying. Sounds like you agree on that. Start there."

"She's mad I got upset about her screaming at a bear. It was just a little one, on the opposite side of a creek."

"Why'd you get upset?"

"I was afraid she'd gotten hurt." He'd imagined blood, broken bones, impending death. "I apologized right away."

"Did you tell her you care about her?"

"Obviously I care about her. I've dropped everything to be with her whenever I can."

"You didn't tell her."

Grant shook his head. "She never would've gotten involved with me at all if she'd thought I was serious," he said. "She broke up with a guy recently who hurt her badly. She hasn't gotten over it. I'm her fun, meaningless rebound guy."

"You're making excuses. Sounds like you're the one afraid of getting hurt."

Grant considered that. It was difficult to hear, a bad sign it was true. "Maybe a little."

"If you want her, go for it. Don't be a chickenshit."

Grant got to his feet but stopped himself from storming off like a child. His grandfather had a point. "Thanks for the advice."

"Are you going to take it?"

After this, he'd never be able to convince his grandfather he hadn't needed his bullying. "Yes."

"Good man. I told Troy you didn't need my help."

"Wait a minute—"

"He seemed to think I bore some responsibility for the whole mess," Grandfather said. "If I'd thought you were going to fall for the girl, I never would've fired her."

All this time, he'd known who Jane was. The old devil. "Troy told you everything, I take it."

"Had you fooled, didn't I?"

Grant sat down again. "You shouldn't fire people like that."

His grandfather pressed his lips together, his face turning red. "That SOB Frank Bostock fed me a line, and I swallowed every bit of it," he said tightly. "I wasn't such an easy mark when I was younger."

"I get it. You thought she'd screwed up. But even if she had, the way you handled it was—"

"Shabby. Yes, I know. In spite of what you might think, I do regret it," his grandfather said. "I was doped up on some pills Rachelle gave me for my cough, could barely see straight. And there were all those young faces around I didn't recognize. I felt old and angry."

Grant remembered the way Jane had looked storming out to her minivan, swearing, right after she'd been fired in front of her colleagues. He'd thought then, and still did, that the swearing was her way of keeping her head up.

"You owe her an apology," Grant said.

With a haughty shrug, his grandfather brought a crumpled

tissue to his nose and honked loudly. "Find a way to get her here, and I'll give her one."

---

AFTER HER COLD NIGHT ALONE, Jane went to the office on Friday morning determined to lose herself in work.

There were clients and meetings and emails, and she kept busy through lunch, trying to focus on her clients' business and not her own. The super burrito she got at the taco truck would have fulfilled her nutritional needs, but she couldn't enjoy it, not even with extra guacamole, and she threw it in the trash.

At four, enduring the scent of refried beans still wafting up from under her desk, Jane felt Sydney tap her on the shoulder.

"Well, this is it." Wrinkling her nose, Sydney looked into her trash basket. "I can't say I'm going to miss the smell of those burritos."

Jane jumped up. "What?"

"I'm giving notice."

"Already?"

"I start at the new place in two weeks." Sydney checked over her shoulder. "But keep your voice down. I want them to hear it from me. That new guy is just over there. He's trying to figure out how to use the printer."

"The broken one?"

"Mm-hmm." Sydney held up her hand and adjusted one of her bracelets, a silver chain with charms made from beaded zodiac symbols—all except Scorpio, which had been her ex-boyfriend's sign. She'd thrown that one down a storm drain.

"Nobody told him to use the one in the conference room?"

"Guess we forgot," Sydney said with a shrug.

Jane laughed. Then she lowered her voice to a whisper. "I can't believe you found another job already."

"I've had some feelers out for months. It was just one of those things that was meant to be."

"You're going to talk to Troy?"

Sydney dropped her smile. "I don't think so. Nicole is gone, so the meeting is with HR." She twirled a beaded ring around her finger. "I expect they'll want me to clear out right away. I might not see you, so here I am."

"They asked Richard to stay two weeks when he quit last year."

"He was leaving accounting altogether," Sydney said. "I'm not. Besides, Nicole thought I was disgruntled. She put it on my performance review. They won't want me hanging around. I bet my password will be changed before I leave the HR office."

"What will you be doing? I thought you wanted to go private or work in tech. Or become a therapist."

"Or all three," Sydney said, smiling. "Maybe in a few years I'll try something new, but like I said, this seems meant to be. They offered me senior manager, a huge raise—huge—and a room with a view. Reverse commute, too. Walnut Creek. I'll finally be able to get a seat on BART every day."

Jane whistled. "Congratulations, Sydney. That's great."

"I'd try to recruit you, but I know it's hopeless."

"Sure, that's why I suddenly took off camping in the middle of the week, because I'm so happy with my job."

"And you lasted one day. And here you are at your desk, working through lunch. In the dead days of summer," Sydney said. "You may not know yourself, Jane, but I do. You're here for the long haul."

Jane looked around to confirm they were still alone. "The fact that I'm here now doesn't mean I'll be here forever."

"Admit it, Jane. You're addicted to Whitman. Just one more day, one more week, one more year. You won't walk away. You're too stubborn to quit. You want to win, and you will." Sydney held out her arms and smiled. "Give me a hug. We might not get a chance later."

Jane wanted to argue, but Sydney was wiggling her fingers impatiently, glancing at the door.

After a short but firm embrace, Sydney left Jane alone with her spreadsheets, coffee, and broken heart. Fifteen minutes later, unable to concentrate, Jane picked up the trash can holding the burrito and carried it to the lunchroom, walking past the new guy, who continued to struggle with the printer.

On her way back, her trash can emptied, she succumbed to her conscience and stopped to tell him, "It's broken."

He barely spared her a glance. "No shit."

"There's another one in the conference room."

"If I need help, I'll ask for it," he said, not turning around.

She resumed walking. Three steps away, she pivoted on her heel and gave him the finger. The guy was hunched over the machine and didn't see her, but she felt better.

"Jane?" Troy asked. He stood in the doorway of the office to her left, his facial expression indicating he'd seen her hand gesture. Sydney stood inside the HR office behind him, absorbed in their conversation.

"The new guy's an asshole," Jane said. "Thought you should know." She continued walking to her desk.

Her heart was pounding. Sure, she was frequently a potty mouth but not at work. And her curses were usually vague, spoken in private, and aimed at inanimate objects.

But she'd just told the boss that the new senior manager was an asshole.

"Come on, Jane," Troy said, a nice guy trying to be tough. "You know language like that is unprofessional."

"No shit," she said.

Hm. Maybe she should go home. Jane smiled at Troy as if it had all been a fun joke and then strode to her desk. She flung the empty trash can under her desk, letting it topple to one side, and packed up her things for the day.

Just as she was slipping her laptop into her bag, she thought better of it and returned it to her desk.

Then she walked out of the office.

And down the elevator.

Across the lobby.

Out to the street.

The aroma of cold burrito was blissfully absent.

Without her laptop, she felt weightless. The bag on her shoulder was as light as an empty water bottle. The kind you bring down to a mountain stream to filter water into.

There was a cart on the corner selling coffee, donuts, bags of chips, other things she didn't usually buy. Today she got the coffee and a pastry with some kind of pink fruit in the middle. She didn't ask what it was.

She was eating the last bite—it turned out to be rasp-berry—when Sydney came out of the front doors of their building, saw Jane leaning against the glass, and came over to her.

"How'd it go?" Jane asked.

"It went." Sydney let out a long breath. "And now I will."

Jane smiled. "How do you feel?"

"Good. Very good."

"Was it hard? You know."

"What?"

Jane didn't know how to mention Troy without being obnoxious. "Saying goodbye. To… Whitman." She raised her eyebrows.

"No problem. I wish I'd done it a year ago."

"Now you can pursue other opportunities," Jane said. "Both at your new job and with a certain someone."

"Oh. Yeah." Sydney sighed. Shrugged. "Not our moment, I guess. He's cute though. Shame."

"What? But— You— I thought you were going to go for it when you had nothing left to lose."

"But now I do have something to lose. This job. It's what I've been waiting for. I'm not going to blow it."

Jane had never thought of herself as a romantic—the idea was laughable—but she was disappointed her friend was going to just... walk away. Jane had the strangest impulse to encourage her to reconsider.

"How about I buy you a drink to celebrate?" Jane asked.

Sydney patted her on the arm. "Sweet, but I've got plans. How about next week?"

Jane nodded, and Sydney strode away, humming to herself.

Just like that. She'd gone for it.

Feeling as weightless as her bag, Jane walked to the BART train, bumping into people who walked too fast, in lines that were too straight, and made her way home.

His Land Rover was gone, his windows were dark, his room was empty.

Pausing with her hand on his door, she didn't feel weightless anymore, only hollow.

What was the relationship advice they were always giving out? You weren't ready for love until you fulfilled yourself. Only after she took charge of her career and day-to-day happiness would she be ready for a serious relationship. Billie was younger than she was but years and years ahead when it came to risk taking and loving. Jane had been living half a life since she was eighteen, always protecting herself, a wounded heart swaddled in Bubble Wrap.

She wasn't ready for a man she could love. Having sent Grant away was proof of that.

But she could fix a few other things.

To her shame, she had to search her email for his current phone number. He picked up on the second ring, which surprised her; she'd expected voice mail. He was a busy, important man.

"Jane?"

"Hi, Dad."

"Is everything OK?"

"Yes, it's fine." Although it wasn't. Oh God, her eyes were filling with tears. She prayed he couldn't hear her emotion in her voice. "Bit of a cold"—she forced a cough—"but good. Listen, I have a favor to ask."

Silence. "Really?"

Her courage wavered. "Is this a bad time? It's not urgent. It's not anything, really."

"It's not a bad time. I was just wasting hours reading the news. You've rescued me."

She smiled at the sincere gratitude she heard in his voice. "Glad to help."

"It was nice seeing you at Billie's party," he said. "I was hoping to see you at the brunch in San Francisco, but I guess she and Ian wanted to keep it small. Not easy to do with our family, is it?"

"No, not easy." Jane paced the kitchen, tempted to take out the cream cheese. "I'm thinking— No, I've decided to move into private accounting. I wanted to ask if you knew any companies I should approach. People I could talk to."

The silence that followed was long enough for Jane to open the fridge and take out the Philadelphia. Loaf, not tub.

"What led you to this decision?" her father asked.

"Look, never mind, you're only the first person I've reached out to—"

"Thank you," he said. "I'm glad you did. I'd love to help. I'll be more effective if I know what you're looking for. What got you to this point? Why now?"

She relaxed. They'd never been close, but he'd never been directly cruel to her. "There are a lot of reasons," she said. "But the main one is I realized my heart isn't in it."

"Your heart?" He cleared his throat. "I see."

Like him, she didn't usually think in terms of heart, but it had been a stressful week. She'd explain in terms he was more familiar with. "They've passed me over for promotion one too many times. The hours are unpredictable, and I'm sick of traveling so much. I want more stability."

"Those are good reasons."

Better than the irrational, touchy-feely, heart-not-in-it reason, she thought as she opened the cream cheese foil. "If you have any ideas, any leads, could you email them to me?"

"Sure. I can do that."

"Thanks." She poked her spoon into the cream cheese, not seriously, just for comfort.

"Can I call you when I have something?" he asked. "I'm old. I still like the old ways."

She smiled. "Sure, Dad. Call me anytime."

"I can already think of a couple people who'd be willing to talk to you," he said. "No guarantees it'll lead to anything."

"Of course not. I've got realistic expectations."

"Don't be too realistic, Jane," he said. "If you want to fly, you've got to shoot for the moon."

Jane was tempted to point out the logical flaws in his metaphor. Birds and airplanes didn't shoot for the moon and would be crazy to try. But he meant well, and she appreciated it.

"Noted," she said. "Thanks, Dad. I'll let you go."

"Sure, all right," he said, but seemed to have more to say. "Jane?"

"Yes?"

"I wasn't quite being honest with you," he said.

"What? What do you mean?"

"I don't usually like talking on the phone," he said. "But it's nice to hear my daughter's voice."

Her throat tightened. She faked another cough. "Thanks." After a pause, she added, "Nice to hear you too."

"I'll call you with a few names," he said. "Promise."

"That would be really helpful. Thank you."

"My pleasure, sweetheart." He hung up.

Eyes burning, she put away the cream cheese.

## 33

"Why won't you do it?" Grant asked.

Troy picked at the label of his beer bottle. "I didn't say I wouldn't do it."

"You can't tell her it's me doing the inviting," Grant said.

"I'm not going to lie to her."

"It's not a lie. Grandfather wants to apologize to her. He can't travel easily, so she'll have to come to him."

Troy reached over the table and stole Grant's uneaten pizza crust. "I'm not going to help you get involved with one of Whitman's best accountants."

"Too late for that," Grant said. "We're already involved."

"There are legal implications. The more I do, the worse it gets."

Grant scoffed. "Legal implications? Come on. Don't be like that."

"I have to be like that. I'm responsible for Whitman. You're not."

"What kind of legal problems could there possibly be in having an employee come visit the elderly founding partner for a light brunch?"

"You know perfectly well it's not the elderly Whitman I'm worried about."

"I don't work there. Never have."

"But you're my brother, and I was just about to promote her. If word gets out you're sleeping together, I'm in a difficult spot. It makes it harder for me to do that."

Grant pushed his plate away. He appreciated Troy's sense of responsibility, but this was more important. "How about you promote her tomorrow and we delay the visit with Grandfather to next week?"

"Sure, because one week will make all the difference," Troy said, glancing at the North Beach restaurant's ceiling.

"Why do people have to know? How would they?"

"These things get around. I'd be surprised if it hasn't already."

"I'd be surprised if they really think Jane doesn't deserve a promotion," Grant said. "Isn't she good? She's been waiting for it too long already."

"I agree. Which is why I'm annoyed you're making it awkward. We just lost a good person last Friday who was upset she hadn't moved up yet. Others will start quitting if they think Whitman hands out promotions unfairly."

Grant couldn't see how he could force Troy to do something he felt was bad for the company so soon after he'd pressured his brother to take charge.

"Fine," Grant said. "I won't be there. Invite her up just to see Grandfather. There's nothing bad for the company in that. He fired her in front of everybody, so they won't doubt he owes her an apology."

"And you'll just happen to come visit Mom at the same—"

"I will not," Grant snapped. "If you think my being there makes your job harder, I won't be there."

"Then why do you care if Grandfather apologizes to her in person? He can send a letter. Call. Much easier."

"Because it would make her feel better," Grant said.

"Really? That's it?"

"You know what that place looks like to people when they visit for the first time. It's intimidating. How would you feel if Grandfather had sent you and Mom away when you showed up after Dad died?"

"Not quite the same." Troy took another bite of pizza crust. "But I get your point. It was bad to fire her like that. That's why I sent you to her house. I regret that now."

"I don't," Grant said.

"If she won't see you again, will you regret it then?"

"No."

Troy regarded him. "Really?"

"Really. It will have been the highlight of my life."

With a snort, Troy picked up his beer. "Right."

"Look at me."

Troy did, a crease forming between his eyebrows.

"I want to spend the rest of my life with her," Grant said.

Troy lowered his bottle to the table. "You're serious."

"That's what I'm telling you."

"I had no idea."

"You weren't listening," Grant said.

"Holy shit." Troy leaned back in his chair. They stared at each other. "OK."

"You'll invite her up to meet with Grandfather?"

"That's what I'll tell her," Troy said.

Grant saw a glimmer of hope. He really didn't want to be like Andrew, lurking around her house for the chance to talk to her. "And…?"

Troy stood, slapping a few bills on the table. "I'll let you know if and when she's coming," he said. "The rest is up to you."

Grant jumped up and hugged him. Bear style.

---

JANE WOKE up Sunday morning with a tattoo. She silenced her phone, shoved it under a pillow, and studied her arm.

She was going to have to cover the fresh ink when she went to see Mr. Whitman. It was on her forearm, still oozing. And it hurt like hell.

Why had she begged Sydney to go out with her yesterday? That woman was a bad influence. She'd woken up Saturday, lonely because she still hadn't claimed her cat from Billie—no, that was the only reason—and had called Sydney, refusing to take no for an answer.

But Jane had to admit it had helped her feel better. Maybe they could do it again soon. Since Grant had moved out, she sweated less about the small stuff. What did it matter if her skin was permanently marked with a tacky (lovely, magical) mermaid? Life was short. Death came for everyone, tattoo or no tattoo.

Her phone began vibrating under the pillow, reminding her of the ordeal ahead. When Troy had called her yesterday, she'd almost told him she didn't need an apology because she was leaving the company soon. That day, however, could be months away, and she couldn't risk losing her job yet. Without a reasonable excuse, she'd agreed to come to brunch that morning at eleven.

It was already nine.

As if the air were molasses and she an elephant shod in cast-iron boots, Jane trudged to the bathroom to get ready.

It was awkward to wash her hair without soaking her fresh

tattoo; she had to arch her back and lean sideways, lathering up with one hand. After the shower, she applied the ointments as instructed, chose a blouse with long, loose sleeves, and was on the road to Marin only a little late. Maybe more than a little.

It was hard to care.

Her sleeve didn't have a cuff, so she pushed up the billowy fabric to give the ink air. Even though the skin hadn't healed yet, she liked how it looked. A lot. In fact, she was already planning her next one. Tats were shockingly expensive though. Maybe she could offer to do the artist's taxes in exchange for a little complimentary artistry.

Just because she was having a nervous breakdown didn't mean she had to be irresponsible about her plans for an early, comfortable retirement.

This time when she arrived at the Whitman estate, she drove through the gates and up to the circular drive without hitting anything. She parked, unable to stop herself from looking unsuccessfully for a familiar Land Rover, and rang the bell.

The estate was as beautiful as ever. The grapevines were heavier, the grass more golden with the coming of autumn. The ancient California buckeye in the center of the round driveway had already lost its leaves.

A woman she didn't know opened the door, although her features seemed familiar. "Come on in. Grant is waiting for you in the garden."

Jane stopped breathing.

The woman gave her a curious look. "You are Jane, right? Here to see Mr. Whitman?"

Swallowing in an effort to squeeze her heart back into her chest cavity, Jane nodded. "Yes, thank you. Jane Garcia."

"Grant is my father-in-law," the woman said, inviting her

in, "so I stopped calling him Mr. Whitman a long time ago. Sorry if you were confused."

"No, it's fine. Of course." Jane followed her over the travertine tile to the courtyard and then back patio.

"He's a little tired today. Don't feel bad if he has to cut the visit short," the woman said.

Jane didn't even know her name. How could she not know her name?

"Thank you, Mrs.....?"

"Brandi. Like the drink but with an *i*."

"Brandi," Jane said. She had his eyes. That was disturbing. "Thanks."

"He asked for the food on trays. Somebody will be bringing that out in about fifteen minutes. Is that good?"

"Sure. Whatever Mr. Whitman likes."

"That's what Grant asked for," Brandi said.

Jane would never be able to think of Mr. Whitman as a Grant. Never. "Sounds good to me."

"There's iced tea on the table out there. I can get you a soda if you'd rather have that. I keep a case of Diet Coke in my fridge."

"Don't put yourself out. Iced tea is perfect."

"That's Grant's favorite," Brandi said, smiled, and walked back into the house.

The oddest feeling crept over Jane. She saw Mr. Whitman waving at her and went over to him in his blue chair. Next to him was a round teak table set with white napkins and silverware.

"Good morning, Jane," he boomed in that low, gravelly voice of his, holding out his hand.

She took it, flinching when he crushed hers. Plenty of muscle strength left in his fingers, that was for sure. "Thank you for inviting me."

"You were brave to come."

"Not at all," she said. "It's an honor."

"You had to worry that I was going to fire you again."

"Are you?"

He lifted his winged eyebrows and made a funny face.

The odd feeling crept over her again, as if she were being played with.

She didn't like it. At all. She wasn't going to put up with his bullying the way she had last time.

"Do whatever you're going to do, Mr. Whitman," she said. "Just do it after we eat. I'm starving."

He laughed, which sent him into a coughing fit.

Warily she handed him a box of tissues from a small cart at his side, in case he needed to spit out anything.

"I knew you were tough," he said. "I hope you didn't lose any sleep over my stupidity."

"Maybe a little." She sipped her iced tea.

He frowned. "I apologize. I do. I'd offer you a promotion, but I think maybe you have other plans."

Her heart skipped a beat. "Why would you think—"

"The way you came here today, not giving a shit. I can tell. You've moved on."

She couldn't admit he was right because she needed her paycheck until she had something else lined up. "I'm still giving Whitman one hundred percent."

"Until you leave." He nodded. "It's my own damn fault. Or maybe not. Maybe you would've left anyway. If *I* were younger, I'd knock on some up-and-coming Techno-Whozit's door with my resume and work my way up to CFO."

That was exactly what she'd been imagining. Ever since Sydney had mentioned the dream for herself, Jane hadn't been able to stop thinking about it. "You would?"

"I would." His gaze drifted over her head to the house. "You met Brandi."

"Yes. Yes I did."

"What'd you think of her?"

"She's very nice," Jane said.

"I'm rather fond of her," he said. "We're only linked by marriage, of course."

Jane remembered the unbearably sad look on Grant's face the few times he'd mentioned his late father. "Of course."

"Only by marriage, but she's still nice to me. You might think it's only because of the money," he said.

"No, of course not."

"Good. I don't think so either. I know it isn't that. She's a good person. My son knew what he was doing."

She smiled, glad to hear he had obviously warmed to his daughter-in-law after the early estrangement. That had to make Grant's life easier. Her Grant, not Mr. Whitman.

She corrected herself. He wasn't her Grant.

"Can I refill your glass?" she asked.

"Don't bother." He was looking behind her. "Grant will do it."

Was there another one? Pulse racing, she turned.

## 34

He was clean-shaven. It was a shocking change from the face she'd known, but he could never hide the scruffy mountain man from her.

She got to her feet and pointed at his face. "What did you do to yourself?"

"Don't you like it?"

She'd missed that voice so much. She frowned at his white kitchen smock. "Why are you wearing that?"

Grant held up a silver tray with covered plates. "Lunch is served, madam."

She turned and saw his grandfather grinning. "I knew something was wrong about this," she said.

"Has he apologized yet?" Grant asked.

She sat down—confused, excited, happy, terrified—and crossed her arms over her chest. The motion bumped her raw skin, and she bit down to swallow a curse.

When the pain subsided, she said, "I'd leave, but your grandfather here would probably fire me again."

"I might," Mr. Whitman said. "Better stay."

"That's the only reason I'm staying," she said. "To save my

job. I don't like being played with."

Mr. Whitman snorted.

"I admire how important your career is to you," Grant said.

She didn't believe him. He thought she was uptight. The type to scream at teddy bears. "Your skin doesn't match."

He rubbed his jaw. The shaved area was several tones lighter than the rest of his face, like a white beard. If she squinted, he looked like Santa.

OK, he was much too young and handsome to be Santa.

She much preferred the beard. It was a crime he'd shaved it off.

"I forgot there would be tan lines," he said. "I'm meeting with my agent in San Francisco tomorrow. The beard was great for headshots, given the subject matter. My agent's going to miss it."

Jane could relate. "Why did you shave it off?"

"To impress you," Mr. Whitman said.

Jane had forgotten he was there. He was smiling, his curved lips exposing a few gold teeth.

"Impress me?" Jane asked.

Grant set the tray down on the table. "Actually, I was trying to buy some time before you recognized me."

It was impossible to stop staring at him. Her fingers itched to stroke the hollow of his cheek, the smooth line of his jaw. "How could I not recognize you?"

He met her gaze. A charge passed between them, and she shivered.

"I don't know," he said. "Maybe because your feelings for me were so shallow and fleeting?"

She looked down at her hands. That's what she'd wanted him to think, wasn't it?

Be careful what you wish for.

"So true," she said. "What's your name again?"

Mr. Whitman laughed, triggering another coughing fit. He reached for his iced tea and looked at his watch.

A fortysomething woman in an orange blouse and denim capri pants came striding out of the house. "Mr. Whitman, there's a call for you."

"Thank you, Rachelle." Mr. Whitman smiled. "On the dot. Love that woman."

Jane wasn't convinced she should be alone with Grant. "You're going inside?" She stood and went over to the table. "But you haven't eaten your lunch."

Rachelle shared a glance with Grant. "The doctor's on the phone. We've been waiting for his call."

"Personal, you know. I'll have to go inside." Mr. Whitman held up an elbow, and Rachelle helped him to his feet. "Sorry to cut it short, Jane."

"I'll take over from here," Grant said.

"You can try," Mr. Whitman said. Then to Jane, "And thus concludes my apology."

As conspiracies went, it wasn't very subtle.

Jane kept her eyes fixed on Rachelle and Mr. Whitman as they slowly made their way up the flagstone path to the house.

"What happened to your arm?" Grant asked.

She looked down. The fabric had stuck to the weeping skin. She stepped to the side, putting the table between them. "You aren't the only one doing body modification since we last saw each other."

"Is that a tattoo?"

"None of your business," Jane said.

Grant frowned. "I'm sorry. It's beautiful. Whatever it is."

"It's a mermaid." A lovely, magical creature. With flowing auburn hair. And fins.

"Do mermaids eat trout?"

She blinked. "What?"

He lifted the cover off the platter. "Fresh fish. Very, very fresh." He strode over and pulled the chair she'd been sitting in over to the table. "Please, it's getting cold."

She hesitated, then sat. A single white dish held three perfect fillets, rice pilaf, and sautéed greens.

"Why are you doing this?" she asked. He didn't owe her anything, certainly not this. If anyone should be apologizing, it should be her.

"The bear ate your pack, so we had to cut our trip short," he said, "and you didn't get to eat any fish from Granite Lake."

It smelled delicious, but she was too agitated to eat. "Will you sit down?" On the opposite side of the table, where she couldn't reach.

He lifted his grandfather's chair, planted it less than an inch from her elbow, and sat down. "Mind if I eat with you? I made two plates."

If she leaned to the right, her arm would press against his. If she tilted her head, she could smell his skin. If she asked, he would kiss her.

"Why are you doing this?" she asked.

His smile creased the white skin of his shaved cheeks. "Aren't you going to ask me where the fish came from?"

Knowing more was too dangerous. Every smile, every inch of him was too dangerous. "I'm afraid to ask," she said.

He flinched but kept smiling. "Come on. Guess."

He was taking such a risk, doing this here with his family watching. She had to give him something in return. "Grant, I… I do care about you. That's… the problem." Her heart began to beat harder, faster. She owed him more, but it was hard to get the words out. Her voice dropped to a whisper. "I'm afraid of caring too much."

"I know," he said.

Just like that. He knew? "How could you know?"

"I'd really like you to ask me where I got the fish."

She took a deep breath. "All right. Where did you get the fish?"

"Granite Lake."

"What?"

Smile fading, he looked down at the plate. "I drove up yesterday."

His words hung there like... like bait on a hook, demanding she ask more questions and realize what he'd done.

She stared. "You... drove up to that same spot, hiked up to the lake"—she held up the plate—"caught these fish, hiked out, drove back home, and cooked them for me here at your grandfather's house—knowing I'd be here because you made that happen?"

"You don't sound happy about it."

She set down the plate and got to her feet. "Don't you get it? I'm trying *not* to fall in love with you. How am I supposed to do that if you do shit like this?"

He got to his feet. "I love how you swear, Jane." He caught her up in his arms. "Say it again."

His body felt better than anything should ever feel. "Let go of me. It's only getting worse."

He grinned, held her tighter. "Jane. I love you."

"Oh, Christ, now you've done it. What the hell's the matter with you?"

He pressed his mouth against hers, lifting her off the ground, and she figured it was a lost cause, she was a lost cause, and kissed him back.

God, how she'd missed this. There was no going back now.

After a few long, hot, sweet minutes, she tilted her head back and frowned at him. "I love you too, damn it."

"I'm sorry." He kissed her again to show her how much.

## 35

The fish was delicious.

Grant assumed it was, anyway. He was too delirious with love and lust to register the taste of anything, but he watched Jane devour it, glancing up at him every few seconds to smile or to tell him it was good.

"Your grandfather is watching us from that window," she said, nodding toward the breakfast room.

"Turns out he's a romantic." Grant ran his hand up and down Jane's thigh under the table. "Who would guess?"

"Turns out *I'm* a romantic," she said. "Never saw that coming."

He laughed. "As I said, I love you, but you're not a romantic."

She opened her mouth to argue, then closed it with an adorable snap. "That's a relief."

"Tell me again about how you love me," he said.

"God help me, it's too soon and I must be out of my mind, but I love you," she said.

It was still a shock. "I thought you cared a little, but this is more than I'd hoped."

"You said you knew already," she said.

"I knew you were afraid of falling for me," he said. "Not quite the same."

"It was hopeless from the start."

"This just gets better and better," he said with a grin. He pushed his plate at her. "Here, have more of the fish. I ate my share while you sat here talking to my grandfather."

She hesitated, then speared a fillet with her fork. "I can't wait until we can eat this at the campfire the way God intended."

"Jane," he said.

"What's the matter?"

"That was the hottest thing I've ever heard in my life." He put his hand over his chest. "Do you have any idea how long I've waited to hear a woman say that to me?"

She pushed away from the table. "Come on, let's get out of here so we can be alone."

"I take it back. That's the hottest thing I've ever heard." He jumped up and took her hand.

"We should clean up."

He cleared the table and carried the tray back to the kitchen. As he'd expected, his grandfather met them just inside the door.

"Things are going well, I see," Grandfather said.

"How was your phone call with the doctor?" Jane asked. Grant walked past them and set the tray on the counter, catching Rachelle's eye and sharing a wink.

"We can drop the charade now." Grandfather slapped Grant on the back. "Did you have to tell her about the trust fund to seal the deal?"

Grant tensed. "Believe it or not, no." He and Jane should've skipped out without saying goodbye. "She's willing to take me as I am."

"You've got a trust fund?" Jane asked, elbowing him in the ribs. "Excellent."

"Of course he does, not that he'll use it," Grandfather said.

"I don't need to use it," Grant said.

"Sometimes you're as half-baked as your father was," Grandfather said.

"I'm as half-baked as you, apparently," Grant said.

His grandfather turned to Jane. "He'll inherit more when I die. A depressing thought for both of us," he said. "His future great-grandchildren will be well provided for, no matter what happens, don't worry about that."

Grant's patience snapped. He'd explicitly told his grandfather not to say anything inappropriate that would make Jane uncomfortable. "I told you—"

"We'll both provide, one way or another, for whatever comes along." Jane took Grant's arm and lifted it over her shoulders. "Won't we?" she asked, tilting her head back to gaze at him.

He never wanted her to stop looking at him like that.

"Jane and I are leaving now," Grant said. If they didn't leave now, he was going to start arguing or kissing, and he'd rather it were the latter, in private.

When they were passing the medieval knight in the dining room, he heard his grandfather shout, "You're welcome!"

Jane laughed. "I could get to like that man."

"Happens to the best of us."

Out front in the sunny drive, they walked to Jane's minivan, parked near the olive grove.

"I was half expecting a Ferrari," Grant said. "To go with the tattoo."

"Mermaids need room for their tails," she said. "Duh."

He caught her up in his arms again and pressed her against the side of the van. "I'm not going to make it to Oakland. It's too far. The Sunday traffic is going to be horrible." He dropped kisses on her throat as he pressed his hips against hers. "I missed you so bad."

Groaning, she arched against him. "Missed. You. Too."

"Don't ever kick me out of your life again."

She grabbed his face in her hands. "Won't," she said, kissing and licking his jaw.

The minivan at their back was a staid, boring companion to their passion.

"By the way, why do you drive this thing?" he asked between kisses, love bites, nibbles, and gropes.

She pulled her arm free, lifted something out of her purse, and squeezed. The rear door slid open.

"Because of all the room," she said.

He looked inside. It was huge. The seats were lowered into the floor. The only cargo was an emergency blanket and a pillow. The windows were tinted.

"I love you," he said.

"I'm sorry," she said, and pulled him inside with her.

EPILOGUE




Six months after Jane gave Grant his own key to the stained glass door, she became an aunt.

His name was Daniel. Billie and Ian called him Dan the Man, Danny Boy, Dino Bino, and Danyeller, but never, not even once, "it."

Daniel was too small (and spoiled) to realize he had an excessive number of aunts and uncles, grandmothers and grandfathers, and countless friends—far more than even the loneliest child would ever need. Jane made sure to stand out, however, by spending more time with him than anyone except his parents.

With all those hours Jane spent with Daniel, limited only by his parents and the demands of Jane's new job as the CFO of an artisanal cheese distributor, Grant would've been lonely. Therefore, he brought his laptop and worked on his novel while Jane played with Daniel.

(Actually, most of the time he only thought about working on his novel. He played with Daniel as much as she did. It was he who came up with Danyeller, in fact.)

To expand his opportunities for procrastination and

writer's block, Grant accepted a position as an English teacher at the community college down the street from their house in the Oakland Hills. He could've aimed for a more prestigious position at a four-year school, but he'd always enjoyed living life on his own terms and didn't see why he should stop now that he was happily engaged to an honors graduate of Spreadsheet University. Unless he needed to provide for Danyeller's infant car seat, he hiked to work on foot.

His book about Fane was already getting a lot of buzz and would be published during next year's holidays. The flap of the hardcover edition contained an author photo taken after Grant was careful to neither shave nor trim his beard for two months. That had been Jane's idea. A fluffy black cat had photobombed the headshot, her pointy ears covering some of the beard. That had been Shadow's idea.

Jane's new company was a web-based start-up that shipped organic Californian cheeses in chilled, reusable foam boxes to customers around the world. Six months after Jane came on board, after implementing her ideas, their profits began to skyrocket.

Before the year was out, they added cream cheese to the product line.

Just because Jane Garcia liked it so much.

# ABOUT THE AUTHOR

GRETCHEN GALWAY is a *USA Today* bestselling author who writes romantic comedies because love is too painful to survive without laughing. Raised in the American Midwest, she now lives in California with her husband and two kids.

Sign up for her newsletter at www.gretchengalway.com to hear about new books, sales, and special goodies!

www.ingramcontent.com/pod-product-compliance
Lightning Source LLC
Chambersburg PA
CBHW051651180726

48284CB00006B/1953